I0566251

The Cliff Hangers: Macy

A Jamie Austen Thriller

TERRY TOLER

Cliff Hangers: Macy
Published by: BeHoldings, LLC

Copyright ©2021, **BeHoldings, LLC**
Terry Toler
All Rights Reserved

All rights reserved. No part of this publication may be reproduced, stored in a retrieval system, or transmitted in any form, or by any means – electronic, mechanical, photocopying, recording or otherwise – without prior written permission.

Book Cover: BeHoldings Publishing
Editor: Donna Toler

For information email: terry@terrytoler.com.

Our books can be purchased in bulk for promotional, educational, and business use. Please contact your bookseller or the BeHoldings Publishing Sales department at: *sales@terrytoler.com*

For booking information email: booking@terrytoler.com.
First U.S. Edition: June 2022
Printed in the United States of America

ISBN 978-1-954710-12-2

This is a work of fiction. All of the characters, organizations, and events portrayed in this novel are either products of the author's imagination or are used fictitiously. Any resemblance to actual persons, living or dead is entirely coincidental.

OTHER BOOKS BY TERRY TOLER

Fiction

The Longest Day

The Reformation of Mars

The Late, Great Planet Jupiter

The Great Wall of Ven-Us

Saturn: The Eden Experiment

The Mercury Protocols

Save The Girls

The Ingenue

Saving Sara

Save The Queen

No Girl Left Behind

The Launch

The Blue Rose

Body Count

Save Me Twice

Powerful Enemies

Deadly Games

Don't Be Careful

Cliff Hangers: Anna

Cliff Hangers: Mr. & Mrs. Platt

Cliff Hangers: The Quarterback

Cliff Hangers: Macy

Cliff Hangers: Not, Not Guilty

Cliff Hangers: The Book Club

Triggers

Non-Fiction

How to Make More Than a Million Dollars
The Heart Attacked
Seven Years of Promise
Mission Possible
Marriage Made in Heaven
21 Days to Physical Healing
21 Days to Spiritual Fitness
21 Days to Divine Health
21 Days to a Great Marriage
21 Days to Financial Freedom
21 Days to Sharing Your Faith
21 Days to Mission Possible
7 Days to Emotional Freedom
Uncommon Finances
Uncommon Health
Uncommon Marriage
The Jesus Diet
Suddenly Free
Feeling Free

For more information on these books and other resources visit
terrytoler.com.

Thank you for purchasing this novel from best-selling author Terry Toler. As an additional thank you, Terry wants to give you a free gift.

Sign up for:

Updates
New Releases
Announcements

At terrytoler.com

We'll send you a copy of *The Book Club*, a Cliff Hangers mystery, free of charge.

1

River Lederman chose his victims carefully.

He always found them in a bar. A hole in the wall dive bar, with no security cameras so his image was never recorded. He never went to the same place twice. In a city like Chicago, that's not as hard as it sounds. Chicago had more than eleven hundred bars. More than enough. He figured he'd be caught or die of old age before he got around to all of them.

Tonight's victim would be number thirteen. Lucky thirteen, he hoped. If things went as planned.

One woman looked promising.

She'd had a little too much to drink and was flirting with everything that moved. Clearly looking for a hookup. A thirty something professional. Stunningly gorgeous. Darkish brown hair. Deep mysterious eyes. Amazingly enough, they looked darker accented by the bright red lipstick that made her impossible not to stare at. She wore designer slacks and an off-white blouse, unbuttoned a couple of buttons, so it barely covered her very impressive chest.

River didn't like the fact that she was so attractive and so forward. He preferred to target women who were unremarkable. A woman other patrons didn't notice. A mousier type.

Something he'd thought about long and hard. So far, he'd always chosen the right victim. Or at least, none of the murders had been tied back to him. Which meant his M.O. was well thought out and working.

It made perfect sense to his analytical mind. When the dead women were discovered, cops would almost certainly go to the last place they were seen. Which would be the bar. They'd ask questions. Show a picture of the victim to the bartender, waitresses, and patrons if they could track them down. For that reason, River wanted his victims not to stand out.

The place he was at that night was perfect. The lights were low. The music blared, and the bar was packed. A lot of people being there might seem counterintuitive. In reality, the more people, the more faces to remember. Or never notice to begin with.

So, River sat off to the side and observed.

He wore a disguise, so if someone did happen to see the victim leave with him, the description given would be of no help to the detective.

He always ordered drinks. A bartender or waitress would remember someone who sat at his or her bar or table but didn't order anything. Those people made the help angry. They took up a table and ordered nothing but water. The bar didn't make anything off those people, and the wait staff didn't get a tip.

So, River ordered a drink and paid cash. He only took a sip or two. He needed to keep his full faculties for the strenuous evening ahead of him. Even his tip was calculated. Too high and the bartender or waitress would look him in the eye and thank him. Too low, and they'd be ticked off and remember him.

On this night, it didn't matter much. The bar was so packed, the bartender and waitresses were barely able to keep up. River doubted that any of them could give a description of any of their customers. When the night was over, they'd fall into bed, and never give him or anyone else another thought.

The woman at the end of the bar was about to finish her drink and no one was around her.

The opportunity presented itself and River walked over and sat down next to her. A voice inside screamed for him to leave the woman alone and choose another victim.

He ignored it.

"Can I buy you a drink?" he asked.

"Sure," she said excitedly.

"One more drink for the lady," River said, raising his hand to the bartender. River stood sideways with his elbow leaning against the bar, so the bartender wouldn't get a good look at him.

"If you're looking for a lady," the woman said with a seductive grin, "you've got the wrong girl."

Perfect.

"I'm Brady," he replied, holding out his hand, giving her one of several fake names he used for these purposes.

She shook it and said, "I'm Macy."

"It's a pleasure to meet you, Macy."

"We'll see," she said. "Somebody is going to be pleased to meet me tonight. It might be you."

The bartender sat the drink in front of her. She lifted it in the air and took a gulp.

Women were so stupid. If River wanted, he could hook up with a different woman every night of the week. Buy them a few drinks, seem like you aren't a serial killer, and they'd come back to his house every time. Once there, killing them was the easy part. Disposing of the body was harder, but he'd gotten it down to a science.

Of course, he was a serial killer. A moniker he wore proudly, often regretting that he had to get caught, to gain the notoriety he deserved. River aspired to become the best ever. That meant the numbers were important. The more women he killed, the more famous he would become.

He studied the famous serial killers of the past. Learned as much as he could from them. They all had one thing in common. They were likable. Women fell for their charm. Other than that, they were unremarkable. Unmemorable. That's how they got away with it. They were your Average Joe. They all had average looks, good jobs, and a little bit of money.

And were nice enough to gain a woman's trust.

Like him.

River fit the profile perfectly.

So did Macy. The victim profile. She was as close to a sure thing as he'd ever seen.

"I'd definitely like to be that guy," River said to her. "Are you going to make me work for it, or do you want to leave now and go back to my place?"

Macy looked around the bar, as if to see if she had any better options. Her eyes fixed back on his. "Well, since you aren't going to make me work for it, it's only fair that I reciprocate. Pay the man for the drink and let's go."

River dropped a ten on the counter. When Macy stood from the bar stool, he checked her out more thoroughly. She was about five feet eight inches tall. Physically fit. Clearly a woman who worked out. Probably regularly attended a cardio class like Pilates or an Elliptical cycling class.

He liked it when the bodies were toned.

River walked her to his car. Something else he'd thought about long and hard before purchasing. White four door sedan. One of tens of thousands on the streets of Chicago.

He opened the door for her.

"Thank you very much," she said. "You're a gentleman."

"I'm sorry. I forgot. You aren't a lady and you don't like gentlemen."

"I'll let it pass this one time," she said with a grin.

Macy was mesmerizing when she smiled.

Tonight was going to be fun.

For him, anyway.

He closed the door behind her. She seemed a little tipsy. He probably wouldn't even have to spike her drink. When needed, he had a drug at his house strong enough to incapacitate his victims. He preferred not to use them. Watching them suffer and then die a slow death fully conscious was a bigger turn on.

The drive to his house took fifteen minutes. He always avoided any of the toll roads which wasn't always easy to do in Chicago. But necessary since he didn't want his or Macy's face on any cameras.

When he got home and put the car in park, Macy bolted out of the car and started walking toward his house.

That made him angry.

He liked to be the one in control. The dominant one. He had a plan. A certain way of doing things. She was rushing things. He liked to build the intensity slowly. Like a symphony orchestra. The first beats of a measure were adagio. Slow. Rhythmic. Soft. Then build the level of energy. Until it reached a crescendo.

River played the French horn in a small local symphony which was why he often compared his work to a symphonic production. In a musical composition the ending was the most important thing.

Like when he killed someone. Thrust a knife into their heart. Or slit their throats. It had to be timed perfectly.

In a way, Macy was ruining it for him. He wanted to kill her on the spot just for that reason alone.

The decision was made. He wouldn't drug her. He wanted her to experience the pain. To be fully aware of his every action. The trick would be not to let her see his anger between now and the time he turned on her.

He also needed to keep her from taking him right into the bedroom. She seemed like she was ready to get to it. That would also spoil his plan. He'd have his way with her, but on his terms. In the way that he liked it.

She was already at his back door. He fumbled with his keys. Hardly able to contain his anger. She hung on his arm.

It annoyed him to no end.

When he finally got the door opened, she pushed past him, and into the kitchen. Walking in before him.

He resisted the urge to strike her on the head. The woman was not only slutty, but rude.

He needed a drink. Making her one, might slow her down a little.

"Can I fix you a drink?" he asked.

"I thought you'd never ask."

"We just got here. When could I have asked?"

He was boiling on the inside. It took all of his self-control not to explode in anger.

"I'm kidding, silly," she said with a smile. "Fix me a drink."

She opened her purse and took something out of it. "Where's your restroom?" she asked.

"Around the corner. First door on the right."

He mixed a couple of drinks. Macy was still in the restroom. He took a big swig of his, then refilled it. Not concerned at all about getting too drunk to carry out his plan. He could hold his liquor. The vodka would tamper down his anger for the woman and keep him from killing her too quickly.

Macy returned from the bathroom and walked over to the counter and picked up both drinks and carried them into the living room.

Hey!

The rage rushed to the surface like a boiling volcano. Who did she think she was, touching his drink?

He had to excuse himself, so he could calm down and not say something he'd regret. "I'm going to use the bathroom as well," River said. "I'll be right back."

When he returned, Macy sat on the couch, with her shoes off, and her feet up and under her.

Why would she put her dirty feet on my couch?

Was she completely void of any manners?

He resisted the urge to tell her off.

Macy handed him his drink and invited him to sit down beside her. He sat down on one of the side chairs instead. Her drink was on the coffee table. At least she had the sense to put it on a coaster.

If she hadn't, he might've choked her to death right on the spot. He took another big swig of his drink.

6

She made a toast and took a sip of hers. He raised his glass then downed his drink in two more gulps.

When he finished, he'd had enough. Time to show this woman who was boss. Give her a lesson she'd never forget. That last thought almost caused him to laugh out loud. The woman only had a few hours left on this earth. By the time she learned the lessons, she'd be dead.

River attempted to stand to his feet.

His legs didn't move.

Alcohol never had that effect on him.

He tried again. His legs didn't respond, even though he commanded them to do so.

Neither did his arms.

He tried to speak, but his lips didn't move. His jaw was locked in place, and he couldn't make a sound. Yet he was fully conscious. Aware of everything that was happening.

An evil smile came on Macy's face. Her eyes twinkled.

A feeling of dread engulfed him.

"Don't even bother trying to move," she said. "You can't. I drugged your drink."

You drugged me!

He couldn't believe what he was hearing.

"Did I tell you that I'm an anesthesiologist at a local hospital?"

No, you didn't.

"We have all kinds of drugs now that let you stay awake during surgery. I gave you one. You won't feel anything I do to you. No pain. Isn't that nice of me?"

He tried to respond but couldn't.

"You'll have to watch though. It won't be pleasant. I like to draw it out."

River's mind raced. He called her all kinds of expletives in his head, but the words didn't make it from his mind to his mouth. He tried to rock back and forth. To somehow shake himself out of his paralytic state.

To no avail.

"You are my eleventh," she said. "Don't you feel lucky to be number eleven?"

River was resigned to his fate.

"Men are so stupid," she said. "They fall for my tricks so easily. They're so predictable. All I have to do is flash them a smile, let them buy me a drink, and they'll beg me like a dog to come back to their house with them. You men are pathetic losers."

She stood up from the couch and slapped him twice on the cheek. He didn't feel it but did have the sensation of his neck jerking to the side.

"I know who you are," she said.

Macy opened her purse and pulled out what looked to be a surgical knife and clamp.

"Let's get started, shall we?" she said with the wickedest smile he'd ever seen.

As ironic as it seemed, he couldn't help but admire her. Maybe she'd be the best serial killer of all time, instead of him.

2

The crime scene was as gruesome as any homicide detective, Cliff Ford, had ever witnessed. That's saying a lot, considering he'd been a senior detective in Chicago for more than ten years.

He was glad he dropped his wife, Julia, at the house. On occasion, she accompanied him to crime scenes, and he often picked her brain on his cases. They were having dinner at a local restaurant when Cliff got the text to come to the location of a murder in a private residence in north Chicago.

Julia was tired and had to get up early the next day. She also wanted to get the babysitter home at a decent hour. Cliff could get tied up on a murder investigation for hours.

A good thing she didn't come with him as it turned out. He wouldn't want anyone to have these images permanently embedded in their brain.

"Tell me what you got," Cliff said to the first cop on the scene.

"Caucasian male. His name is River Lederman. I found his wallet on his person. That's how I identified him. From his driver's license. The victim is forty-three-years old. Computer programmer. The man is jacked up."

"I can see that."

"How do you know he's a computer programmer?"

"One of his business cards was in the wallet."

"Okay."

"It's some kind of ritualistic killing," the cop explained. "The victim was tortured. What a way to go."

Cliff did a quick visual three-sixty scan of the scene. He already had gloves and booties on, so he started walking around to get a general lay of the home.

The man was killed in the living room.

Cliff studied the victim, resisting the urge to turn his head away. Even after ten years, some things about his job were still hard to take.

The victim was of average build. Not muscular, but not scrawny either. Big enough to fight back. Cliff wondered how a man that size could be tortured in that manner without any arm or leg restraints.

Too much alcohol or some kind of date-rape-drug came to mind.

The house was a modest one-story older home that looked to have been recently remodeled. A typical Chicago residence. The man probably made just below six figures.

"How was he discovered?" Cliff asked the cop who was still following him around waiting for him to ask more questions.

"A coworker phoned it in. She also confirmed that the victim was a computer programmer. She shared the cubicle next to him. When he didn't show up for work, she reported it to her boss. They tried to reach him but weren't able to."

"So what did they do when they couldn't get in touch with him?"

"Not a thing. Nobody followed up on it for a couple more days. Eventually, that same coworker took it upon herself to come to his house after work to check on him. His car was in the driveway, but he didn't answer the door. That seemed strange to her, so she phoned it in."

"I'd like to talk to the woman."

Cliff wondered if the victim had any family nearby and why he wasn't discovered sooner.

"I've got all her information."

Cliff got it from him and wrote it down in his little black book. Along with a few notes.

The cop stood there patiently.

"What happened next?" Cliff asked.

"My partner and I responded to the call. I observed blood on the floor through one of the windows in the back. I entered the premises and found the body. Then we secured the scene."

It seemed as though everything had been done by the book to that point.

"Good work, officer. Any sign of forced entry?"

"No sir. The back door was unlocked. That's how I entered the premises."

Cliff stared at the body for a good minute. He wasn't a forensics expert, but by the smell and the condition, he estimated the man had been dead for three days. That matched the information the coworker provided. The medical examiner would give him a more precise determination.

For the next twenty minutes, he went through his routine. Observing. Making mental notes. Writing down anything that seemed important.

Two drinks were on the coffee table. Cliff pointed that out to the cop.

"That means he wasn't alone," the cop said.

Cliff laughed.

"Those wounds aren't self-inflicted. I already knew he wasn't alone. Let's hope we have DNA and fingerprints on those glasses."

Cliff bent down and examined the glasses without touching them. He noticed what appeared to be red lipstick on one of the glasses.

"It took a lot of rage to do this," the cop said. "Do you think it's a crime of passion?"

Cliff shook his head.

"This isn't a crime of passion," he said. "Angry lovers don't torture their victims. Not like this. The movie *Misery* being an exception. Actually, the abuser in that movie was a fan of a novelist. Not a lover. Still."

Having voiced it, Cliff thought that scenario might apply here. The killer might be some kind of sicko with a deep-seated resentment for men. He felt the need to clarify his statement to the cop. "Actually, it is a crime of passion in a sense. It's just that the anger toward men was likely caused by someone else."

"Why do you say that?" the cop asked.

Cliff wondered if the officer aspired to become a detective with the type of questions he was asking. If so, he'd help him out. Cliff was wet behind the ears once as well.

He explained his reasoning. "In a typical crime of passion, the wounds are violent. Random. With no thought behind them. Typically, we'll see multiple stab wounds or multiple gunshot wounds. Overkill, so to speak. In this case, the killer was methodical. You used the right word earlier. Surgical."

Cliff wrote that word down in his notes and then continued with his thoughts which were helping him form a theory in the case.

"The killer was likely abused as a kid. By a man. A father or stepfather. An uncle or next-door neighbor. A pastor or priest. Could be anybody."

"So you think the victim didn't know his killer?"

"I think they knew each other. Just not for very long."

"Maybe a romantic hookup?"

"Maybe. But not in the traditional sense. I think the victim was targeted. Stalked by a predator. Probably randomly. Maybe at a grocery store. A gym. A bar, perhaps."

Cliff searched his thoughts for more ideas.

"The victim had to know the killer since there's no forced entry. They were also having a casual drink together. The victim trusted the killer enough to let her in his house."

"That makes sense."

"This person was a professional," Cliff added. "I'd bet the change in my pocket that the killer has killed before."

"A serial killer?"

"I can't rule that out."

Cliff made a mental note to search the files for unsolved murders. This scene was so unusual, any similarities to another murder would most likely be more than a coincidence.

"He's one sick man," the cop said.

"He?"

"I assume it's a he."

"Never assume anything."

"Aren't most serial killers men?"

"Yes. But not all."

"Is a woman capable of doing all this?"

"You'd be surprised."

The cop did have a good point. Most serial killers were men. But the red lipstick gave him pause. That told him the killer was probably a woman. It's possible the victim had a few drinks with a woman, and she left. Then somebody else came in and killed him.

But that didn't fit with his theory. He was convinced the victim was drugged. Probably from something in his drink. Forensics would have to confirm it, but from looking at the scene, his gut told him that the person drinking from the second glass with red lipstick on it was the killer.

"Definitely a man," the cop said. "That's what I think."

Cliff was getting annoyed by all the speculation, so he sent the cop to a different room to look for more clues. That didn't mean he didn't continue the speculation in his own head.

A scenario was forming in his mind.

The man met the killer in a bar for a hookup. When Cliff saw the killer in his head, it was a woman. Easy enough to prove. If not by the lipstick, by the fingerprints and DNA which were almost certainly on the glasses. The lab would be able to identify the sex of the person drinking from both glasses and would be able to tie one of the glasses to the victim.

Which also told him something important. The killer made no attempt to hide her identity. She didn't wear gloves. Was perfectly willing to leave an impression of her lips on the glass. That meant he wasn't going to find a DNA or fingerprint match in the database. She'd never been arrested.

It also told him something else. The killer wanted him to find those clues. Almost like she was leaving her signature behind so all her kills could be tied together. Like she wanted her number known.

Cliff was convinced he had a serial killer on his hands. Not hard to prove if he found similar cases. That's the first place he'd look.

He continued to run the scenario in his mind. They came back to the victim's house. Had a couple of drinks. He corrected himself. Probably one drink. Somehow, the killer was able to sneak a drug into the victim's drink.

That's where it got hinky. A detective's slang term for strange.

Why the long-drawn-out torture session? That didn't seem like something a woman would do.

The wounds on the body also looked like they didn't come from a common knife. More likely from a scalpel or something similar.

Was the killer a wanna-be doctor? Cliff couldn't imagine a real doctor getting her kicks from cutting somebody open, considering she did it several times a day.

What about a nurse? She'd have access to drugs.

An anesthesiologist?

What about a medical student?

Cliff looked back at his notes. The victim was forty-three. A typical medical student would be in her twenties. Would she leave a bar with a man twenty-years older without him being suspicious?

Probably. He'd be excited to bring her home. The chance for a dream hookup with a young hottie would be exciting for an older man, nearing a midlife crisis.

Cliff wondered if the victim had been married before. He didn't see this as the work of an ex.

It could be the work of a scorned husband. A doctor whose wife was having an affair. He caught them together. Was there another victim out there somewhere? The wife?

Then he remembered the lipstick. That scenario only worked if the doctor came in after his wife left.

But what about the drugs in the drink? The woman had to put them there.

Cliff rubbed his eyes roughly. All the scenarios screaming in his head were giving him a headache.

This was the problem with serial killers. A detective's worst nightmare. The victims were usually random. That made the killer much harder to catch. There wasn't a rhyme or reason to their madness. No established pattern to predict future behavior.

While he wouldn't rule other scenarios out, the serial killer thread seemed the most likely one to pursue. He could be wrong, but those were his first impressions. More often than not, his first instincts turned out to be right.

The beat cop interrupted his thoughts. Cliff was so deep in thought he didn't realize the cop had come back in the living room.

"Detective, I think I found something," he said excitedly.

"Show me."

The officer led him into an office. On the desk was a computer. The computer was already on.

Cliff frowned at the cop. It wasn't his job to turn on a computer and search it.

"I moved the mouse by accident, and it came on," the cop said, probably anticipating Cliff's unease with his actions. "This is what came up."

On the main screen were video files. Named after women. Right in plain view. Not hidden behind a password.

Cliff was curious, but why was the cop practically giddy?

"I clicked on one," the cop said, answering the question in Cliff's mind. "You won't believe what's on it."

Cliff was so curious as to what was in the files, he didn't bother chastising the cop for overstepping his bounds and doing a detective's job. When Cliff clicked on one of the files named Darla, a video came up. He enlarged it so it fit the whole screen.

It appeared to be shot from a phone rather than a camera. The man in the video was the victim in the other room and had the phone pointed at himself.

"I want you to meet Darla," the man said.

He turned the phone away from himself.

Cliff's mouth flew open so far, it would've continued widening had it not been constrained by his jaw muscles.

A woman was strapped to a chair. The same chair the victim was found sitting in.

What Cliff watched in horror was every bit as gruesome as the scene in the other room.

He could only assume the other video files contained more victims. He counted twelve of them.

He did have a serial killer on his hands.

Only this time, the sadistic killer got a taste of his own medicine.

Became the one tortured and killed.

Cliff corrected himself.

He probably had two serial killers.

One was dead.

The other out there to kill again.

A woman.

What were the odds?

3

Two days later

The Lieutenant over all the homicide detectives in Cliff's office, had an open-door policy. Along with several rules. Only walk through that open door if you had something important to tell him, never sit down until instructed to do so, speak only after spoken to, and get in and out of there as quickly as possible.

Cliff violated the second one. He walked into the Lieutenant's office and sat right down in the one side chair across from his desk. The Lieutenant's head was down and he was writing something. While he obviously knew Cliff was there, he didn't look up, and pretended to be ignoring him. Mostly for effect.

Whatever the Lieutenant was working on couldn't possibly be as important as the information Cliff was about to give him. If his boss knew that, he'd stop what he was doing immediately.

Nonetheless, Cliff waited patiently until he was spoken to, careful not to violate more than one rule at a time. Eventually, the Lieutenant looked up and frowned. Followed by a passive aggressive statement related to the intrusion.

"What are you doing, Ford? I'm in the middle of something."

"I'm solving cases. That's what I'm doing."

"That's what we pay you to do. Thanks for letting me know you're doing your job. Because of that, I won't fire you. I'll keep you on for another week."

The Lieutenant looked down and started to write again. A smirk escaped out of the side of his mouth as he almost smiled at his joke. He seemed to be enjoying the hoops he was making Cliff jump through.

"I solved twelve cases over the last two days," Cliff blurted.

That got the Lieutenant's attention. He lifted his head, sat his pen down on the desk, and leaned back in his chair.

"Alright. I'll bite. What ya got?"

"I solved the Midway Butcher cases," Cliff said proudly.

The Lieutenant's right eyebrow raised a good half inch above the other one. His lack of a verbal response was Cliff's cue to explain.

"There was a murder two nights ago," Cliff said. "A man named River Lederman."

"I'm aware. I heard it was pretty gruesome. I figured the Butcher did it."

Not many things went on in that office that the Lieutenant didn't know about. He made it a point to familiarize himself with every case.

"River Lederman is the Butcher," Cliff said.

"I thought he was the one murdered?"

"That's right."

"The Butcher got butchered?"

"Kind of ironic," Cliff said.

The Lieutenant sat back in his chair and stared at the ceiling.

"I found evidence in his house that tied him to the twelve unsolved Midway Butcher murders," Cliff enthused.

"What kind of evidence?"

"The mother lode. I've got DNA. Fingerprint matches. The instruments of torture he used when he committed the crimes. Gloves. Knives. Zip ties. Rope. Bloody clothing. Keepsakes he kept that belonged to the victims. The sicko even videotaped all his murders. Every one of them is on his computer."

"Good work, Cliff. This is going to make a lot of people happy," the Lieutenant said with no emotion.

The Lieutenant would be genuinely relieved even if he didn't show it in his stoic demeanor. This was a headline case. The media was having a field day with the fact that a serial killer was on the loose in Chicago and his detectives had unsuccessfully tried for four years to find him. It reflected negatively on the Lieutenant and the whole department.

"Did you talk to Gerke?" he asked.

Lou Gerke was the lead detective on the Midway Butcher cases.

"I did talk to Lou. He would've been here, but he's in the process of notifying all the victim's families."

"A lot of women in Chicago between the ages of twenty and forty will sleep better tonight."

Cliff nodded. He could see the wheels spinning in the Lieutenant's mind. More than likely, a press conference would be called. The mayor, commissioner, and the lieutenant would take a victory lap. Thankfully, Cliff wouldn't be invited. Gerke might since he was lead detective. It didn't matter to Cliff. He preferred to remain behind the scenes.

"So, that's what I've been doing," Cliff said. "Getting my ducks in a row."

"Is it a slam dunk?" the Lieutenant asked. Meaning, was the case actually solved. The last thing he'd want was to get in front of the media and get it wrong.

"A hundred percent."

"Scratch what I said earlier. You can keep your job for at least a month then."

"I appreciate that."

"Any leads on who murdered Lederman? He deserves a medal."

"She deserves a medal," Cliff corrected. Phrased in a way for ultimate shock value. Which he accomplished. The Lieutenant's eyebrow made a second journey up his forehead.

"Butcher was killed by a woman?" he asked, incredulously.

"Yes. Although, she doesn't deserve a medal," Cliff said. "Lederman was killed by the Clown Slayer."

"What? How do you know?"

Both of the Lieutenant's eyebrows raised this time. Like he didn't believe it.

"Her DNA is all over the place. I've got red lipstick on a glass. The Butcher's wounds were made with a scalpel. She's definitely the one who killed the Butcher."

The Lieutenant ran both hands through his mostly bald hair. Most police supervisors went their entire careers without dealing with a serial killer. Chicago had been terrorized by two over the last few years. A man who preyed on women and a woman who killed men. Both with savagery usually only seen in horror movies.

"Imagine that," the Lieutenant said. "Did she leave behind any clues as to her identity?"

"No. But there's a lot of evidence to go over. I figured Sammy would be the one to follow up on it."

Sammy "the Possum" Poser was the lead detective on the Clown Slayer murders.

"We need to get right on it."

Cliff let out a sigh. Reminded of the fact that a detective's work was never done. Solve one case and another one was on the desk crying out for attention. From the Lieutenant's perspective, tell the press you caught one serial killer, and the follow up question would be, why haven't you caught the other one?

"Is it a coincidence?" the Lieutenant asked.

Cliff knew what he was asking. He'd already been wondering the same thing. Did they know each other? Were the two serial killers working together? Did one turn on the other? Was it a random meeting? Did the Butcher simply choose the wrong victim? If so, how did she get the better of him?

"I don't know," Cliff said, honestly. "Too early to tell."

According to Sammy Poser and Lou Gerke, many in the department wondered if the two were related. The prevailing opinion was that they weren't. Cliff didn't know enough about either case to form an opinion. Didn't matter anyway. In a matter of minutes, he could wash his hands of the whole matter. A special division of the department handled serial killers. Cliff wasn't a part of that team and didn't want to be. His experience was handling individual homicides.

"I assume you talked to Possum," the Lieutenant said.

"I did and filled him in."

Sammy Poser was nicknamed Possum for a number of reasons. Good and bad. He was crafty like a possum. An excellent detective, known for outwitting killers like possums outwitted hunters.

More to the point, Sammy was known for his obsessive self-grooming. Apparently, possums were notorious for always cleaning themselves as well. The other detectives used the opportunity to rag on him. In that vein, Sammy fit the persona perfectly. He was a strapping good looking man with a full head of hair. Which he constantly combed whenever he saw a mirror.

Rumor had it that his police locker was full of hair products.

"Did Sammy confirm it's her?" the Lieutenant asked.

"Yes. Everything fits the M.O. The red lipstick. The wounds to the victim. It's her. It's only a matter of time until DNA confirms it."

The Clown Slayer was given the moniker because red lipstick was always found at the scene. The killer's signature. The men in the department had other off-colored names for her. The Cleavage Cleaver Killer. The Red Widow Maker. Cereal Killer. Sicker Mom, Heart Breaker. Home Wrecker. To name a few.

"I've got all my files in order and am ready to hand them off to Sammy," Cliff said.

The Lieutenant shook his head from side to side. "I want you to work with him on this case. He could use a partner."

"I don't have any experience with serial killers."

"This will give you some. I'd like a new set of eyes on it. Sammy hasn't made much progress. The numbers keep adding up. I think Lederman makes ten killings now. You're the best I have at solving homicides."

Before Cliff could offer an objection, the Lieutenant explained, "Detectives working serial killers sometimes get caught up in the big picture. They get overwhelmed by all the murders and evidence and try to solve all the cases at once. You're not like that, Cliff. You're good at solving one murder. In my view, if you solve one, you solve them all. Focus on Lederman. That's the freshest."

"Will Sammy have a problem with me invading his space?"

"If he does, then have him see me. I doubt it though. He'll appreciate the help. He's a good guy. Get to know him. Spend some time together away from the office. You'll become friends. You'll be partners for a while. He's got a new girlfriend. Introduce her to Julia. They'll hit it off."

"Julia's busy with the new baby."

The Lieutenant waved his hand dismissively.

"That's what babysitters are for."

Cliff laughed. "Tell that to Julia. She won't leave the baby. Not even to go out to dinner. You know how new mothers are."

"That's temporary. Before long she'll be begging you to take her out. You get my point. Get in Sammy's back pocket. Become his new best friend. I think the two of you can learn a lot from each other."

"Will do."

At first, Cliff was hesitant. Now he was excited for the new opportunity. His mind was already spinning like a computer since he was back on the case. He had mentally checked out of it. He was all in again.

"One other thing," the Lieutenant said.

"What?"

"It might be dangerous."

Cliff laughed. "Every time I strap on my gun, I realize how dangerous it is."

The Lieutenant leaned forward in his chair. His facial expression turned as serious as a surgeon about to perform open heart surgery.

"Sammy's been getting death threats from the Clown Slayer. Menacing stuff. She knows who he is. Where he lives. She threatened his girlfriend. That's part of why I want you on the case. So he has backup."

Cliff's heart skipped one, maybe two beats. An anxiety suddenly flooded his emotions.

"You know my history," he said.

"That's why I'm telling you. This case could get dicey."

Cliff's first wife was killed in a drive-by shooting. The murder committed by a gang called the Strikers. Retaliation because Cliff had put one of their own away for murder.

He married Julia a few years later. She got in the crosshairs of one of his cases as well. Cliff was investigating a high-profile murder. One night, he and Julia were attacked by rioters while Cliff was tracking down a lead. Julia was in a coma for a week. The doctors didn't know if she would survive.

He almost lost a second wife because of his job.

Because of that, Julia had taken a lower profile on his cases. She used to go with him to look at a crime scene or interrogate a witness or suspect. Not anymore. Not since they had a child. Risky enough that one parent put his life on the line every day. They couldn't risk the baby growing up without both parents.

The Lieutenant was essentially giving him an opportunity to decline the case. Normally, he didn't have that option. Cases were assigned and he lived with it.

This was different. That gave Cliff pause. If the Lieutenant thought Cliff's life was in danger, and possibly Julia's, then the threat was more serious than Cliff had even imagined.

Everything inside of him screamed not to take the case.

"I'll help out," Cliff said reluctantly.

"Keep Julia out of it and you should be okay," the Lieutenant said.

"I will."

"Watch Sammy's back. This lady is dangerous."

"If we solve the case and arrest her, then we don't have to worry about it."

"That's the spirit. Now go do just that."

Cliff got up and left the office. Wondering if he was making a big mistake.

4

Rita had changed their lives. For the better.

The nine-month-old baby girl was named after Julia's sister. Since the baby was born, Cliff had been much better at getting home from work on time. Their new family routine was set and working well.

They had dinner together at six. Cliff spent an hour or so playing with Rita while Julia had time to herself. After that, they bathed Rita together and got her ready for bed. She was always in bed by eight. Most nights, she slept through the night. They felt very fortunate.

After the baby was asleep, they started to unwind and spend time with each other. To the extent they could, considering they were both exhausted. Regardless of how tired they were, a conversation was mandatory. It kept them connected, even if only superficially. The weekends were when they had more time and energy for each other.

That night, they stayed in the living room to talk. If they went into the bedroom, they'd both start yawning, and have a hard time staying awake.

"How was your day?" Julia asked.

"I had a good day," he said. "I solved a case that made the Lieutenant happy."

Cliff was determined not to mention the serial killers.

"That's good. Rita and I had a good day, too."

Fortunately, Julia avoided any probing questions about work. She yawned which caused the same reflex in him. She seemed satisfied keeping things light as well.

They talked for about twenty minutes. After they ran out of things to say, Julia went and drew a bath for herself. Cliff went to the kitchen table and pulled out the Clown Slayer file. The case file was thick but well organized. Sammy had done a good job highlighting the important information.

Cliff zeroed in on an FBI profiler's report. A while back, the Lieutenant brought in an FBI expert to give them an idea who they might be looking for. Reading the report gave him a new kick of energy.

The first part of the report discussed women serial killers in general. The statistics were shocking. One in six were female. Sixty-four total through the history of the United States from the 1800s to today.

The violence wasn't always against males. Half of the killers murdered at least one female. Shockingly, a number of their victims were children or the elderly. Cliff would've thought women would have more compassion for the most vulnerable in our society.

Profit and revenge were the predominant driving motives. Some women killed large numbers to steal social security or welfare checks. Some robbed their victims. A smaller percentage did it for control. A majority had a strong hatred for men. Sex wasn't generally a motive.

A surprising number of female serial killers were health care workers.

Cliff scrolled through some of the pictures of past notorious women who killed large numbers of victims. Most were older. Less attractive. Hardened. Almost all had been abused as children. Many were prostitutes.

The part of the report about the women's approach to killing brought a smile to Cliff's face, even though the subject matter was chilling. Female serial killers tended to be more efficient. Less messy. The crime scenes were less bloody.

Cliff could see that. Women would tend to be better prepared. More meticulous.

Surgical.

The Clown Slayer was all of those things. Cliff tried to form a picture of her in his head. He didn't picture someone older. Haggard looking. He pictured young and vivacious. For whatever reason.

Julia suddenly walked in.

Cliff closed the file quickly. She obviously noticed.

"What are you working on?" she asked.

He hesitated.

Julia sat down in one of the kitchen chairs next to him with her elbows on the table and her knees under her. Cliff got a whiff of the familiar flowery scent of her bath crystals.

"You wouldn't be interested," Cliff said dismissively.

His wife had just spent the last hour relaxing in a hot bath. He wasn't about to talk about such macabre things as a female serial killer who tortured her victims.

The crime scene photos were in a file on the table. Cliff nonchalantly picked them up and stuck them in the accordion file. The action wasn't lost on her.

"This is just work stuff," Cliff explained. "I got assigned a new case."

"Why don't you want me to see it?" she asked.

"It's pretty gruesome stuff."

"I know what you do for a living, Cliff. You solve murders. You used to take me to the morgue, for goodness sake."

Cliff shrugged his shoulders.

"You're a mother now," he said sheepishly. "I want to protect you from the gruesome stuff."

A huge smile formed on her face. "Trust me. I've seen some pretty gruesome stuff coming out of both ends of your daughter."

That caused them both to laugh, releasing a little of the tension. Cliff did miss those times when they used to joke around and she'd help him with cases. It seemed like their lives had become too serious.

"Tell me about the case. It must be a big one. That's a lot of paperwork."

As if talking about female serial killers was going to help them become less serious.

Really, how could he talk to her about it? The Lieutenant's admonition aside, his baby was sleeping in the next room. It was after nine o'clock. They should be in their bedroom kissing. Snuggling. Whatever. Winding down. Not discussing depraved women who butchered men. That discussion was the things nightmares were made from.

"I'm not sure I should go into it," Cliff said hesitantly. "It's a murder. You know. It's pretty bad."

"It's okay. I appreciate that you're trying to shelter me from your work. But I miss it."

"I miss talking to you about work as well. I'm just not sure this is the one to discuss."

"I'm bored. I spent the whole day talking to a baby. The only conversations I have now include the words goo goo and gaa gaa. I don't remember the last adult conversation I had. Probably with the checkout lady at the grocery store. My vocabulary is shrinking. I talk in small syllables now. I'm becoming a blabbering mom. I'd like to have a grown-up discussion for a change."

Cliff rubbed his eyes, trying to buy time to come up with an excuse.

Julia pushed his shoulder playfully.

"Come on. Let me help. I haven't done anything productive for society in months."

"You're raising our child! That's productive. And you take care of me."

Julia rolled her eyes.

"You know what I mean," she said. "I miss work." Her lips twisted into a frown. "Not work per se. I miss being a part of the action. I miss challenging my mind."

Julia had taken an extended leave of absence from her work. She used to run a shelter for battered and abused women. After the baby was born, she decided to stay home and be a full-time mom. She'd eventually go back to work once the baby could go to a mother's day out program or start kindergarten.

She persisted. "Come on, Cliff." Her voice was shrill and whiny now.

"Okay."

What could it hurt? He'd leave out the most horrific details.

"I solved the Midway Butcher cases," he blurted out.

Julia's tired eyes widened.

"That's huge, Cliff. I'm so proud of you. I didn't think you handled serial killer cases."

"I don't. I lucked into it. Somebody murdered him. I went to investigate and was able to tie him to the other murders. The Lieutenant was thrilled."

"I can imagine. You deserve a little luck every now and then. I'm glad to hear you finally caught him."

"He was killed by another serial killer."

"Wow!" Julia's mouth gaped. "That's weird."

"Tell me about it. That's what I'm working on now. My job is to find his murderer."

"Why are you working on it? I thought you only handled homicides. Aren't serial killers handled by another department?"

"The Lieutenant wants me to look at it. He thinks I might be good at it."

"Are you sure you want to? You're getting into some heavy psychological stuff. These people are sick."

"I'm not sure I do. But the Lieutenant insisted."

Cliff didn't want to tell her why. Sammy's life was in danger, and he wanted Cliff around to have his back. She'd only worry. He could hardly blame her, since he had a little bit of trepidation about the whole thing as well.

Especially after reading more about serial killers. They didn't want to get caught, but they were willing to take a lot of risks. Cliff doubted the Clown Slayer would think twice about killing Sammy or his girlfriend.

Fortunately, the killer didn't know about Julia and Rita. Cliff wanted to keep it that way.

"How many victims are there?" Julia asked.

"Ten. Including the latest one."

"That's a lot."

Julia picked up the FBI profiler report that was still lying on the kitchen table. She turned to the first page. Then looked up.

"The serial killer is a woman?" she said in disbelief.

"Yep. She's called the Clown Slayer."

"Why's that?"

"She wears bright red lipstick. That's her signature. Serial killers like to leave a calling card, so to speak. So that we know it was them. It's like a game. They want to get credit for the murders and leave clues daring us to catch them. The killers take pride in the numbers."

Julia nodded. Her head was now buried in the report. Cliff kept talking knowing she had the ability to multitask. Better than anyone he'd ever met before.

Cliff told her everything he knew about the killer and victims.

Julia looked up from the report and stared off in the distance. Deep in thought. "I'm not sure this report is right," she finally said.

"An expert with the FBI wrote it."

"I know. But it says the killer is timid, vulnerable. Lacks self-confidence. Might have a learning disability."

"I read that."

"It says she has below average intelligence. I don't see that."

"What do you see?" he asked.

She kept reading. Summarizing aloud as she went along. "The Clown Slayer is socially inadequate. Unskilled. She has a low birth order status. Was disciplined harshly as a child. Lives alone. Works near the crime scene. That doesn't sound like your killer to me."

Cliff resisted the urge to argue the point. Instead, he simply explained the rationale behind it. "The profiler differentiated between an organized and an unorganized crime scene. According to the report, these murders are classified as disorganized. Apparently, this fits the profile of a disorganized killer."

"It sounds to me like she was an *organized* killer," Julie retorted. "Didn't she use a scalpel? Didn't you say the wounds were surgical?"

"I tend to agree with you. The crime scene was a mixed bag. It looked messy and random. But it seemed to have an organization and precision about it. A method to the madness so to speak."

"What if the crime scene was made to look disorganized?" Julia said. "What if the killer knows about profiling and is trying to manipulate the scene to throw you off track?"

"That's possible."

"That'd make her highly intelligent. On the genius end of the scale."

Cliff nodded.

Julia continued. "The profiler said that the woman was a prostitute in her background. An exhibitionist. Which is why the bodies were left in clear view and weren't disposed of."

Julia shook her head from side to side.

"I disagree. I see the opposite. From what you described, I see a woman with a lot of self-confidence. Above average in beauty and intellect. I'd say she is a professional worker. Skilled in a craft. With a good job."

"Why do you say that?" he asked with an inflection of curiosity in his tone.

"The red lipstick," Julia said matter-of-factly. "The women I know who wear red lipstick are trying to make a statement. They are bold. Aggressive. Red lipstick is associated with power and strength."

"The profiler acknowledges that but says the killer applies the lipstick after the fact. After the victim is dead. That shows her insecurity. She gets bold when it's safe to be in control and confident. She writes on the wall with red lipstick. Or on the dead body. It's a power move, but after she's accomplished the deed, and there is no more threat."

"You said the lipstick was on the drinking glass. That means she was wearing it."

"I suppose. She could've applied it to her lips after the victim was dead."

Julia shook her head again.

"All of her victims are professionals. Good looking. Why would they take a frail, timid, mousy middle aged woman home with them?"

"That's a good question. Maybe because she'd be easier to get into the sack."

"I'd say your killer is attractive, employed, educated, cunning, with a lot of self-control. Meticulous. Ruthless. I'd even call her charming. She seduces her victims. They are eager to let her. Because she's beautiful. That's why they take her home with them. They are proud to be seen with her."

Cliff didn't respond. He sat there thinking about what she said. It sounded right. He couldn't discount the profiler's opinion, but when he pictured the murderer, she looked more like what Julia was describing.

"The profile says the woman was likely abused as a child," Cliff said. "Maybe she's attractive but also insecure and timid because of the abuse."

"I've seen the ladies who come into the shelter who've been battered. Not once were they wearing red lipstick. They are highly anxious. Desperate. They are rock bottom in self-esteem. They feel bad. Like it's their fault. They don't have the strength to get away from their abusers. Much less kill ten men."

Julia continued. "The profiler said that seventy-four percent of women serial killers do it for the money. What's the financial motive here?"

"We haven't found one. There were no signs of a robbery."

"I think the killer does it for a different reason. Revenge is my guess. She doesn't need the money."

Cliff remembered the death threats sent to Sammy and his girl-friend. The woman was brash. Willing to follow the lead detective on the case. Not afraid to contact him.

Julia was right. This lady had confidence.

"Here's the most chilling sentence in the entire report," Cliff said.

"What's that?"

"The Clown Slayer is living in plain sight."

5

Cliff worried that getting Julia to leave Rita with a babysitter for an evening to have dinner with Sammy and his girlfriend would be more difficult than getting a full confession out of a murder suspect. Turned out, she was into it and took no convincing at all. In fact, she was downright giddy about it and had been since the day Cliff mentioned it.

"I didn't think you'd want to leave the baby," Cliff had said to her.

"Are you kidding me?" she replied. "The opportunity to get out of the house and be a normal person for an evening. Why wouldn't I want to do that?"

"We would've done this sooner if I'd known you wanted to. We need to communicate more."

"You know where to find me. I'm always here at the house. Communicate away."

Even finding a babysitter wasn't hard. A young woman at church worked at the nursery and watched Rita on Sundays. The college student was already familiar with Rita and was dependable. She was even available during the day.

Julia started picking out what to wear four days before the scheduled dinner. According to Sammy, the restaurant he chose was on the dressier side, which made Julia even happier.

"I get to wear a dress," she said. "I haven't worn a dress in months."

Cliff looked at his watch and let out a groan that Julia couldn't hear. They were thirty minutes from needing to leave and his wife still hadn't decided on what to wear.

"Does this dress make me look fat?" she suddenly asked Cliff out of the blue.

She was trying on the third of four dresses she had picked out for the occasion. At that moment, she was standing in front of the full-length mirror and kept looking at herself from all angles. Turning sideways. Pressing her stomach in. Trying to flatten it with her hand.

"This dress makes me look fat, doesn't it?" she asked for a second time when Cliff didn't answer.

He'd rather smash in the door of a suspect's house with his gun drawn than respond to that question.

It did make him smile.

Julia looked amazing, considering she'd just had a baby nine months before. While she wasn't back to her size zero or her eight BMI, she probably never would be. Cliff couldn't tell much difference in how she looked, but Julia could.

He understood. A few pounds had crept into his midsection over the past two years. Julia never mentioned it, even though he felt self-conscious when he took his shirt off. Before they were married and before Rita was born, the two of them were workout fools. Obsessive in their fitness regimens. Since Rita, there wasn't the time nor the energy.

Julia got more exercise than Cliff. Every morning, unless it was raining, snowing, or the temperature was bitter cold, she put Rita in a baby carriage and took her for a two-to-five-mile brisk walk.

Cliff could only join them on the weekends. The rest of the week, he was too busy to work out. His gym membership had gone mostly unused. As each birthday ticked off, he noticed it harder to lose the weight and regain the level of fitness he once enjoyed. He probably never would. He was okay with it.

More so than Julia. Apparently.

She let out another painful groan.

"I can't go!" Julia said, with the exasperation of a grounded teenager.

Cliff still hadn't said anything. He knew it best to keep out of the conversation she was having with herself.

"I don't have anything to wear!" she said in her most whiny voice. "Everything I have is form fitting. I can't do tight anymore. I need loose. My baby pooch is showing. I look like a kangaroo."

She let out an exaggerated sigh and disappeared into the closet. When she came out, she held another dress up to her body and examined it in front of the mirror. Then let out a sound of disgust.

Cliff still refused to get sucked in.

"What are you smiling about?" she said to him.

He couldn't help himself even though he'd tried to keep it off his face. "This brings back old memories," he answered. "B.R. Before Rita. You had a hard time deciding what to wear back then as well."

He'd seen this circus juggling act before.

"This is different. All my clothes are for young skinny girls!" Julia exclaimed. "Who haven't had a baby? I'm too old to wear these dresses. I need a whole new wardrobe. Ugh. I'm going to have to start shopping in the old lady's section."

Julia disappeared into the closet again. She reemerged holding a sweater.

"I can wear slacks with a sweater," she said. "That'll hide my big fat belly."

Cliff walked up to Julia and put his arms around her. "What you have on is perfect?" he said. "You look amazing."

She frowned.

He took the sweater out of her hand and stood beside her while they looked in the mirror. Julia was wearing a black dress with sleeves that went below her elbows. The dress was slightly above her knees. Form fitting, but not overly tight.

Her hair was only three quarters dry. Her makeup wasn't done. While they still had thirty minutes until they had to leave, they weren't to the point of picking out shoes yet. That alone could take the full half hour.

Cliff started to get nervous that they'd be late. Then forced in a breath. In the past, Julia had always made it on time. Maybe with only seconds to spare, but she was always ready at the appointed time.

That was then. He wasn't sure if he could count on the same thing now. Post pregnancy. Post Rita. They were in uncharted territory. He needed her to make a decision on the dress. His mind raced to try and figure out how to make that happen.

"I think you should wear the dress you have on," he said. "It's perfect. You look as beautiful as you did the day I met you."

"That's sweet."

She put her arms around his neck and kissed him. "But you have to say that," she said dismissively. Then abruptly turned back toward the mirror.

Her eyes suddenly widened.

A smile came on her face. That was an encouraging sign.

"There's one good thing about having a baby," Julia said, pushing up on her chest. Her tone had noticeably changed.

"What's that?" Cliff asked.

"I have cleavage now. Have you noticed?"

He had.

"Since I started breastfeeding Rita, I'm bigger. I'm filling this dress out nicely. This dress does look good on me."

Cliff couldn't help but smile again. When he first met Julia, she was an A cup. Exacerbated by the excess exercising and that's just how God made her. She had bemoaned that fact on more than one occasion.

Having the baby had reapportioned her body in a good way. Cliff could see what she was talking about. She did look good in that dress.

Julia went back into the closet and returned with shoes on con-firming she was going with that dress. She had two different styles of shoes on her feet.

A wave of relief came over him. Once they crossed that line, she never went back.

"Which one do you like the best?" she asked.

This wasn't Cliff's first rodeo. It didn't matter which one he picked, she'd choose the other. It didn't bother him anymore, that's just how the game worked.

"The one on the left foot," he said, figuring she'd like the other one better.

"Okay."

Julia turned and went back in the closet. Surprisingly, she re-turned wearing the shoes he'd picked out.

Apparently, the old rules didn't apply.

He felt better now that they had a dress and shoes. That was nine tenths of the battle.

"I'm going to jump in the shower," Cliff said, realizing he only had twenty minutes to get ready.

"You're so lucky," she said. "You can be ready in five minutes."

"Probably six," Cliff said, "since I don't know what I'm wearing."

Julia pushed him toward the bathroom. She gave him a funny face that looked more like a scowl except that he knew she was only kidding.

He felt comfortable leaving her alone. Julia would be ready on time.

The babysitter was already there as well. She'd come early so they'd be able to get ready without distractions.

Cliff got his shower and was dressed with time to spare. They went into the front room, where the young woman was on the floor with Rita. The baby was lying on her stomach kicking her legs. It wouldn't be long until she started crawling.

After going over the instructions for the third time, and Rita hav-ing endured far too many kisses from her momma, they were in the car and on their way. About halfway there, Julia asked, "What do we know about Sammy and his girlfriend?"

"I don't know much. I've never met her. Knowing Sammy, she's a knockout."

She nodded.

Julia had met Sammy several times. At Christmas parties and around the station when she visited Cliff there.

"What's his girlfriend's name?"

"I don't know."

"Cliff Ford. You didn't ask her name! Oh Cliff. What kind of a detective are you? You're such a man. We girls need details."

"What do you want me to do?"

"At least ask for the name of the person we're having dinner with."

"I did ask. I think. Or he mentioned it. I just don't remember what it is. Candy or something like that."

"Candy? I don't think so. She's probably not a stripper. I bet she knows my name."

"That's different. Sammy has met you. He already knows your name."

"I'm embarrassed."

"I'm sure we'll find out her name."

"Hopefully, when Sammy introduces us, he'll say it. I don't want to have to ask."

Cliff wanted to change the subject.

"Sammy and I agreed that we're not going to discuss work," he said.

Julia made a gesture of locking her mouth and tossing the key away. "That's fine by me. I don't want to talk about murders and serial killers with someone I just met. She might be squeamish. "

Cliff shook his head from side to side. "Apparently not. Sammy says his girlfriend... Katie Ann,"

Julia rolled her eyes.

"Apparently, she likes to talk about work all the time," Cliff continued. "She's very inquisitive. Murders interest her."

Carol Ann. Kellie Ann. Sammy's girlfriend's name was something like that.

They arrived at the restaurant and Cliff pulled into the valet stand.

"This is a fancy restaurant," Julia said, as the valet opened her door. "I'm glad I'm wearing a dress and not that sweater."

They'd never been there or even knew about it. Sammy picked it out. Cliff wasn't wearing a tie, but did have a jacket over his polo shirt even though Sammy assured him a jacket wasn't required.

Once inside, they found Sammy in the bar area. He stood to his feet when he saw them. A stunningly beautiful girl was immediately at his arm. The two of them looked like they'd just stepped out of a GQ magazine.

Sammy kissed Julia on both cheeks. Ignoring Cliff.

"Let me introduce you to Cami Ann," Sammy said.

Oh. That's right.

It suddenly rang a bell.

"My mom's the only one who calls me Cami Ann," she said with a pleasant smile. "I'm usually in trouble when she does so. Most people just call me Cami."

Her smile was wide and mesmerizing. Cami had dark brown hair and deep rich eyes.

"Or just call me Cam."

Cami held out her hand and Julia shook it first, then Cliff. Her grip was strong. She looked him right in the eye. She was probably five foot eight and appeared to be extremely fit. Cliff was careful not to look down. She definitely had a lot more going for her in that area than his wife and wasn't afraid to display it.

Not distastefully. Just more provocative than how his wife dressed.

"I put our name in with the hostess," Sammy said. "Can I get you guys a drink?"

Both Julia and Cliff declined. Julia sometimes had wine at dinner. Cliff rarely drank. Being a detective, he always felt like he was on call even when he wasn't. He never knew when a situation might arise. Both Sammy and Cliff were required to carry their weapons and badges at all times. They were both packing heat at the restaurant. If a situation did come up for some reason, he didn't want alcohol to be in his system.

Then he remembered. Julia wouldn't drink either because she was breastfeeding. She hadn't had alcohol in more than eighteen months.

Sammy seemed satisfied with the answer even though they hadn't provided an explanation. It appeared that Sammy and Cami were on their second drinks.

The hostess came into the bar area within a couple of minutes and notified Sammy their table was ready. She led them through several rooms to a nice table in the back.

They hadn't been seated for ten seconds when a waitress came and took their drink orders. Cliff and Julia ordered water. Sammy ordered a bottle of wine.

The conversation was casual but friendly until the waitress returned with drinks and bread. Mostly the girls talked and the guys listened.

Cami seemed nervous. As did Julia. But they hit it off immediately. Cami was personable. She asked about the baby. About Julia's work at the women's shelter. Where Julia was from. How long they'd been married.

Cami had a way of making Julia feel like she was the only person in the room and Cliff could tell that this was good for Julia. It took a while before Julia could turn the conversation back on Cami.

"What do you do for work?" Julia asked Cami.

The waitress interrupted that question to take their order.

"Can you give us a couple of more minutes?" Sammy said.

The lady left and the conversation came to a halt for a few minutes while they pored over the menu. They didn't see the waitress for several minutes.

Julia leaned forward. "I think the waitress won't come until we all close our menus."

The girls still had theirs open. They both closed them, and the conversation resumed.

"What were we talking about?" Sammy asked.

"They asked what I do," Cami answered.

"That's right. Where do you work?" Julia asked.

"I work at Chicago Memorial Hospital."

"That's nice. What do you do?"

"I'm an anesthesiologist."

The waitress appeared ready to take their order.

6

They finished their dinner and declined dessert.

With their mouths no longer full of food, the conversation picked up steam. Mostly between the girls. Cami was engaging and friendly. Julia was as excited to be out of the house as a dog who'd been let out of a crate. She didn't want the evening to end so she kept the conversation moving.

Cliff looked at his watch several times, but the girls were oblivious to it.

"Where did the two of you meet?" Julia asked, looking at Sammy and then at Cami, although Cliff expected Cami to be the one who answered. Sammy had lost interest in the conversation a while back.

"I was stalking him," she said, jokingly. She took Sammy's hand in hers.

"She showed up on the doorstep of my apartment one day," Sammy said with a wide smile. He was on his second drink after the bottle of wine. His eyes were starting to gloss over.

Another reason Cliff wanted to leave. Sammy was getting drunk and as long as they were sitting there, it's clear he'd have a drink in front of him.

Members of the department who tracked serial killers often had drinking problems. Understandable. The stress to find the killer and prevent more murders, combined with the gruesomeness of the crimes, paid an emotional toll on the investigators. To cope, many of them turned to some form of addiction.

Cliff was already feeling the stress of the Clown Slayer case and could see why the detectives might use alcohol to medicate. His individual cases were stressful enough. In this case, it felt like the weight of the entire city of Chicago rested on their shoulders.

"That's not exactly how it happened," Cami said, interlocking her fingers with Sammy's. "I happened to be in his neighborhood, and we bumped into each other. We had an instant connection and here we are. Six months later, he still hasn't dumped me."

"And I don't plan too," Sammy said, raising his glass in the air. "Why would I? Look at you."

He downed the last of the drink in his glass not seemingly bothered by the fact he was drinking alone.

Cami smiled and winked at him. "Thank you. You're not so bad to look at yourself. I think I'll keep you around a little longer."

They both ran their hands through their own hair at the same time. The two would be neck and neck in a contest to see who had the shiniest coif.

Sammy looked around for the waitress. Presumably to order another drink. Cliff was glad she was nowhere in sight.

"Where did you go to med school?" Julia asked Cami.

Cliff resisted the urge to look at his watch again. It'd be too obvious.

"I got my undergraduate degree from the University of Nebraska," Cami said.

"Is that where you grew up?" Cliff asked, so he could be part of the conversation and manipulate it into ending as soon as possible.

"I grew up in Omaha. I'm a Midwest girl. I went to med school at the University of Minnesota. Did my residency in the Twin Cities. Then I moved to Chicago a few years back."

"Will you ever go back to Nebraska?" Cliff asked.

"I hope not. I love Chicago. I've become a big city girl."

Cami reached into her bag and produced a thin tube of lipstick. She applied the bright red to her lips.

Cliff now understood what Julia meant the night before. Cami was the kind of girl who could pull off the color red on her lips. Maybe the Clown Slayer was a beautiful model type after all.

Cami deposited the lipstick back in her bag and leaned forward in her chair and put her elbows on the table. Her look and tone turned serious.

"Cliff, I hear you're working on the Clown Slayer killings with Sammy," she said.

Cliff felt a grimace approach his face, but he beat it back. They'd successfully avoided the topic and he thought they might get through the evening without broaching it. He quickly scanned his thoughts for a way to end the evening and avoid it altogether.

The waitress arrived at the table at that moment and Sammy ordered another drink. Not the interruption Cliff was looking for. They weren't leaving anytime soon.

Cliff let out an indiscernible sigh. He still didn't want to answer the question but didn't see the harm in confirming information Cami already knew.

"Yes, Sammy and I are partners on the case. Although, he's still the lead detective."

"He tells me that you don't think the FBI profiler got it right," Cami said. She turned her head to the side in an inquisitive manner.

Cliff winced. Was there anything Sammy didn't tell her? He shouldn't judge. He'd shown the report to Julia.

"We're still working on a profile," Cliff said. "These things are complicated. Profiling is not an exact science."

"This woman is fascinating, isn't she?" Cami said.

"That's not exactly how I'd characterize it, but she is an enigma for sure," Cliff responded.

"I agree with you," Cami said. "I don't think the profile does her justice. I think the killer is someone pretty. Like Julia."

Julia blushed. Her cheeks became a brighter red than Cami's lips.

"It's hard to say," Cliff said. "There aren't very many female serial killers. Profiling is difficult for someone this emotionally depraved.

It takes a sick person to do what this woman does. How do you profile that?"

Cami didn't respond but Cliff thought he perceived a slight but controlled grimace.

"I feel sorry for the killer," Julia said, in a compassionate tone. "She must've had severe trauma in her past to do what she's doing."

"Who knows why people do what they do?" Cami said.

"Maybe she was abused as a child or something," Julia said. "I used to see it all the time at the shelter. Women who are abused have deep emotional scars that can turn into hatred and anger. Even violence. I've seen women actually kill their abusers, but it's rare."

"That's because they feel helpless in our male dominated society," Cami said.

Cliff didn't want to go down that rabbit hole.

A sudden silence allowed the last comment to linger over the table like a puff of smoke from a cigar.

"Do you think the woman is offended by the moniker, the Clown Slayer?" Cami asked. "That's kind of disrespectful don't you think?"

"I haven't thought about that," Julia said. "But you're right. Women don't like to be called clowns."

"The killer doesn't know that name," Cliff answered sternly. "That's a name we came up with internally in the department. The press hasn't picked up on it. Please don't ever repeat it."

"I won't," Cami said.

She sat back in her chair and moved her head from side to side in a stretching motion. Maybe she was ready to go as well.

"I won't either," Julia said.

Cami didn't drop it, signifying she wasn't ready for the conversation to end. "The name doesn't really fit the woman anyway. Midway Butcher was better. So typical. The man serial killer gets the better name."

Cliff couldn't tell if Cami was serious or kidding.

"As if any name is good enough for this sicko," Cliff retorted. He didn't like the direction the conversation was headed. That's the second time Cami had gotten in a dig toward men.

"I agree with Julia," Cami said, ignoring Cliff's comment. "It seems like there's a better name for her. Just because the woman wears red lipstick doesn't mean she's a clown."

That's not exactly what Julia said.

The waitress brought Sammy's drink and sat it down on the table. Number five if Cliff was counting. Plus the bottle of wine which he split with Cami. Sammy seemed perfectly content to stay out of the conversation.

Cliff should take his lead.

Sammy took a big swig of his drink. There's no way Cliff was going to let Sammy drive home.

Cliff wasn't sure whose turn it was to speak, so he said what was on his mind against his better judgment.

"I don't care if the woman feels disrespected or not," Cliff said, roughly. "She doesn't deserve any respect. She's a cold-blooded killer. And a coward."

"Why do you say she's a coward?" Cami asked, as her eyes widened somewhat. "It seems like it takes a lot of courage to go back to a man's house, overpower him, and then kill him. Sounds like she's brave."

"She doesn't overpower them. She drugs them. That hardly makes it fair. It's not like she's skilled at what she does. Anybody can overpower a victim if he's unconscious."

Cami must've sensed that Cliff was getting annoyed because she lightened the mood.

"We should call her the Dating Game Killer," Cami said, jokingly.

"That's already been taken," Sammy said, perking up somewhat. He was clearly drowsy from the alcohol.

"A man in the 1970s killed between fifty and two hundred and thirty women," he continued. "He appeared on the *Dating Game* when he was in the midst of his killing spree."

"What happened to him?" Julia asked.

"He was sentenced to death but died in prison before they could fry him."

"Lady in Red," Cami said with a sly grin. "That'd be a good name."

"What about Jack... the Zipper?" Sammy said, laughing loudly. So much so, that a couple at the next table, looked over at him.

Sammy was partially slurring his words and acting silly. "Oh... that's right. He's a she. What's the girl's name for Jack?"

He laughed again. Then glared at the patrons sitting at the adjacent table for looking at him a second time.

"What about The Lipstick Killer?" Cami asked.

"Already been taken," Sammy interjected again. "William Heirens. 1945. Killed three women in Chicago."

"You really know your serial killers," Julia observed.

"It's my job."

"Why are you so interested in the woman's name, Cami?" Cliff asked.

"She fancies herself as a sort of amateur sleuth," Sammy answered.

"It's more of a morbid curiosity," Cami said. "I watched a lot of horror movies growing up. It's interesting to watch it play out in real life."

"I don't find it interesting at all. It's a tragedy. And how did we get on this topic?" Cliff asked. "This is not exactly normal fodder for after dinner conversation."

"I like it," Cami said. "It's interesting."

"I like it, too," Julia said. "Cliff and I used to talk about his work all the time."

"You girls are sick," Cliff said, trying to interject some humor.

"What you men do is much more interesting than what I do twenty-four hours a day," Julia said. "All I talk about are teething and baby rattles."

Cliff got a smirk on his face.

Julia saw it and glared at him.

"Do you know why most serial killers are men?" Cliff asked.

Julia rolled her eyes with exaggeration.

"I must warn you," Julia said to Cami, "my husband has a joke for every subject."

"I'll take the bait. Why are serial killers always men?" Cami asked.

"Because women like to kill one man slowly over many years."

Julia punched Cliff in the shoulder.

Cliff smiled broadly.

"That's horrible," Julia said.

"Why are there no female serial killers?" Cliff asked, wanting to build on the momentum. The lighter mood was better.

"Please stop, Cliff," Julia pleaded.

"Because after the first kill, they have to tell somebody," Cliff said with as wide a grin as possible.

Cami didn't laugh and didn't seem amused by the jokes. In fact, she seemed angry as her jaw clenched and her forehead furrowed.

"It seems like you're making fun of the woman," Cami said roughly. "All women for that matter."

"I was just joking," Cliff said, trying to backtrack.

"Lighten up, Cami. He was only trying to be funny," Sammy said.

"It's not funny," Cami said, turning the mood awkward in a matter of seconds. "Men have been making fun of women for centuries. Because they think they're better than us. They get paid more money for doing the same job. Did you know that male anesthesiologists at the hospital make fifteen percent more than women? Can you believe it?"

Cliff had clearly hit a nerve.

"That's not what I meant—" Cliff said before being interrupted.

"Men kill women all the time," Cami said. "I don't hear you making jokes about them. They abuse women left and right. Physically and emotionally. But it's the women who are stereotyped and called depraved."

"I was only making a joke."

"It's not funny. Men think women have limited job skills. That our place is in the kitchen. Having babies. We're identified as sex objects. We didn't even have the right to vote for the first hundred years of our country. Women are oppressed in our society."

"I consider my wife my equal," Cliff said defensively.

"Maybe in words. Not in action. Not really. The attitudes that oppress women are still prevalent. Men think women are biologically inferior."

"You are weaker physically."

Cliff immediately regretted saying it.

"Then why do women live longer than men," Cami argued.

"Because we're married to women," Sammy quipped, then let out a drunken giggle.

Cliff grimaced, even though he was thinking of the same joke but had the sense not to let it out of his mouth.

Cami was clearly fired up and Sammy's comment had only thrown more gasoline on the fire.

Now Cliff really wanted to get out of there.

"Did you know that more women survived concentration camps than men?" Cami said, raising her voice further. "That's because we're stronger."

"I'm not disagreeing with you," Cliff said. "All I'm saying is that killing men is not the answer. It doesn't make women stronger. The Clown Slayer is a pathetic excuse for a woman. I think she's weak. Lacks self-control. I pity her."

"I don't think she wants your pity," Cami retorted, bitterly. "I think she wants to be admired."

"Why would I admire someone who murders men?"

"Because she's strong. She refuses to be dominated by men. The woman who does this is proving to the world that men aren't stronger. Women are. If given the chance."

"Men are superior in some ways," Cliff said, no longer able to keep his mouth shut. "Women are superior in other ways."

"I'm not trying to prove women's superiority," Cami retorted with a volley of her own. "Women aren't more moral than men, we're just not as corrupted by power. Women don't have the need to prove their masculinity. Men do. Which is why they exert power and domination over women."

Cliff looked at his watch.

"Is that my cue to shut up?" Cami asked angrily.

"No. It's just that it's getting late, and we have a babysitter at home."

"Is your babysitter a girl?" Cami asked.

"Yes."

"My point exactly. Girls are put into certain roles from childhood, and they can never break out of it."

Julia was eerily silent.

"This is not a problem we're going to solve in one evening," Cliff said. "Will you excuse me? I need to use the restroom."

Cliff couldn't get out of there fast enough.

When he got back to the table, the waitress had dropped off the checks. Cliff slipped a credit card out of his wallet. Sammy had already done so.

Interesting how Cami wanted to be equal to them but made no attempt to pay the check. Cliff wasn't about to point it out.

On the drive home, Julia was unusually quiet.

"This was an interesting evening," Cliff said.

"Yes, it was."

"Cami will probably never want to see us again."

"We're actually getting together for lunch this week," Julia said. "She wants to meet Rita."

"Really?"

"We arranged it while you were in the men's room."

That didn't sound like such a good idea.

7

One week later

The problem with tracking serial killers was that an investigator needed for them to kill another person in order to create more clues. It wasn't like a normal homicide investigation. Normally, ninety-nine percent of the time, murder victims were killed by someone they knew or happened to come in contact with, and if there were multiple victims, the killings were related in some way.

An investigation of that sort generally involved finding out who had motive and opportunity. Then determining if they had an alibi. If they didn't, you kept digging. Even circumstantial cases could be proven beyond a reasonable doubt by using common sense.

In the Clown Slayer cases, common sense wasn't as helpful. No one in her right mind would kill men in this manner. She likely didn't know her victims, so the normal motives didn't apply. The three R's as Cliff called them. Revenge. Robbery. Romance.

The Clown Slayer murders were random. Without rhyme nor reason. Knowing motive wouldn't solve the case. That made finding the opportunity the most important thing. A connection existed between the victim and killer, but it wasn't obvious, and likely occurred on the spur of the moment.

The killer had to meet the unsuspecting victim, then form enough trust in a short period of time for him to feel comfortable bringing her to his house. Once there, she had to get him to offer her a drink so she could drug him. Then she had to kill him in a lengthy ritualistic style and disappear like a puff of smoke in the wind without anyone seeing her. A tall task that only someone with a high level of intelligence could pull off. Which made it a battle of wits.

The Clown Slayer was literally a needle in a haystack as big as Chicago. Two hundred and thirty-four square miles. Eight million people. There simply wasn't a small pool of potential suspects to question or check alibis.

All they could do was look for a pattern. A tedious and frustrating process.

In Cliff's mind, his talents were wasted on this investigation. The Clown Slayer had only killed ten people. Only, being the pejorative word. Ten was ten too many, but to put it in perspective, more than thirty homicides were committed in Chicago over the weekend. In one week's time, Cliff could solve six or seven of them.

But the Lieutenant had him focused on the Clown Slayer. For whatever reason, a serial killer got more attention from the powers that be. They'd rather solve the one higher profile case than the thirty. At least it felt that way.

Probably because of the media. The news outlets loved reporting on serial killers. Sensationalizing them. The public fed on the drama. The citizenry were terrified but also fascinated. If the media played it right, they could create an obsessed viewership who would watch the events unfold twenty-four seven.

With media attention, came politicians looking to show their faces on television. When the politicians were involved, all the time, money, and resources moved heaven and earth to make it look like they were doing something.

So it wasn't Cliff's call. The case was his to work indefinitely and, after a week, he was up to speed on the entire file.

Sammy and Cliff sat in a meeting room assigned exclusively to them. That's where they kept all the files. On the wall, a map pinpointed all the locations of the murders. A second map tracked the cell phone activity of the victims leading up to the murders. A third bulletin board had the word *Suspects* pinned to the top of it.

That board had nothing on it. Frustratingly void of anything. So, Cliff drew a crude picture of a clown and pinned it on the bulletin board just so it wouldn't be such a reminder that they were failing.

At the large conference table, Sammy and Cliff discussed patterns. "To catch a serial killer, you have to think like they think," Sammy said.

"That'll take some getting used to," Cliff said. "I think like an investigator."

An investigator was what the Lieutenant wanted on the case which was why Cliff was there. The Lieutenant's advice was to focus on River Lederman's murder which was what Cliff was going to do.

"I've been thinking about it," Cliff said, in his investigator voice, "and the question in my mind is, where did she meet Lederman? That's the pattern. We find out where she met him, then we can probably discover where she meets all the men."

"Could be anywhere," Sammy replied.

Cliff shook his head.

"Not really. She can't meet them where there are security cameras. That rules out public places like grocery stores, convenience stores, fitness gyms, work, or public transportation."

"Thousands of people come in and out of those places every day," Sammy retorted. "She might be more comfortable meeting them someplace where there are a lot of people. Like a grocery store. Remember the profiler's report. She's hiding in plain sight. Lederman went to a grocery store after work."

"The killer has to know that we can track the victim's movements," Cliff argued. "By their cell phones. By credit card receipts. Witness testimony. Chicago toll roads. If Lederman went to a grocery store, he probably paid with a credit card. That'll be time stamped. All we have to do is look at the security cameras and see if Lederman interacted with someone in the store. The killer is not dumb enough to show her face on a grocery store security camera."

Sammy wrote something down. Probably a note to check out the security cameras at the grocery store. Something already on Cliff's things-to-do-list. She might not be dumb enough, but Cliff would check anyway.

"She could've been in the parking lot and followed him home," Sammy said, more spit balling than anything. He surely knew that wasn't the most plausible scenario.

"There's no forced entry at any of the victim's houses," Cliff replied. "She had a drink with him. That's how she drugged him. A victim's not going to invite a perfect stranger into his home and then have a drink with her."

"If she's pretty enough."

Cliff frowned. He didn't mind the devil's advocate game to an extent. Once it got totally out in left field, he tried to bring common sense back into the equation. Cliff looked at the board with the circles. "The cell phone movement is the key to this thing. We have to track those."

"We've already done that with the first victims. We know their last cell phone pings. So that narrows it down to a certain radius."

Sammy pointed at the board. "Within each circle are hundreds of places where they could've met," Sammy added.

Cliff shook his head for a second time.

"I don't think so. Think about how difficult it would be to kill ten people and not get caught. The meeting has to be clandestine. It has to be at a place where the killer can keep her face off the camera."

"A prostitute maybe? On the street where there are no cameras."

Cliff shook his head again, for a third time. He was the one playing devil's advocate now. But this was productive. The conversation was helping him solidify what might make sense in his own mind.

"The victims all brought the woman back to their homes," Cliff said. "Who brings a prostitute home with him? They go to a hotel or do the deed in a car or a park somewhere."

"That means it's a hookup."

"Yep. Which tells me they met in a bar."

Sammy's eyes were distant, and he was deep in thought.

Cliff continued with his own imagination driving the narrative. "A bar is dark. There are a lot of people around. No one is going to remember them. She can make herself inconspicuous. Hide in plain sight. She spots a victim and strikes up a conversation. He buys her a drink. They talk. She knows what questions to ask."

"What about online?" Sammy said, interrupting his train of thought.

"I thought of that. But you've got the Midway Butcher. He's never going to give his address to a victim. We also didn't find any dating apps on his computer."

"None of the other victims either."

"The woman we are looking for is a control freak. You can't kill ten people and not get caught without being meticulous in your preparations. She has to control the narrative and the circumstances."

"So, how does she seize control?"

"By meeting in a bar. That's the most logical. That way she can choose her victims. She feels them out. She has to get him to invite her to his house. Not to a hotel. Or in the car. It has to be someplace where she can drug him and then carry out the murder over a long period of time without being seen."

"If the man doesn't invite her to his house, then she doesn't follow through."

"Exactly. He has to be single and living alone," Cliff said. "Any red flags and she aborts. It's probably happened a dozen or more times."

"Answer me this," Sammy said. "How does she know there aren't security cameras in the victim's house?"

"She doesn't. But that's easy to deal with. She can destroy the tapes once she kills the victim. And, if she gets to the house and the situation is not ideal, she can always abort and not follow through with the killing. Maybe the guy has a roommate. Maybe a neighbor is on the street and says hi. She can keep her options open until the last minute."

"Other houses in the neighborhood could have cameras that she might not see."

"And they do. But it's late at night. It's dark out. In all of the killings, no one sees a second car. So, she leaves the bar with the victim. That means she leaves her car at the bar."

"That also means she has to get back to the bar."

"We need to check and see if any ride services picked up someone in the vicinity of the murders," Cliff said. "On the nights in question. They'll have a log. I would go out by a one- or two-mile radius. She won't catch a ride right in front of the house."

"Hopefully the driver will remember the ride and which bar he dropped her off at."

"Mark my words. It'll be a different bar each time. She can't go back to the same one. Someone will remember her."

"Now you're thinking like a serial killer," Sammy said with a sly grin.

"I'd rather not be."

"Which bar? That's the question. It's not like we haven't thought of that before. I looked it up. There are eleven hundred bars in Chicago."

"She'll pick a bar without a security camera."

Sammy grimaced. "That narrows it down to eleven hundred bars. Most bars don't have security cameras inside."

"Some of the higher end ones do. The seedier places don't have them. People go there for anonymity. To do drug deals. Carry on adulterous affairs. Those are the bars to focus on. That's why the Midway Butcher was there that night. Looking in a bar for a victim."

Cliff paused to decide his next move.

"I'll focus on this latest murder," Cliff said. "I'll look for a bar that fits the description in that circle. Then I'll check out security footage around the bar and see if I can catch the victim's vehicle on camera. We might get lucky and catch a glimpse of the killer on a streetlight or something."

"Now you're thinking like an investigator."

"Let's go over River Lederman's cell phone records."

Cliff stood and walked to the bulletin board with the circles that indicated the cell phone radius on it.

Sammy shuffled with some papers.

"We've got him at work for most of the day," Sammy said. "Then he goes to the grocery store and then home."

Sammy stood from his chair and marked a spot on the cell phone map. "This is the cell tower where Lederman was from ten to ten thirty on the night of his murder. He left that area, and then went back to his house."

Cliff picked up a marker for the whiteboard.

"Let's write down what we know," Cliff said.

"The murders always occur on Wednesday or Thursday nights," Sammy said. "At the victim's home."

Cliff wrote that down on the board.

Sammy continued. "We've got the red lipstick. DNA profile. Fingerprints. Fibers. That'll make it easy to investigate suspects. We simply ask for a DNA swab. We can rule them in or out that way."

"The killer uses medical instruments and a paralytic drug," Cliff said. "That tells me the killer is likely involved in healthcare."

"Cami said those drugs aren't easy to come by," Sammy said. "And the killer would have to know the right dosage to give to the victim. Too much, and she'd kill them right away. Too little, and they won't be immobilized."

That confirmed what Cliff was thinking. The person had some medical training.

"We had a good time at dinner," Cliff said, changing the subject momentarily. "I hope I didn't offend Cami with my jokes."

Sammy waved his hand dismissively in the air.

"No worries. She's not easily offended. She's opinionated. That's one of the things I like about her."

"Okay. I'm glad we're good. Maybe we can do it again sometime."

Cliff turned back to the whiteboard.

"Back to the bars," Sammy said. "Remember that Lederman was wearing a disguise. If you show his real picture, they won't recognize him. Maybe someone will remember a girl."

Cliff laughed. "I'll ask them, 'Have you seen a pretty woman flirting with a man and then leaving with him?' I can hear the answer now. 'Yes. Dozens of them every night.'"

"She wore red lipstick."

"That doesn't narrow it down much. Julia wears red lipstick sometimes. So does Cami. We don't even know that the woman wore it at the bar. She might've put it on later."

"Welcome to my world. That's the nature of a serial killer investigation," Sammy said with resignation. "Sometimes we just need a break. Somebody might remember her."

It seemed like they picked up some momentum at the meeting. They continued on for another couple of hours. When the clock neared five, Cliff packed up his things and headed home.

When he pulled onto his street, he saw a strange car in front of the house that he didn't recognize. The garage was detached and around back. He pulled in and went inside.

"Honey, I'm home," he said. "Whose car is out front?"

Cliff walked through the hallway leading from the back entrance into the open living room, kitchen, and dining room.

"Hello, Cliff," Cami said. "Welcome home."

Cliff's mouth flew open. Cami was sitting on the living room floor playing with Rita.

8

To say Cliff was surprised to see Cami in his house was like saying his parents would be surprised if he got an A on a calculus test in high school. More shocked than anything else.

Cliff knew Julia was making plans to get together with Cami. He just didn't know it was today and that Cami would be at their house when he got home from work.

He recovered quickly and consciously changed his demeanor from confusion to friendliness. He'd already gotten off on the wrong foot with this woman and didn't want to compound things by having the wrong reaction now.

"Hello, Cami," Cliff said with a fake smile. "I didn't expect to see you here."

"I'm off today."

"Oh."

"Wednesdays and Thursdays. Those are my days off."

Cami stood athletically from the floor, picked up Rita, and walked toward Cliff, holding his daughter on her hip. She wore black leggings, sneakers, and a long-sleeved white tee, with red markings on it. She looked even more toned and fit than when he'd seen her in a dress at the restaurant the week before.

"Look who's home," Cami said to Rita in a tone used to talk to babies. "Daddy's here. Can you say Dada?"

Cliff sat his satchel on the floor and took Rita in his arms. He kissed her cheek and felt his heart warm. Like it always did. Rita was excited to see him and laid her head on his shoulder. One of the highlights of his day was walking through the door and having his two girls greet him.

Something was missing from this picture.

Julia.

Where was she?

"Your daughter is so adorable," Cami said, as she reached over and affectionately touched Rita's hair, then stroked it.

"Fortunately, she looks like her mother," Cliff replied.

"I noticed that!" Cami said with emphasis. "She does look like her mother."

Rita had Julia's dark hair and eyebrows and Latin American complexion. Cliff could also see his wife's passionate nature coming out in Rita as well. At times, Rita could be as fiery as a stoked grill doused with kerosene. At the moment, she was as calm as a turtle dove.

Not sure what to say next, Cliff looked around the room again trying to spot Julia who he had expected to appear by now. Her car was in the garage which meant she was home. Or at least she should be.

"Your wife and I had lunch," Cami explained, as if she sensed his uneasiness. "Then we went to the park and came back to your house."

Cliff nodded, avoiding eye contact. "Julia said the two of you were going to try to get together sometime. She didn't mention it was today."

"It was a last-minute thing."

It felt really uncomfortable being in the room alone with Cami.

Still no sign of Julia. He thought she would've heard him drive up or walk in.

"Where is Julia?" Cliff asked, in as casual a voice as he could muster.

"She's in the office on the computer."

"Thank you."

That sounded and felt awkward, but Cliff left Cami standing there and walked toward the office with a purpose. Cami followed but then peeled off when he got to the entryway.

"Hi, honey," Cliff said to Julia. Then let out a breath he didn't realize he was holding.

Why did he feel relief when he saw her?

His wife's head was buried in the computer.

"Hello, dear," she said, looking up. She smiled when she saw him holding Rita.

Julia hit a few keystrokes, then stood to her feet. She spanned the few steps between them quickly and kissed him. Then poked Rita a couple of times in the tummy. Rita let out a giggle and turned her head away, trying to hide on Cliff's shoulder. Julia persisted. Rita looked back at her mom and laughed when the poking turned to tickling.

Cliff loved his daughter's laugh.

"What are you working on?" Cliff asked. The detective in him was always just below the surface. He was one of those who didn't like not knowing something.

Like why was his wife on the computer? Which she never was.

Why wasn't dinner ready? Like it usually was.

Why was Cami in their house? When she never had been before.

His inquisitive mind wanted to know.

But he treaded lightly. His questions at home sometimes sounded detective-like. Making the switch from work voice and demeanor to husband and father voice was a challenge sometimes.

Early on in their marriage, Julia pointed out his tendency to sometimes question her like he would a suspect. Changing that behavioral trait was hard since he didn't always know when he did it. Eventually, he got better at it. Or at least Julia didn't complain about it as much as she used to.

This felt like one of those times when he could fall back into it. His annoyance and curiosity were both bubbling below the surface competing with each other to make an appearance on the scene. Thankfully, she didn't keep him guessing.

"Let me show you what I'm doing," Julia said. She walked back over to the computer and sat down. He followed her and stared over her shoulder. Still holding Rita.

"I'm working on our family tree," she said, excitedly.

That might be the last thing he expected her to say.

"Cami told me about this website," Julia continued. "It's called *Generation Tree*. It's really awesome. It's an ancestry thing. You can make your own tree. Look. You can even contact relatives and merge their trees with yours."

A tree with names and pictures popped up when she clicked on a tab at the top of the page with her mouse cursor. His name was on a limb connected to Julia's. Rita had her own branch attached under them.

Cliff was impressed.

"Look what I did. All in one afternoon," Julia said, like a kid who'd just discovered a new toy. "I've gone back four generations on my family tree. All the way to my great, great grandparents who lived in Cuba. Isn't that fascinating?"

It actually was.

"We can add to the tree when we have more kids," she added. "When Rita gets married, we can put her husband next to her."

"Thirty years from now!"

Julia twisted her face into a frown. "Right. *When* Rita has kids, thirty years from now or whenever, we'll start her own tree."

Cliff couldn't believe they were talking about Rita's kids. A topic he had hoped wouldn't come up for many years. He already had a plan. When a boy came to date his daughter, he'd have his sidearm on his hip. Tap it a few times. Make sure the boy knew what would happen if he touched his daughter in the wrong way.

"This tree is preserved for many generations to come," Julia said, snapping him out of the future he was already dreading. "Neat idea, huh?"

"I like it. I've seen the commercials on television for this company. It looks like you've put a lot of work into it."

"I'm not done. I want to go further back in my family's history."

"How can you do that? Do they have records that go back that far?"

She nodded. "There are all kinds of ways to find your ancestors. Everything is online now. And *Generation Tree* connects to all different kinds of databases. I can search through immigration papers. Death certificates. Baptismal records. Marriage records. Some documents go back to the Middle Ages. How cool is that?"

Cliff wasn't sure how going back that far was important unless you came from royalty, but he humored her, nonetheless. "You've been busy," he said. "That's awesome."

"I can do your family tree as well. All I have to do is enter your relatives into a tree. When I do, a notification will come up and a male or female emoji will appear by their names if they find a match. That's called a notification. It means they might've found one of your relatives."

Cliff didn't know much about his ancestry and had never asked.

"We can work on that together sometime," Cliff said. "It'll be fun."

He meant it.

Rita began to fidget, so Julia took her from Cliff.

"What's for dinner?" he asked.

"I know. I'm sorry. I got so involved in what I was doing, that I lost track of time. So, I ordered a pizza. It should be here shortly. I invited Cami to join us. I hope you don't mind."

He did, but what could he say?

"No. I don't mind. She said you guys had lunch together."

"Yes. We went to the *Salad Emporium*. Then we took Rita to the park. Cami is really good with her. She doesn't have kids of her own but works with kids at her work. You know, kids having surgery. Things like that."

Julia tapped Cliff on the chest. "You should go get freshened up. You smell like a police station."

A few minutes later, after having showered and donning casual clothes, Cliff was more relaxed. While in the bedroom, he heard the doorbell ring which meant the pizzas were there.

The three adults sat at the kitchen table and Cami fed Rita in her highchair. She did seem good with her.

"How was work today?" Julia asked Cliff.

"Same old, same old," he responded.

That wouldn't be a good enough answer if they were alone. He wondered if he'd get away with it since they had company. Julia knew his work was sensitive and that he didn't like to talk about it in front of other people.

Since Cami was dating Sammy, Julia might not think it mattered. Especially since they had talked about the case at dinner the week before.

Cliff and Julia discussed that. The conversation with Cami made Cliff uncomfortable. He thought she overreacted to his jokes. Julia didn't really defend Cami but did say that people sometimes misinterpreted his attempts at humor.

It didn't take long for Cami to bring up the case again. "Sammy said you were making progress on your case," Cami said.

Cliff really didn't want to say, so he decided to be as vague as possible.

"I guess you could call it progress. It's slow moving. We have some leads we're pursuing."

"Like what?" Cami asked.

"Looking for patterns."

"Have you changed her name yet or do you still call her that awful clown name?"

"She's still the Clown Slayer."

"I think you should change it to the Red Lipstick Killer."

"Sammy said that's already taken," Julia interjected.

Cliff laughed. "It's not like the names are copyrighted. It kind of makes sense. The Red Lipstick Killer of old was from Chicago. So is our girl. The murders were gruesome like the ten we are dealing with. The killer left messages on the mirrors of his victim's homes in red lipstick. Our girl leaves red lipstick behind as her signature."

"What kind of messages did the Red Lipstick Killer leave on a mirror?" Julia asked.

Cliff looked at Rita and wondered if he should say in front of a nine-month-old-baby. Both ladies looked at him like they really wanted to know.

He took a deep breath. "One of the messages said, 'for heaven's sake, catch me before I kill more. I cannot control myself.'"

"That's creepy," Julia shuddered.

"Not everything is similar between the cases," Cami argued. "He's a man. The person you are looking for is a woman."

"They both use red lipstick and are both from Chicago," Cliff said. "That's close enough."

"I think she deserves her own title," Cami blurted. "I've been thinking about it. Instead of Red Lipstick what about Lady of the Night?"

"She doesn't really act ladylike," Julia said.

Cliff was glad Julia was the one who vocalized what he was thinking.

"The Monster of the Midway was one of the names we considered," Cliff said.

"Isn't that name taken as well?" Cami said. "I've heard of it before."

"The Monsters of the Midway were famous Chicago Bears football players," Julia said, proud that she knew the answer.

"Yes. The 1940 and 41 Bears were called that," Cliff explained. "Because of their ferocious defense. They also won an NFC Championship. In 1985, the name was revived when the Bears defense was dominant again."

"I think I prefer Lady to Monster," Cami said.

"I like the Clown Slayer," Cliff said.

Cami grimaced.

Cliff changed the subject, and the rest of the evening was mostly pleasant.

9

Cliff could finally get out of the office and into the field. Not that pushing papers wasn't important in an investigation, it's just that he preferred to interview witnesses, develop and pursue leads, and breathe cold, brisk, fresh air as opposed to the moldy stale air in the station.

If he were ever relegated to a desk job, he'd quit.

His intention was to retrace the Midway Butcher's steps based on his cell tower location pings. The grocery store was his first stop. As expected, he didn't find anything there. The store manager offered up their security camera footage without an objection or demand for a warrant and Cliff found the Butcher roaming the store on the day in question.

Cliff didn't see anything suspicious. Inside the store, no one paid attention to the Butcher, and he wasn't searching for a victim. Buying groceries seemed to be his only aim. The outside cameras showed him drive away but didn't pick up anyone following him.

Cliff was certain the Midway Butcher met his intended victim later that night. Probably at a bar. On a piece of paper in his car were eight addresses of bars within the targeted circle. That's where Cliff would focus his activity.

He quickly ruled out the first three bars he went to. One had a security camera in the parking lot and one pointed at the entrance. Another was in a busy strip shopping center with dozens of other businesses. The third was out of business.

The fourth on his list was promising. The parking lot was in the rear and only one light bulb above the back door illuminated the entire area and was on even during the middle of the day. The bar/restaurant/tavern opened at noon and closed at two a.m., seven days a week.

Cliff sat in the parking lot and observed. An underwhelming number of patrons came in and out over the next hour. He suspected the tavern did most of its business at night after people got off work. Especially on Friday nights which was payday for most of the laborer class who seemed to be the type of clientele this bar attracted.

Sammy said Cliff needed to think like a serial killer. So, he tried. He imagined the Butcher doing the same thing he was doing. Sitting outside the bar scoping things out. Determining whether or not to go inside.

It seemed counterintuitive. Why would the Butcher go inside a dive-bar like this? He was a middle-class, white-collared professional. Not one person entered who even remotely matched his profile.

Cliff was thinking like an investigator using common sense and not like a serial killer. The Butcher would go there because his victims weren't on his socio-economic scale. After more observation, it became apparent that the women who entered and exited the bar fit the profile of the Butcher's victims perfectly. Thirty-five to forty-five years of age. Rough around the edges. Thin. Smokers. Not unattractive, but not knock-out gorgeous.

None wore red lipstick.

Half of them had no makeup on at all. It did look like the kind of place the Butcher would look for a victim based on the pictures of the thirteen victims he had murdered.

Did the Clown Slayer fit the same profile? Not according to Julia and Cami.

That gave him pause. Something about the visual didn't make sense if she was as pretty as they suggested. This didn't seem like the kind of place a beautiful professional woman would frequent.

So, Cliff shifted gears. He tried to put himself into the mind of the Clown Slayer.

He thought the moniker fit the killer perfectly. Cami's opinion aside, the woman serial killer was a clown. He looked up the definition. A clown was someone who wore exaggerated makeup. You could pick a clown out of a crowd of a thousand people. A woman wearing red lipstick in this bar would be similarly noticed.

Cami was right about another thing. The woman wanted to be noticed. She had a need to be respected. She thought more highly of herself than most. That's the reason for the death threats on Sammy and Cami's lives. The woman wanted to be recognized and feared. She might even know about the Red Lipstick killer of the last century and was copying him.

Did she want to be compared to men serial killers or to women who killed in high numbers?

A question for another time.

Assuming she was above average in looks, what would the woman serial killer be thinking if she was sitting in that same parking lot observing this clientele? What questions were running through her mind?

Would she go inside a bar like this? Wouldn't she want to go to a higher end club other pretty girls frequented? So she wouldn't stand out in the crowd.

No.

Cliff felt his mind spinning. Processing the data.

Those establishments would have security cameras. She'd have competition in those bars. There'd be lots of pretty women. Getting one of the men to take her home would be harder. A lot of the men would be there with their buddies. In this bar, she'd have her pick of victims. Almost everyone who entered was alone.

Any number of the men Cliff had seen entering and exiting would likely chase anything wearing a skirt. Figuratively speaking. Not one of the women who had entered was dressed in anything nicer than faded blue jeans and a tee shirt. Nevertheless, the men who frequented these kinds of sleezy establishments were probably used to paying for sex.

What would they think when a pretty woman walked in?

They'd think they were the luckiest man on earth if she talked to them. If she asked to go home with him, no strings attached, he'd be thrilled out of his mind. A freebee from a woman out of their league would have the men in the bar salivating.

The path of least resistance.

It'd be easy for the Clown Slayer to pick up men at a bar like this.

Would she have that same effect on the Butcher? A working professional with an above normal IQ.

Obviously.

The Butcher did get fooled. He picked her up and took her home. Even deviated from his normal profile. Assuming the Clown Slayer was beautiful. If she wasn't, then this bar made even more sense.

Cliff felt a jolt of excitement.

His pulse picked up its pace. He was onto something. Cliff got out of his car with a pep in his step.

When he opened the door to the bar, the rush of stale air laced with mold and cigarette smoke stopped him in his tracks and nearly took his breath away.

He stood in the doorway for several seconds before going all the way inside. Cliff wasn't used to being around cigarette smoke. The *Chicago Clean Indoor Air Act* prohibited smoking, even in bars and taverns. The owner of *Bob's Tavern* obviously didn't care. Neither did the patrons who filled up half the bar stools with a drink and an ashtray sitting in front of them.

Several people looked at him, including the bartender. Cliff closed the door. Without the outside sun, the bar was dark, and it took a moment for his eyes to adjust. When they did, he felt like he'd stepped back into the 1950s or into a time capsule.

If the word dive bar was in an encyclopedia, a picture of *Bob's Tavern* would be next to it.

In the back was a long bar that took up the entire wall. Behind it was a bartender along with the alcohol. A mirror took up the entire back wall and went from counter to the ceiling.

Cliff didn't rush over to the only occupied part of the establishment. He loitered near the entrance where he found framed pictures of Al Capone, the Rat Pack, and famous Cubs baseball players on the left wall. A few of them were signed and personalized to Bob.

Video Slots lined another wall on the other side of the restaurant part of the establishment. Older looking metal tables with white and black checkered tablecloths were placed throughout the dining area. Along with uncomfortable looking metal chairs.

A number of vintage alcohol signs hung on the walls and looked like they'd been there for decades. The only well-lit area was a separate room with a pool table and dartboard.

Satisfied he had the layout memorized Cliff approached the bar. His badge and gun were clearly displayed on his hip, so he didn't bother flashing his credentials. Everyone in there knew what he was. It wouldn't have been more obvious if he had a neon sign flashing the word *Cop* on his forehead.

Cliff smiled, hoping they'd see this as a friendly visit.

The patrons at the bar had inconspicuously put out their cigarettes. Something Cliff welcomed, even though he had no intention of harassing them about breaking that law.

"What can I get you?" the barkeep asked.

"Nothing. Thank you. I'd like to ask you a few questions."

"What about?"

The man was twenty something and the youngest one in the bar by a pretty good margin. Probably a college student. He had a shadowy beard. Decent looking. Cliff put his elbow on the bar and leaned into it. From his vantage point, he had a good view down the bar. The patrons sitting on the stools had their heads down and weren't making eye contact with him.

They were even older than Cliff had realized. Scruffier. Their faces carried the weight of years of alcohol abuse and probably several divorces. More than likely unemployed which was why they were in the bar drinking in the middle of the day.

Cliff took a picture of River Lederman out of his pocket and showed it to the bartender. He wanted the young man to know right away that he had a specific reason for being there and it wasn't related to targeting him. A bartender would be nervous when law enforcement entered the premises. A cop could be looking for any number of things that could get a bartender in trouble. Selling drinks to a minor. Dealing drugs. Skimming money out of the till.

The young man took the picture in his hand and looked it over. To at least give the impression he was cooperating. Maybe really looking at it.

"He doesn't look familiar," he said and slid it back across the bar at Cliff.

"Do you work on Thursday nights?" Cliff asked.

"Usually."

"Were you working two weeks ago? Not last Thursday, but the one before that."

He looked off in the distance clearly thinking.

"Yeah. I was."

"So, you would've been behind the bar between ten and ten thirty that night?"

"Yeah. I suppose so."

Cliff slid the picture back toward him.

"Take a look again. See if you remember a guy like that on that Thursday night."

He picked up the picture and looked it over again.

"I can't say that I've seen this guy. He doesn't look familiar."

"That's okay. What about a girl? Do you remember a woman who might've been here that night?"

"We get a lot of women in here."

"I'm sure. What about someone you've never seen before? Someone new."

"Maybe. It's possible. That was a few weeks ago. I've slept since then."

"Me too. Although, I have a nine-month-old daughter. We don't sleep as much as we used to."

Cliff was trying to maintain a friendly tone.

"Think about it. It's important. Did you see a woman? A real looker. She might've been wearing red lipstick."

His eyes widened.

"I do remember a woman like that. She sat down on the far end. She ordered a vodka tonic if I remember right."

Cliff perked up. He was beginning to think he'd run into a dead end. Now he wasn't so sure.

The bartender chuckled. "I've been doing this for too long. I remember what people order more than what they look like."

Cliff gave him a slight nod of the head. "This woman. What did she look like?"

"Kind of pretty. I don't know. Really pretty, I guess."

"Did you talk to her?"

"Not really. Other than to take her drink order. I don't hit on girls in the bar if that's what you mean. I have a girlfriend. This lady was older than me. Maybe thirty-four or so."

Cliff could feel a slow boil of excitement percolating inside of him. Like a volcano in the early stages of an eruption.

"What color hair did she have?"

"Brown. I think. Dark brown."

"What color eyes?"

"I don't know what color eyes my own girlfriend has."

"But you remember the red lipstick."

"Yeah. Bright red."

"Was she talking to anyone?"

"Come to think of it, she was talking to a man. She left with him."

"Take another look at that picture. Could that be the man?"

"Maybe."

"What if he had a mustache and was wearing glasses?"

"That might've been him."

"Was anyone else working that night?"

"No, just me. We have three people behind the bar on Friday nights, but I can handle Thursdays by myself. You know. I get all the tips that way."

"Do you have a security camera in this place?"

"Yeah. But it doesn't work."

Cliff took out a five and laid it on the counter.

"You've been very helpful."

"Thanks."

He had a lead.

Cliff took a deep breath once he got outside. His clothes reeked of cigarette smoke.

He got back in his car and thought about the development. Could be nothing. Could be something. How could he confirm that it was his man?

By checking the security cameras on adjacent buildings. He found one. The owner was cooperative.

River Lederman drove an older black Lexus with tinted windows. Cliff spotted it on archived footage heading southbound from the bar at 10:32 on the Thursday night in question. He couldn't see any of the occupants because of the tinted windows but did confirm the license plate number belonged to River Lederman. The Midway Butcher.

His energy increased along with his optimism. A lot of things came out of his efforts that afternoon. He now knew the Clown Slayer's M.O. She went to bars to find her victims.

Julia had also been right. The woman was pretty.

10

Upon closer scrutiny, Cliff realized that the Clown Slayer murder cases hadn't been investigated as thoroughly as he would've liked. Several things he expected to see in the file were missing.

The killings started two years before. An investigator named Pete Riser was initially assigned to the case. Sammy took over for him six months ago. He simply picked up where Riser left off and worked under the same assumptions.

What if those assumptions were wrong? It might explain why Sammy hadn't made much progress in the case over those six months even though half of the ten victims were murdered in that time frame.

One of the primary theories driving the investigation before Sammy got involved was that the murders were random. Therefore, no effort was made to conclusively rule out a connection between the victims and the killer, or a connection between the victims.

One of the first things Cliff would've done was prove they were random. At least to the extent possible.

Joe Gerke, who investigated the Midway Butcher cases, did a pretty good job documenting in the file why all twelve murders committed by the Butcher were random. From that, Cliff concluded that the Midway Butcher's attempt to kill the Clown Slayer was a random act stemming from a chance meeting at *Bob's Tavern*.

Did that mean the murder of the Midwest Butcher by the Clown Slayer was random?

Not necessarily.

The woman killer could be operating under a different set of mo-tives and strategies. Probably was. While a random act of violence seemed like the most obvious theory, Cliff didn't like to make assump-tions. He certainly didn't want to pour valuable time and resources into a thread that hadn't been fully vetted.

So Cliff did some of his own research focusing first on the killing of the Midwest Butcher. One thing he found was that the Butcher had a criminal record. He was accused of sexual assault in college. He pled no contest and was given a six-month suspended sentence and two year's probation.

From those criminal records, Cliff learned the Butcher had been sexually assaulted by an uncle when he was a boy. The abuse hap-pened for several years until the uncle was caught and sentenced to jail. That's part of the reason why the Butcher got a lighter sentence. He was a victim as well as a perpetrator. That and he was a first-time offender.

Cliff expected to see something like that in the Butcher's past. Most serial killers were abused at some point in their lives. The FBI profiler suggested the Clown Slayer was likely abused at some point as well. Probably by a man. Which would explain the intense anger that came out in the killings.

Cliff kept digging. He wanted to know if the Butcher had any-thing in common with the Clown Slayer's other victims. That's where he ran into problems. Pete Riser hadn't done the work necessary to confirm or deny any connections.

So, Cliff asked the Lieutenant for additional staff and the request was approved based on the information gathered at *Bob's Tavern*. His boss wanted to see progress on the case before he assigned more resources to it and placing the Butcher's car at the bar was just what he was looking for.

A plan formed in Cliff's mind. The additional staffers would du-plicate his efforts and canvas the bars within the cell tower circles for each of the other nine Clown Slayer victims. They'd also look for security cameras around each bar. Then take it a step further than Cliff had.

Cliff wanted them to document every vehicle that entered or exited the bar on the day of the murders. Then cross check the vehicles to see if the same one entered or exited one or more of the other bars on the days of the other murders.

If the theory that the murders were random was correct, the Clown Slayer met her victims at the bars, left with them, then killed them. That meant her car was likely present at every bar. With good-old-fashioned detective work, they might break the case wide open.

The huge undertaking would take four to six weeks.

But what if the victims were targeted and not random? A lot of manpower to expend if the working theory wasn't correct. So he wanted some of the staffers to work on filling in some of the background information on the Clown Slayer victims.

Cliff voiced his concerns to Sammy who was skeptical.

"I've been going over the cell phone records of all the victims," Cliff said. "What if the Clown Slayer didn't meet them all in a bar?"

"Like you said, she had to meet them someplace without security cameras."

Cliff shuffled some papers around.

"I'm looking at victim number three, Joseph Pinion. His cell phone pinged continuously at the same tower near his house. He never left the area."

"He might've gone to a local bar within the circle."

"Or he might've never left his house."

"Or he might've left his cell phone at home."

"That's a lot of might'ves."

"What's your point?"

"If he never left his house, then he was targeted," Cliff explained. "The Clown Slayer knew the victim in some way. That makes it no longer random. If it's not random, then they had a connection. We need to know what that connection is. It also may mean she had a connection with the other victims."

Sammy frowned, then sighed. "Maybe she followed him home from a bar."

"Victim number seven, Noel Armstrong, wasn't killed at his house. His body was found in a dumpster."

"He was married with two kids. She couldn't go back to his house."

"Exactly. That means she had to deviate from what she was used to. What was so special about Armstrong that she wanted to kill him anyway and take more risks? Why not just move on to another random victim who fits her proven methods?"

"Maybe she liked him. The fact that she didn't kill him at his house, doesn't mean she didn't pick him up at a bar and take him someplace where she could kill him."

"How did she drug him?"

"Maybe she took him back to her house. Maybe she killed him in her car. Maybe she had some booze in the car with drugs already in it."

"That's a lot of maybes."

"You know as well as I do that, early on in an investigation, speculation is often all we have to go on."

"All I'm saying is that some of these killings don't fit the same M.O. as the Butcher killing."

"You're the one who came up with the theory."

"I know. I still like it. But I want to make sure things fit before we sink a lot of time and manpower into it."

"What else have we got? We have to start somewhere."

"There's another thing that bothers me," Cliff said pensively. "Nobody looked into the victims to see if there was a connection."

Sammy bowed his back in defensiveness. "Riser concluded that the murders were random. I agree with him. I didn't see the need to go back through all the cases and waste manpower trying to prove a negative."

Cliff didn't say anything while he gathered his thoughts.

Sammy continued before Cliff could respond. "Some background was gathered on the victims. For instance, they didn't work at the same location. None of them went to the same church. They didn't live in the same neighborhoods. Every time there was a new victim, Riser went back to the older cases and asked the relatives if they knew the victim. Just to see if there might be a connection. They all said no."

"He never ran a criminal background check on any of the victims."

That's one of the first things Cliff did with the Midwest Butcher. That's how he found the sexual abuse charge.

Sammy shrugged.

"He never ran their DNA through a database," Cliff added.

"The victims all had IDs on them. He knew who they were. It wasn't like he needed to identify them."

"I would've run a criminal background check. To see if any of them had a record."

"Have at it," Sammy said.

"I'm not saying there's a connection. I just want to rule it out."

"Knock yourself out. Run whatever background checks you want to run. I think you're wasting your time."

"Victim number five was killed in the afternoon," Cliff argued.

"People go to bars in the afternoon."

"His cell phone never left his house either."

"Maybe he walked to a neighborhood bar."

"There were signs of forced entry at his house."

"It wasn't conclusive. A window in a back bedroom appeared to be shimmied."

Cliff might not be impressed with Sammy's investigative skills, but he was impressed with his knowledge of the facts. He seemed to know the individual cases backwards and forwards.

"Riser decided it wasn't tampered with since the lock wasn't broken," Sammy added.

"I get that. Let's assume it was tampered with and the Clown Slayer was waiting for the victim at the house."

"What if she was? Where are you going with this?"

"That means she targeted him. Why?"

"Who knows?"

Cliff closed up the file in front of him.

"That's all I'm saying. We've got three victims who don't perfectly fit the working theory that she met them in a bar."

"Nothing ever fits perfectly."

"I know."

"The murders can still be random."

Sammy's cell phone rang interrupting the spirited exchange.

"Sammy Poser," he answered.

His eyebrows immediately furrowed, and his jaw clenched. Whoever was on the other line had created concern which was evident in his demeanor.

"I have no comment," Sammy said and abruptly hung up the phone.

"Who was that?" Cliff asked.

"A reporter with the Chicago Tribune," he said slowly and deliberately. "He was asking if I wanted to confirm that we are investigating a woman serial killer."

Cliff's heart almost jumped from his chest. He'd been dreading the day the media would get wind of the investigation. So far, they'd been able to keep it under wraps.

"I wonder how he heard about it," Cliff said, in the same slow drawl.

The Lieutenant suddenly appeared at the doorway of their conference room. His face was as serious as a heart attack. He must've gotten the same phone call.

"I need the two of you to go down to the Chicago Tribune," he said, confirming Cliff's suspicions.

"I just got a call from a reporter at the Tribune," Sammy reported.

The Lieutenant grimaced. "Of course, you did. I wonder how he knew you were the lead detective on the case."

"What's going on?" Cliff asked.

"The Tribune got a letter. From someone who claims to be a woman serial killer. I need you to go down there and see if it's valid."

"We're on it."

Cliff bolted out of his chair. He took his suit jacket off the back of the chair and slung it over his shoulder. "I'll drive," he said to Sammy.

They rushed out of the station and were at the Tribune's office building within ten minutes. They were led to a seventh-floor conference room. Within two minutes, three people entered the room and made introductions. The editor, the reporter who called Sammy, and an attorney.

The editor did the talking for the newspaper. Cliff would speak for them. Sammy would take notes.

"As you know, we received a letter in the mail," the editor said.

"Do you know when?" Cliff asked.

The reporter had a file sitting in front of him. He opened it and handed Cliff a photocopy of an envelope with a postmark dated six days ago and a company stamp showing it was received four days ago.

"Why did it take so long for you to contact us?" Cliff asked.

"I just opened it today," the reporter said. "I read the letter and took it directly to my editor."

"I called your Lieutenant immediately," the editor said.

Cliff nodded, satisfied with the response. "How many people handled the letter?" he asked.

"All mail comes into our postal room in the basement," the editor said. "It's sorted. Then delivered to the various departments. By a mailroom employee who pushes a cart. I'd guess four or five, not including those in this room."

"In my case," the reporter said, "I have a tray on the corner of my desk. That's where my mail is deposited. I don't always open my mail every day. That's part of the reason for the delay."

"The letter is addressed to you," Cliff said to the reporter. "Any idea why?"

He shrugged his shoulders. "I'm a news reporter. The person probably got my name off our website or read one of my articles."

"Can you confirm that we have a serial killer on the loose in Chicago?" the editor said.

"I can't officially comment on an ongoing investigation."

The editor could read between the lines. Cliff had just confirmed an investigation. The Lieutenant had directed him to do so. If the letter turned out to be genuine, the story was going to be front page headlines anyway. Even if it wasn't legitimate, the reporters were going to start digging and would verify an investigation. This way, the department could get ahead of the story and control the narrative.

"Are you willing to go on record with any information?" the editor asked.

"Let's see the letter first," Cliff said.

The lawyer had a file as well. He opened it and pulled out a zip lock bag. Inside the clear plastic was an envelope. Cliff assumed the letter was inside. The attorney handed the bag to Cliff who gave it to Sammy who set it to the side.

"I assume you made a photocopy of the letter," Cliff said, looking at the reporter.

He opened his file and pulled out several sheets of paper and passed them to each person at the table.

The entire room was eerily silent as they all read the one-page letter. Typed by a word processor. Double spaced. Clear and precise.

Which matched what Cliff knew of the killer.

Dear Whoever Reads This,

I can no longer keep silent. I've killed eleven men. Why don't the police tell you about me? Because I'm a woman?

So the police know it's really me, I'm going to give you information only they know. Ask them about the red lipstick.

I will kill again. I have already identified victim number twelve. You can't stop me from killing him. Eventually, you may catch me, but not anytime soon. Just so you know, I'm not evil.

The Requiter

Sammy looked over at Cliff. Their eyes met. They had to be thinking the same thing.

Eleven men?

11

Lunch with Cami was becoming a normal occurrence for Julia and something she looked forward to. Usually on Wednesdays or Thursdays, since Cami was off work those days. This Thursday, they decided to do something different and go to the indoor mall in the Magnificent Mile shopping district. The upscale section of high-end shops that ran from the Chicago River to Oak Street in the downtown area.

Julia hadn't been there since she'd had Rita. For one, she didn't have anyone to go with, and two, Cliff and Julia were down to one income. She took an indefinite leave from work and a detective's salary was barely enough to make ends meet, much less spend at upscale shops.

Julia didn't even buy expensive things when they had two incomes. She certainly wasn't going to do so now. That didn't mean she didn't enjoy looking.

After an hour of more walking than buying, each lady had one light shopping bag to their credit. Julia bought a new tie for Cliff. At some point, the Clown Slayer case was going to make the news and Cliff suspected he'd be in front of the cameras when it did. He could always use more ties.

Cami got a new pair of running shoes. Julia considered a pair of shoes for Rita, but she'd outgrow them in a matter of weeks, not months, so she resisted the urge even though they were the cutest shoes she'd ever seen.

They took a break from shopping and ate a small lunch at the food court. The conversation flowed nonstop through the meal. Rita had fallen asleep in her stroller giving them a welcomed opportunity to focus on each other rather than the baby who demanded all of Julia's attention when she was awake.

"Do you have any brothers or sisters?" Julia asked.

Cami grimaced slightly flattening out the dimples on her face and creating lines in the otherwise perfectly contoured cheekbones. A noticeable sadness filled her eyes to the point she had to look away.

"I have two sisters," Cami said slowly and in a somber tone. Her voice almost cracked as she said it. "One has passed. I don't have any brothers."

"I'm so sorry to hear that about your sister," Julia said, feeling her own rush of grief. "Same with me. I don't have any brothers. I have two sisters. Had."

Julia paused and the words sunk in like a weight in water.

"My sister was killed in a drive-by shooting a couple of years ago," Julia explained. "Her name was Rita. We named squirt over there after my sister."

Julia pointed at her daughter who was sound asleep and oblivious to all the noise and chatter around them. The food court was bustling and the din required them to raise their voices to hear each other.

"I'm sorry," Cami said sincerely.

Julia let out a sigh. "My *daughter* Rita is going to be a lot like my *sister* Rita. Fearless and feisty."

"Those are two good qualities for women to have in this world. It's nice that you could name your daughter after your sister. I'm sure she'd be proud of the gesture."

Tears welled up in Julia's eyes. She blinked twice to push them back.

"How old was your sister when she died?" Julia asked.

"Fifteen. She was my younger sister."

"What happened to her?"

Cami changed positions in her chair. Then lifted her drink and took a sip. After she swallowed hard, she said, "I don't really like to talk about it."

Julia understood. She rarely talked about her sister's death. Only with Cliff and her other sister, Anna. So she decided not to press the subject.

"My other sister, Anna, lives in New York," Julia said. "I don't get to see her as much as I'd like. Where does your sister live?"

"She lives in Seattle," Cami replied.

"Is she younger or older?"

"Older."

"Do you ever get to see her?"

"Not much. Our parents still live in Nebraska. We get together at the usual times. Thanksgiving. Christmas. Not every year. But as often as we can."

The conversation had clearly taken a somber tone. Up to that point, things had been fun and cheery. Superficial really. Julia decided a more serious discussion was good. They'd get to know each other better. Take the next step in their friendship.

"Are you close with your family?" Julia asked.

A new frown formed on Cami's face. She continued to resist making eye contact and either stared down at her empty plate that once held a slice of pizza or off in the distance at the shops and other patrons. Going deeper was clearly hard for her. It would be for Julia as well if she weren't the one asking the questions.

"I am close to them," Cami said. "I guess. I don't see them as often as I'd like. Things haven't been the same since my sister died. My parents took it hard. I took it hard."

Julia saw Cami's jaw clench in anger. Julia felt that same outrage sometimes about her own sister's death. Cliff had helped her channel that into more productive emotions. Rita's killer was in jail and Cliff had put him there. That's the only satisfaction she could find in the whole sordid and unnecessary tragedy.

"Rita's death hit our family hard," Julia said, struggling with her own vulnerability.

They didn't seem to be able to get away from the sadness. Naming their daughter after her sister had a downside. When she talked about Rita's death, it felt strange saying her daughter's name in the past tense.

"It's a dangerous world we live in," Cami said. "Speaking of a dangerous world, how is Cliff doing?"

Cami's tone changed. Her body language perked up as she sat forward in her chair with renewed energy showing on her face. She clearly wanted to change the subject. By that point, so did Julia.

Although, talking about Cliff and the serial killer case was another touchy subject and not necessarily pleasant. Cliff had warned her not to talk about the Clown Slayer case with Cami or anyone else for that matter. He could get in trouble if the Lieutenant found out.

If Sammy wanted to talk to Cami about the details, that was his business. It didn't feel appropriate for the two ladies to do so. Julia understood why.

"I don't know what's going on with the case, honestly," Julia said, evasively. "We don't talk about it as much as we used to. The serial killer case has him tied up in knots. Even when he's with me, he's not with me. If that makes sense."

"It makes perfect sense. Sammy's the same way. Sometimes I'll say something, and he just stares off in space like I'm invisible."

Julia chuckled. "I think all men do that whether they're a detective working on a big case or not. Men are born with the ability to tune us out."

Cami nodded then rolled her eyes. It seemed like she wanted to say something snarky, but resisted the urge.

"Do they have any suspects?" Cami asked instead.

Julia didn't respond so Cami continued.

"I don't think they do. Sammy doesn't talk about it much anymore. I think the stress is getting to him as well."

"What about your job?" Julia asked, in her own lame attempt to change the subject. "I think it would be quite stressful. Do you ever worry about getting the wrong dosage in the anesthesia?"

"Not really," she said. "I'm a detail-oriented person. You have to be in my line of work. There are safeguards in place to ensure that doesn't happen. Actually, what happens more often are adverse reactions to the drugs. It's one of the leading causes of death in America."

"How did we get on such gruesome topics?" Julia asked.

"I think it's my fault," Cami said with a slight nervous chuckle. "Comes with the territory, I guess. I work in a field with a lot of tragedy and death. So do Cliff and Sammy. You did as well when you worked at the shelter. I'm sure you saw your share of tragedy. The four of us are pretty serious people who chose intense and stressful professions."

Julia only nodded, hoping not responding would put an end to the topic.

Rita was starting to stir anyway.

"Do you want to stroll down the mall?" Julia asked.

With a nod of the head, the ladies stood and packed up their stuff. They deposited their plates and cups in the trash bin and began to walk down the mall corridor. Julia pushed Rita in the stroller, and the women discussed fashion as they made their way slowly past the windows of several high-end clothing stores.

Ahead on the right was an electronics store. Julia picked up the pace toward it.

"Cliff has been wanting a new television," Julia said. "One with a really big screen. It seems like a waste of money to me. We don't watch that much TV. But I've been thinking about getting him one for his birthday. I heard the prices are going down."

"Sammy has one. Ninety inches, I think."

"That's huuuge," Julia said, exaggerating her tone. "I don't think Cliff wants one that big. What do you guys like to watch?"

"Sammy likes detective shows. He's obsessed with them."

"Cliff won't watch them. It reminds him of work. He says it's not relaxing."

"I can see that. I don't like to watch medical shows. When I do, I'm always nitpicking them. I notice all the things they get wrong. Dosage. Procedures. Those kinds of things."

"Tell me about it. Cliff's always saying real life is nothing like television. In the real world, cases aren't solved before the last commercial. Like the Clown Slayer. They've been looking for the woman for two years. She must be good to avoid getting caught for this long."

"Are they still using that name? The Clown Slayer," Cami asked with disapproval in her tone.

"Yeah. I think so."

"The woman is good," Cami opined. "I don't think they'll catch her any time soon."

"If I know my husband, he'll catch her. It's only a matter of time."

They arrived at the front of the electronics store and Julia stopped. "See. A TV like that would be a waste of money." She pointed to the one in the window. "When Cliff is watching a whodunnit, he tries to figure out who the murderer is. He talks non stop. So much so that I can't follow what's going on. It's not really enjoyable to watch it with him."

"What do you like to watch?"

"Like I said, we don't watch much TV. Especially now that we have Rita. The only thing we really watch together is sports. Even then, more often than not, we go out to a sports bar. Cliff likes to watch games with people around. He likes the excitement of it. It's the next best thing to actually being at the game. Which we can't afford to go to right now."

"Sammy loves the White Sox."

"Cliff is a Cubs fan. I don't care either way. I just go along to support him. I don't think we'll be watching much sports until he solves this serial killer case."

"Your husband seems like he's a good detective," Cami said.

"One of the best. His instincts are good. Did you know he's the one who solved the Cole Dillinger murder? The Chicago Bears quarterback who was murdered."

"I did know that. I know all about his career. I looked him up on the internet. I wouldn't want him after me," Cami said with a slight chuckle and then a grin.

"Don't kill anyone and he won't be," Julia said with an even larger smile.

They both laughed, awkwardly. Julia realized it was a stupid thing to say. A silence ensued. The socially inept comment lingered over them like the smell of an exhale from a cigar.

Julia turned and faced the large screen television displayed in the window.

"Cliff would like something like that," Julia said. "But he doesn't have a room of his own. Rita's room was supposed to be his man cave. I don't know where we would put a TV that big. I guess on the wall in the living room. It seems too big for that small of a room."

"Hey!" Cami said, grabbing Julia's attention. Then grabbing her arm.

Julia looked over at Cami and saw that her eyes had suddenly widened to the size of quarters.

"Isn't that your husband?" Cami said, pointing at the television.

Julia's jaw dropped when she focused on what Cami was pointing at.

A news conference was on the television set. A breaking news banner scrolled along the bottom of the screen.

Cliff's Lieutenant stood behind a podium with a microphone. Behind him were five men. A uniformed cop, a man she recognized as the Police Commissioner, the Mayor of Chicago, and Sammy.

Cliff stood next to Sammy off to the side. Almost out of the picture.

A headline flashed on the screen.

Chicago Police Discuss Possible Serial Killer.

12

Cliff stood in the background behind the podium where the Lieutenant had just read a prepared statement announcing the investigation into the Clown Slayer.

"I'll open it up for questions now," the Lieutenant said.

Cliff shifted his weight from one foot to the other. Press conferences like this made him nervous. Not so much being in front of a crowd of reporters. He'd grown accustomed to that over the years. But because he knew the killer was watching. She was somewhere out there. On the other side of the lens.

Cliff tried to picture her.

Where was she? What was she doing? Who was she with? What was she thinking?

Because of that, he made continual eye contact with the camera, and glared with intense resolve. As if somehow, he could intimidate the killer through the lens.

Cliff couldn't help it, even though doing so only called attention to himself. Sammy had gotten death threats. Being present at the press conference let the killer know that he was associated with the case now as well.

He wasn't worried for his own safety but for his wife and daughter. How could he protect them? Did they need protection? She hadn't killed any women or children yet, that he knew of, but it didn't mean she wouldn't. Especially if backed into a corner.

But how could he protect Julia and Rita when he didn't know who the killer was? The Clown Slayer could be anyone. She could walk right up to Cliff on the street, and he'd never know it was her. He wasn't with Julia twenty-four hours a day. The killer could make contact with Julia and she wouldn't even know it.

Hiding in plain sight.

He didn't even have a description of the killer other than that she wore red lipstick. He didn't know her height. Weight. Hair color. Eye color. Age. He knew nothing other than a general description given to him by the bartender at *Bob's Tavern*. Unreliable at best.

Cliff did know what she was capable of and it sent a chill down his spine just thinking about it.

The woman was an enigma. Cunning and skilled at murder and covering her tracks so she wouldn't be caught. Two years of investigation and they were no closer to catching her than the day they started the hunt.

Cliff had to make a conscious effort to hold back his frustration so the killer couldn't see it on his face.

"The letter said that she has killed eleven men. Can you confirm that?" a reporter asked the Lieutenant.

The identities of the ten victims had been released.

"I can only confirm ten victims at this time."

The mention of an eleventh victim in the letter had Cliff worried. He believed another man had been killed. His body just hadn't been discovered yet.

The letter had been released to the general public. After Cliff and Sammy returned from their meeting with the newspaper, the team met in the conference room to discuss a plan of action. Releasing the letter had been an easy call. The newspaper was going to release it anyway.

The actual letter was at the crime lab. Hopefully, by the time the news conference was over, they'd have confirmation that the DNA and fingerprints on the envelope and letter matched.

They also knew which postal facility handled the letter, by the postmark. Not that the information was helpful. Thousands of people went through that post office every day.

"Do you believe these killings are random?" a reporter asked.

The Lieutenant clutched the podium with both hands. "We do. Yes."

Cliff wasn't so sure.

"We believe that the Clown Slayer meets her victims in a bar," the Lieutenant added. "She befriends them. Gets them to take her to their home. That's where she kills them. In a savage and brutal manner."

"Does she drug them? Is that how she overpowers them?"

"I cannot confirm or deny that information at this time."

They also agreed to be as vague as possible on the details. Holding back things that only the killer knew was standard procedure in a murder investigation. Things such as drugging the victims and the use of medical instruments to savagely brutalize the bodies.

"The Midway Butcher was one of her victims," a reporter asked. "Did she know him?"

Something Cliff was wondering as well.

"We don't think she knew the victims beforehand."

Cliff wasn't so sure. The killer said in her letter that she had a twelfth target in her crosshairs. That meant targeting to him. It's still possible that the victims were randomly chosen, but he was more anxious than ever to begin digging deeper to see if he could find a connection between the victims.

Unfortunately, he feared it'd be too late for victim number eleven. It'd be too late for twelve as well, if Cliff didn't get a break soon.

"The killer signed her name The Requiter. Why are you calling her the Clown Slayer?"

"That's the name we assigned to her."

"Apparently, she wants to go by a different name."

"I don't care what she wants. She doesn't get to choose what we call her," the Lieutenant said roughly. "We chose the Clown Slayer because she leaves a message at each scene in red lipstick."

Cliff liked the tone. The Lieutenant was telling the killer that she didn't control them. Cliff glared at the camera lens again as if he was making eye contact with the killer.

If the killer was with someone at that moment, maybe the press conference would spark something in that person and they'd call the office with a lead.

"So that must mean that you believe the letter is authentic," a reporter shouted above the others. "Since the killer mentioned red lipstick."

"We're waiting for crime lab results, but we believe at this time that the letter is from the killer."

"What do you think the name Requiter means?"

"I don't know."

Something that intrigued Cliff as well. The name, Requiter, could mean several things. He had looked it up. It meant to avenge. To return something in a similar fashion.

Requiter suggested revenge. That the killer was giving the men what they deserved or what they'd given to someone else.

For two years, the investigators had been going under the assumption that the killer was a bloodthirsty evil maniacal psychopath. Who killed men for the thrill. Or had been abused by men in her past and wanted to punish the victims for what her abuser did to her.

Was that the point of the name?

Did she feel like all men deserve to be punished or did the men she kill have something in their past that she knew about? Did those men hurt her or someone else and she wanted to hurt them in the way that they hurt their victims?

The word intrinsically meant that the killer was responding to something the victims had done.

Did the killer know that the Midway Butcher was a serial killer? Was that why she targeted him?

If so, how did she know, when the police didn't?

"Do you have a motive?" a reporter asked, recapturing Cliff's attention.

"We think the woman was likely abused by a man in the past. She has a demented and sick hatred for men. That much is clear. That's the likely motive."

Cliff wished he had a more definite motive.

"Do you have any suspects?" the reporter asked.

"Not at this time," the Lieutenant said. "But we're asking the public for their help. We have a tip line. Here is the number."

He read it off.

"We are offering a $25,000 reward for any information that leads to the arrest of the Clown Slayer."

Cliff was worried. This was why he didn't want the media involved. That tip line would be flooded with calls. Especially since there was a reward offered. Every wacko within a hundred miles would be calling the line.

Their job just got a lot harder. They'd have to follow up on every tip that came in. Fortunately, the Lieutenant would give them even more resources and staff now that the press was involved.

The upside was maybe one of the tips would lead to an actionable lead and an arrest.

"That's all I have at this time," the Lieutenant said, and the press conference abruptly ended.

Thankfully.

The group returned back to the office and went straight to the conference room. The crime lab results were already back. A quick turnaround. The media being involved had lit a fire under Cliff's bosses. The Clown Slayer was now the number one priority case in their division.

Cliff opened the envelope with the results.

"The DNA matches," he said. "The letter was definitely written by our girl."

"That's what we expected," the Lieutenant said.

Cliff also wanted to run DNA tests on all the victims. He then wanted to run the results through the database to see if he got any matches. To see if any of the victims could be tied to cold cases.

Doing so was like throwing spaghetti against the wall and hoping it stuck. The crime lab wouldn't like it. Their current caseload had them swamped. Getting results might take several weeks as current cases had priority.

Cliff spent the rest of the afternoon gathering the samples anyway and took them to the crime lab. Then went to the Lieutenant's office to let him know he was headed home.

The glare of his Lieutenant let Cliff know he wasn't happy. He probably was expecting Cliff to burn the midnight oil now. In Cliff's mind, the investigation had been going for two years. Longer hours weren't going to make a difference now. It'd only increase the frustration. He'd spend more time once he had some valid threads to pursue.

He was determined not to deviate from his routine, even if it made his boss mad. He'd go home, play with Rita for an hour, have dinner with his wife, then work on the file if he had the energy.

When Cliff drove up to their house, he was thankful he didn't see Cami's car. Julia had said they were having lunch that day. He wasn't in the mood for company and Cami grilling him for information on the case.

Julia and Rita were at the door to greet him which immediately made him feel better.

After spending a few minutes with them, he got a shower, and changed into more casual clothes. Then spent his hour playing with Rita, while Julia prepared dinner. After they ate, they gave Rita a bath together, then got her to sleep.

After all that, the last thing Cliff wanted to do was work on the Clown Slayer file. So, they sat down on the couch. Both exhausted.

"Cami and I watched your press conference," Julia said.

Cliff hadn't expected that. He had preferred not to talk about the case, but now he was curious.

"How did you do that?" Cliff asked. "I thought you went to lunch with Cami."

"I did. We watched it together. It was on a television at the mall. One of the employees in the electronics store turned up the sound so we could hear it."

"The newspaper got a letter from the killer," Cliff said. "We had to go public."

"I got you a tie. You can wear it at the next press conference."

"Did you read the letter?"

Julia nodded.

"What did you think?"

"It's interesting. Not what I would've expected. The woman didn't sound insane to me."

"You haven't seen the crime scenes. The woman is driven by a rage I've never seen before."

"She says she's not evil."

"I would tend to disagree. What she does to those men is evil."

"A woman scorned."

"That's just the thing. Who scorned her? What is she so angry about?"

"All women have been hurt at some point in their lives by men. A father. A boss who sexually harassed them. You can't walk down the streets of Chicago without being whistled at."

"Does that make you want to kill them?"

"Sometimes," Julia said with a smile, so he'd know she was kidding.

"Tell me about your lunch date with Cami."

"It was good."

"How's she doing?"

"She's good. She opened up a little. I told her about Rita. My sister, Rita. Apparently, Cami had a sister who died young as well. She didn't go into specifics, but it sounded like it might've been tragic. Like Rita's murder."

"I'm sorry to hear that. Did ya'll go to the park afterwards?"

"No. Cami had to rush off. After the news conference, she said she had to get home. There was something she had to do."

"I'm glad you had a good time."

"We did."

The conversation about the killer died out.

The rest of the evening was spent with each other. Relaxing. The Clown Slayer was almost out of his mind for a couple of hours.

Cliff finally fell into bed around eleven. Two hours past his normal bedtime.

He had just nodded off when his cell phone buzzed.

Sammy was calling.

"What's up?" Cliff said with a tone halfway between annoyance and anger.

"We got a tip," Sammy said. "It may be something."

Cliff sat up in bed.

"A man called it in on the tip line," Sammy said. He said there's a woman in a bar wearing red lipstick. Acting suspiciously. She's at the *Hideaway Saloon*. She's there right now."

"I've heard of it. Text me the address. I'll meet you there."

"Should we take the cavalry?" Sammy asked.

"No. I don't want this out on the police scanner," Cliff said. "You and I will go and check it out. Could be nothing."

"Could be something."

"Right."

Cliff hung up. Then rubbed his eyes until he was awake.

"Who was that?" Julia asked.

"Someone may have spotted the Clown Slayer at a local saloon."

"I hope so."

Cliff got dressed, kissed his wife goodbye, and raced off to meet Sammy at the bar.

On the way he remembered something.

Today was Thursday.

13

Cliff arrived at the *Hideaway Saloon* just before midnight. Sammy hadn't arrived yet which gave him time to check things out.

The outside of the seedy looking dive bar looked similar to *Bob's Tavern*. Both buildings had seen better days. The lighting was inadequate and did nothing more than cast eerie shadows over the entrance and the back parking lot, which was overflowing with cars. The saloon had no visible cameras nor did the buildings around it.

The area was industrial. Adjacent were several abandoned warehouses and office buildings. The nearest establishment open for business was several blocks away. Even the streetlights in front of the saloon were out. More than likely the work of the owners or patrons who preferred to conduct their business in the dark.

The kind of place conducive for nefarious activities.

Was the Clown Slayer inside that bar?

Driving over, Cliff wasn't optimistic. A bartender saw a woman wearing red lipstick. So what? Thousands of women around Chicago were in a bar that night wearing red lipstick. Even if it was a Thursday night, that didn't mean the Clown Slayer was on the prowl for victims.

She'd killed ten men in a little over two years. Eleven, if Cliff believed what the letter to the news media said. Which he did.

Even at eleven, that meant she killed less than once every two months. It'd only been two weeks since they discovered the body of the Midway Butcher. If she were to kill again, she'd be accelerating her pattern.

Something which wasn't unusual. Most serial killers killed more frequently as they became more comfortable. More skilled. Effective. Efficient. Brazen. Arrogant. Certain they wouldn't be caught.

Cliff had to be open to every possibility.

One thing was for sure, though, tip or not, Cliff wasn't going to spend his Wednesday and Thursday nights chasing a ghost. Jumping out of bed and losing sleep every time someone saw a woman wearing red lipstick.

The Lieutenant would say to follow every lead, no matter how inconvenient. That's the main reason he was there.

While Cliff waited for Sammy, he walked around the entire building. Several patrons entered and exited. He kept out of sight so he wouldn't be seen. His vehicle was parked on the street a block away. The government-issued undercover car stuck out like a swollen elbow.

As did the badge and gun on his belt. He preferred no one inside the bar knew that a cop was on the premises until he and Sammy were inside. If the killer was there, he didn't want her tipped off.

Cliff let out a huge sigh, trying to calm his mixed emotions. On the one hand, this did seem like the type of place the Midway Butcher sought out his victims and eerily similar to where the Clown Slayer enticed the Butcher to take her to his house. On the other hand, what were the odds that the first tip would lead them to the killer?

Slim to none.

Why was his heart fluttering? Why was adrenaline flowing through his veins like a firehose on full blast? Like he was headed for a confrontation or an arrest. While his mind was pessimistic, his emotions boiled on the inside like water in a teapot ready to set off the whistle.

What if she was inside?

Cliff needed to be ready. Just in case. Fully awake and engaged. Sometimes, investigations needed luck. Leads often came from the most unusual sources and at the strangest times.

Whatever happened, he'd have a hard time sleeping that night.

About that time, Sammy pulled into the parking lot. The lot was full, so Sammy double parked behind someone. Didn't matter. They probably wouldn't be there that long. If Clown Slayer was inside, no one would be permitted to leave anyway. Not until they'd been questioned.

Cliff emerged from the shadows. Sammy exited his vehicle and filled him in on what he knew. Cliff went over what he had observed over the last few minutes while he waited for Sammy to arrive.

They stood in the parking lot assessing their options.

"How do you want to play this?" Cliff asked Sammy. Cliff had more experience apprehending suspects, but Sammy was the lead investigator. Technically it was his call.

"Let's go in and see what we see," he replied. "The bartender's the one who called in the tip. Someone named Charlie. I'll ask for him and have him identify the woman. Hopefully, she's still here. I'll signal you. You approach her and I'll watch your back."

"I can do that."

"You take the lead from there," Sammy continued. "Ask for her I.D. Or whatever. Handle it however you want. If you think it's nothing, cut her loose. If it's worth pursuing, then decide what to do next. I'll support you. One hundred percent."

Cliff knew what he meant. Approaching a potential suspect in this situation was tricky. Killer or not, the woman had fourth amendment rights meant to prevent unlawful searches and seizures. Things had to be done by the book or Cliff and Sammy could find themselves in trouble.

While Sammy rattled off a few more things, Cliff was deep in thought, considering how to handle it on the inside. He was well within his rights to approach the woman. That wasn't the problem. As detectives, they could approach anyone in public at any time and ask questions. Even ask to see an I.D. Probable cause wasn't necessary.

But the woman could refuse to cooperate and walk away. That's where things could get dicey. There's nothing Cliff could do about it unless he thought a crime had been or was about to be committed.

He might have to make a split-second decision. If he made the call to detain her, he'd better be sure she was the Clown Slayer or had a good reason to suspect so.

How could he possibly know? A woman wearing red lipstick wasn't enough evidence to question an uncooperative individual.

If he had something more concrete, he could enforce what was called a "Terry" stop. To invoke a Terry stop, he'd need a reasonable suspicion that she had committed a crime or was about to. He didn't need probable cause in that instance either. He could go as far as to search her if he had a reasonable fear for his safety or even a suspicion that she was armed, engaged, or about to be engaged in criminal conduct.

Reasonable being the operative word.

Better to ask forgiveness than permission?

Not in this instance. Cliff couldn't fly by the seat of his pants. Most of the time, his actions weren't scrutinized. In this high-profile case, every decision would be analyzed ad nauseum by everyone involved. He had to be prepared to justify his actions.

The only way he'd really know if she was the Clown Slayer would be to take her down to the station and give her a DNA test. To do that he'd need to arrest her, unless she went voluntarily. If she were the killer, there's no way she'd consent to going to the station.

To force her to go, he needed probable cause. Even with it, a judge would question his motives and reasoning. Cliff had to reasonably believe that she was the Clown Slayer. Not only did he have to believe it, but he had to convince the judge after the fact that a reasonable person would believe it.

Otherwise, even if she were the killer, the entire case could crumble and any evidence they gathered could be deemed inadmissible.

Those constitutional safeguards were there to protect the general public. Cliff didn't have a problem with them. He just never went into these situations without reminding himself of all the ramifications. Ending up on the wrong side of the law because of a misstep had ruined many careers.

Satisfied, he'd thought things through, Cliff led the way to the entrance without saying anything else. He opened the door and let Sammy enter first.

As expected, the inside of the bar was dark. Country music blared from a jukebox. A few people danced on the dance floor on the other side of the room. One strobe light allowed the dancer's faces to be seen better than those sitting at the tables. Cliff estimated that about seventy-five people were in the bar.

Two bartenders stood behind the bar serving drinks. Each stool was taken by a patron. A few people stood at the bar or leaned against it talking to those sitting on the stools.

After a scan of the entire premises, Cliff didn't immediately see the woman in question.

"Wait here," Sammy said to Cliff as he walked toward the bar.

Several people were already eyeing them warily. Cliff avoided eye contact but stood with his back against the wall so no one could sneak up on him. From his vantage point, he had a clear view of both exits in the main area.

Sammy was engaged in a deep conversation with the bartender. The man pointed toward the sign above an open doorway that said *Restrooms*. Above the sign was a green exit sign.

When Sammy returned to Cliff's location, his voice exuded excitement. "She's still here," he said. "The bartender said he saw her go to the restroom. Right after we walked in."

A nervousness caused Cliff's body to twitch. The only exit he didn't have covered was the one off the bathroom.

Had the woman seen them and was hiding? Was she trying to get away? Did the exit off of the bathroom have an alarm? *Probably not.*

Questions swirled in his mind like white water rapids in Colorado.

Cliff didn't wait for instructions. He made a beeline for the doorway that led to the restrooms. As he rounded the corner into the hallway, he heard a door slam shut.

To his right were two doors that said men and women. Those doors were too light to make such a loud sound. At the end of the hallway was another exit sign on the wall with an arrow pointing to the right. That's where the sound of a door shutting had come from.

Cliff headed straight for it. He peered around the corner rather than bolting around it. Just in case.

At the end of another shorter hallway was a door. The exit sign above it was burned out. As were the lights in the hallway. Cliff yelled back to Sammy. "You wait here," he said. "See if the woman comes out of the bathroom. I'll check outside."

"You got it."

They didn't have radios, so they'd have no way to communicate with each other once Cliff went through the door.

He threw it open. It took a second or two to get his bearings. The exit door led to the side street and the area was dark.

Cliff shifted his head from right to left scanning the street for any sign of the woman. It took nearly ten seconds before he saw a flash of movement out of the corner of his eye.

To the left.

He gave chase. Following the stealthy figure he could barely make out in the darkness.

After a few paces, it became obvious that the one fleeing was definitely a woman. He could tell by the gate and the longer hair which bounced around behind her head.

She had a slim build. Above average height. Athletic. She ran with a purpose. Cliff struggled to keep up.

Cliff shouted at her "Chicago P.D.! Stop!"

His lungs burned as he tried to catch his breath.

The woman ignored the command and kept running. He sprinted after her.

She was fast and had a head start. Over the first thirty or so yards, he didn't gain on her. When she angled to the right, it led them into a maze of abandoned buildings. That's when he got closer. Close enough to shout again for her to stop.

She didn't.

Cliff quickened his pace. His heart pounded in his ears.

Nine months ago, he would've been able to keep up a faster pace than this. Since Rita was born, he hadn't been working out regularly and he was feeling it. His legs burned from the sudden and intense pressure he was demanding from his body.

They were now on a straight concrete driveway at the back of the buildings. Loading docks were to his right, along with several dumpsters filled with trash and debris.

Cliff was gaining ground. She glanced back occasionally to see if he was still behind her. She was far enough away that he couldn't clearly see her face. Not well enough to pick her out of a lineup.

The woman abruptly stopped. Cliff maintained his pace and gained ground quickly. She hopped on one leg and took off one of her shoes. Then switched legs. Hopped and removed the second shoe. Then staggered to regain her balance.

Cliff stopped and pulled his gun and ordered her face down.

She looked at him. Still too dark to make out her face.

"On the ground! Now!" he ordered.

She spun and abruptly took off running again. Faster this time. Too far away to get off a shot, and he wasn't about to shoot someone who wasn't a physical threat to him.

Rather than continuing straight, the woman turned right. Out of sight now. Cliff slowed his pace when he got to the edge of the building. He carefully led with his weapon, slowly peeking around the corner.

The shadowy figure of the woman penetrated the deepening darkness. Further away than before. Cliff holstered his gun and gave chase again. If he didn't hurry, she'd get away.

He strained to go faster. Every muscle in his body screamed for him to stop.

His shoes were hard to run in as well.

She rounded another corner. Cliff didn't bother to stop this time. He bolted around it with a purpose. What he saw brought a smile to his face.

The woman was cornered. At the end of the concrete driveway was a large fence. At least ten feet high. She had nowhere to go.

She didn't slow down, though.

To his surprise, the woman approached the fence and leapt onto it. She sprung over it like a monkey. Dropping the ten feet to the ground, landing on her feet on the other side.

For a moment, she faced him. He couldn't see her face because of the poorly lit area.

She spun and took off running again, not bothering to look back.

Cliff jumped up onto the fence but lost his grip and fell backwards. He couldn't scale it wearing his dress shoes which were slick on the bottom. By the time he took them off, she'd be gone.

He slapped his hands together in disgust. Then bent over to catch his breath.

The woman disappeared into the darkness.

Once he could breathe again, Cliff paced around in a circle, mad at himself for letting her get away.

Then he saw it.

On the ground next to the fence was a shoe. One of the high heels she'd been wearing. The lady must've dropped it when she scaled the fence. Cliff took a pen out of his pocket and lifted it up by one of the straps. Careful not to touch it.

Then walked back toward the bar, carrying his evidence.

"She got away," Cliff said to Sammy who was frantically searching for him.

"Did you get a good look at her?" Sammy asked.

"Nope! I didn't see her face."

Cliff wondered if he'd ever be that close to her again.

14

One week later

The Clown Slayer sent two more letters. One to the newspaper and one directly to the station addressed to Cliff. Sammy had just returned from the newspaper's offices with the letter they received in an evidence bag. Cliff donned gloves and read it to himself while Sammy read the one addressed to Cliff.

Dear Tribune Reporters,

The police lied to you at the press conference. You deserve answers. I'll give them to you.

Reporter: Can you confirm she has killed eleven men?

Them: We can only confirm ten victims.

Me: I can confirm eleven.

Reporter: Do you believe the killings are random?

Them: Yes.

Me: No.

Reporter: Does she drug them?

Them: We cannot confirm that at this time.

Me: I can confirm it.

Reporter: Did she know the Midway Butcher?

Them: We don't believe so.

Me: I knew he was a serial killer.

I hope this is helpful. Don't even bother asking the detectives any questions. They can't even find the eleventh victim.

Signed: The Requiter

P.S. I AM NOT THE CLOWN SLAYER. RED LIPSTICK HAS NOTHING TO DO WITH IT.

Cliff sat the letter back down on the conference table in the strategy room. His initial response was anger. He tamped that down. Information was power in an investigation. The killer had unwittingly given him a tremendous amount of information.

The killings weren't random. She knew the Midwest Butcher was a serial killer. The name, Requiter, was important to her. For whatever reason. She was also clearly on some kind of mission. She wanted to be understood. Respected. Honored. Like she was doing everyone a service and didn't want to be characterized as an evil monster.

"This is one of the most bizarre things I've ever seen," Sammy said, interrupting his thoughts.

Cliff nodded.

"She's basically mocking us," Sammy added.

Cliff ignored how that comment made him feel, even though it was true. His frustration level was high. Not only did he miss his opportunity to capture the Clown Slayer at the bar but she was turning the whole thing into a media circus. She'd turned it into a chess game with Cliff as one of her pawns.

Events were unfolding at a rapid pace. He felt the weight of it. That's why he didn't like working on this case. Solving murders were often frustrating. That wasn't the problem. In a normal investigation, he didn't generally have to worry about the killer killing again. If he didn't catch him or her right away, it wasn't the end of the world. He'd eventually bring the killer to justice.

In this instance, he was in a race against time. The Clown Slayer would kill again. And again. And again. Over and over until he stopped her.

Unfortunately, it didn't feel like they were getting anywhere. It seemed like they were driving on the freeway going two hundred miles an hour headed in the wrong direction. They were making good time but didn't know where they were going.

There was nothing he could do about it other than catch her. So, he tried to wrap his mind around the content and what it meant to the investigation. That's where he needed to keep his focus. Otherwise, he'd drive himself crazy if his emotions got out of control.

Cliff picked up the letter addressed to him and read it again.

To: Detective Cliff Ford,

Must I do everything for you? Obviously, you need my help. Here you go:

S B Q T   N H Q C N W L Q O   (W Y D R Q O   Q H Q Z Q W)

Signed: The Requiter

P.S. You should've caught me when you had the chance.

Cliff sat the letter down on the table. He fought back the rage building inside of him. *You should've caught me when you had the chance.* This letter obviously confirmed that the Clown Slayer was the one in the bar that night. The one he chased.

He had relived that night over and over again in his mind. Searching for answers. Beating himself up over what he should've done differently.

After the Clown Slayer bolted over the fence, Cliff went back to the bar carrying the woman's shoe which she had dropped. Sammy and Cliff both agreed searching for her was futile so they stayed at the parking lot of the *Hideaway Saloon* and waited until three in the morning thinking she'd have to return for her car. If she didn't, whatever vehicle was left in the parking lot had to be hers.

One by one, all the vehicles left. No sign of the woman. That meant she either rode to the bar with someone or caught a ride service. They checked, and none of the local companies had a record of dropping anyone off at the bar earlier that evening.

Cliff wanted to have a sketch artist meet with the bartender and come up with a composite drawing of the woman and release it to the media. The Lieutenant wouldn't sign off on it until they got the DNA and fingerprint results back from the crime lab. Which should come at any time. They should've had them already, but the lab was backed up and slower in providing the results than usual.

"What do you make of the two letters?" Sammy asked, breaking the silence in the room that had gone on for too long.

"The letter to me has some kind of code in it," Cliff said, pensively. Still deep in thought.

"How do we decipher it?" Sammy asked.

"I don't know," Cliff replied. "We don't even know if it's from her. Could be from a copycat."

"You and I both know it's from her," Sammy said. "We'll run the DNA tests and confirm it, but it's definitely our girl."

Cliff sighed. He knew Sammy was right.

"She said you should've caught her when you had the chance," Sammy continued. "She's obviously talking about the bar. Don't you think?"

Before Cliff could answer, the Lieutenant appeared in the doorway. He'd heard about the letters. He wouldn't be happy, and from the look on his face, he wasn't. While he hadn't said so directly, he was clearly disappointed in them for letting the woman at the bar escape.

"What do the letters say?" the Lieutenant asked roughly.

Sammy handed him the box with the gloves they used for examining evidence. The Lieutenant waved his hand dismissively.

"Just read them to me."

Cliff read them aloud. By the time Cliff was done reading, steam was practically rising from the top of the Lieutenant's head. His jaw was clenched so tight, it'd take a crowbar to pry it open. The woman was making his detectives look like fools and he didn't like it.

Investigators liked to control the narrative. The last thing they wanted was for the Clown Slayer to begin to gain a following. Become a cult figure that a fringe segment of the population rooted for.

"What do you make of it?" the Lieutenant asked in a surprisingly subdued tone.

"Let's take them one at a time," Cliff said. "The letter to the news-paper. Two things are interesting to me. She says the murders aren't random and that she knew the Midway Butcher was a serial killer. That tells me she has a connection to the killers and a motive."

"What does it mean though?" the Lieutenant asked.

"She doesn't kill for sport or for the fun of it," Cliff responded. "There's a deeper motive. Once we find out what that is, it'll make it easier to catch her."

"What do you think it is?"

"I'm looking into it," Cliff said. "I'm trying to find a connection between the victims. That's the key. I took DNA samples of the nine victims down to the crime lab. I'm waiting on results. They're backed up. We still don't have results back from the shoe."

"What about this eleventh victim she keeps talking about?"

"We don't know who that is."

The questions from the Lieutenant were coming rapid fire.

"How could she know that the Midwest Butcher was a killer when we didn't even know it?" He asked the same question that had been rattling around in Cliff's mind since he read the letter.

"I think she was probably working with him," Sammy interjected. "They killed people together. They were probably lovers. Bonnie and Clyde. He ticked her off and she killed him."

Cliff shook his head no. The Lieutenant must've seen it.

"You don't agree with that, Cliff?"

"That's a viable theory," Cliff said. "But that's all it is. A theory. There's nothing to prove it as of yet. Something definitely worth pur-suing, though."

"The letters are misdirection," Sammy continued. "She's trying to throw us off our game. The killings are random. Same with the Butcher. He met the victims in a bar. Brought them home and killed them. She helped him."

"Then how come her DNA and fingerprints aren't at any of his crime scenes?" Cliff asked. "For that matter, none of the Butcher's DNA is at her crime scenes. That leads me to believe that they were separate serial killers and not operating together. Maybe she knew him or maybe she didn't. That's what I have to find out. The connection."

A slight rap on the door interrupted them. The Lieutenant was closest to the door and opened it.

Julia and Cami burst through the threshold bringing immediate energy to the room. The Lieutenant had a sudden broad smile and kissed them both on the cheeks.

"How are my two favorite girls in the world?" he asked. The Lieutenant was a flirt and didn't even pretend not to be.

"Aww," Cami said. "We're out causing trouble. We thought we'd save you the trouble and turn ourselves in."

Cami held her wrists out. "Do you want to handcuff me?" she asked.

"No. But I'm sure Sammy does," the Lieutenant said with a lustful grin which turned into a smug look of pride at his quick-witted remark.

Julia rolled her eyes slightly. Imperceivable to anyone but Cliff. He deduced that she was glad she had someone else besides her for the Lieutenant to fawn over.

Cami patted the Lieutenant on the chest. "You need to get your mind out of the gutter."

"It's too late for that," he said with a deep chuckle.

"What are you doing here?" Cliff asked, in an attempt to put a stop to the banter.

"We came to take you two to dinner," Julia responded. "We figured you could use a break."

Cliff looked at Sammy, then at Julia, and then said, "Sure. We can do that. We're about done here."

The girls had gone shopping that afternoon and Cliff assumed Rita was still with the sitter. He actually preferred a nice evening at home alone, but they didn't get many opportunities to go out since they had Rita. This would be a nice break.

The Lieutenant left the room and closed the door behind him. The girls shouldn't be in the evidence room. Since the Lieutenant didn't say anything, neither did Cliff.

Julia walked over and gave Cliff a kiss. Cami walked straight to the table.

"What's this?" she asked.

Before Cliff could react, Cami picked up the letter from the Clown Slayer off the table. The one addressed to Cliff.

"No! No! No!" Cliff said. "Don't touch that! It's evidence."

She quickly sat it back down. "I'm sorry," she said, like a kid in trouble at school.

Cliff gathered both letters and put them back into the evidence bags. Barely able to contain his annoyance.

"What are they?" Cami asked. "Is it a letter from the woman?"

Sammy nodded.

"Can I see it?" she asked.

"You can look at it," Sammy said. "Just don't touch it."

Cliff didn't think letting her look at it was a good idea. "Let's check out the letters," Cami said to Julia.

Before Cliff could object, the two of them sat down at the table. Sammy handed them each a letter which they read through the evidence bag. After they finished one, they traded and read the other.

"The letter to me has some kind of code in it." Cliff said. "We don't know what that code is."

"It looks like a cryptogram to me," Julia said, matter-of-factly. "A cryptogram is a word puzzle."

Cliff knew what it was but hadn't thought of that.

"Do you have a piece of paper and a pencil?" Julia asked.

Cliff reached for his yellow pad, tore off a piece, and handed it to her along with a pencil that had been stuck behind his ear.

"This is fun," Cami said enthused. "I'll help."

"This shouldn't be too hard to solve," Julia said. "I'm good at puzzles."

"Let's see if you can do it," Cliff said.

"You start by looking for common letters," Julia said, more to herself than anyone else.

"The most common letter in the alphabet is the letter e," Cami said.

Julia nodded in agreement. She wrote out the entire code onto her piece of paper.

S B Q T N H Q C N W L Q O W Y D R Q O Q H Q Z Q W

"Look at this. The letter q appears seven times in the words," Julia said. "By far the most."

"Put an e above each of those letters," Cami said.

Julia did so.

"I like to look at the end of the words. There are two O's," Julia said. "After words two and three."

"Since they are next to the E's," Cami said, "that means they're probably not a vowel. Most words don't end in two vowels."

"That means they must be a consonant," Julia said.

She touched the pencil to her cheek and stared off into the wall on the other side of the room. Clearly thinking.

"What are the most common consonants?" Cami asked.

"T, S, and R are common. So is N," Julia replied. "But T wouldn't normally be at the end of a word. S and R would be, though."

"So would N," Cami said.

"It could be someone's name," Cami said.

Julia's eyes widened and her mouth gaped open. "What if it's victim number eleven's name?"

Cami gasped in an exaggerated tone. "The very last word might be eleven. It fits. If Q is E."

Cliff's mouth would've gaped open if he weren't so stunned.

"That means H is L, Z is V, and W is N," Julia said, then wrote it above the letters.

"There are several W's, so that helps with the rest of the puzzle," Cami said.

"Let's assume that O is R, since N is already taken," Julia said. "Two words end in O."

She wrote the letter R above the two coded letters in pencil.

"It could be Alexander!" Cami said.

"That fits!" Julia replied excitedly. She filled it in on the sheet of paper.

"Do you think that's the victim's last name?" Cliff asked.

"Alex or Alexander could be a first name," Sammy said.

"It comes second in the order," Julia replied. "I think it's the last name."

Julia's head was buried in the piece of paper as she kept working on solving the code.

She suddenly looked up. "I've got it! The last two words are Number Eleven."

"Alexander is victim eleven's last name," Cami said.

"So what's the victim's first name?" Sammy asked.

"I don't know. We only have one letter in the first name. The letter E," Julia said.

Cliff had an idea. He pulled up his laptop and logged in to the system's database. He flailed away on the keyboard until he found what he was looking for.

"Joseph Alexander," Cliff said.

"Who's that?" Sammy asked.

"There's an unsolved murder in the database," Cliff replied. "It goes back twenty-two months ago. The man's name is Joseph Alexander."

"Joseph doesn't fit the first name," Julia said.

"Joey does," Cami said. She pointed down at the paper.

Julia wrote it down.

"I bet that's it," Cami said. "I bet he's victim number eleven. Joey Alexander."

How in the world did she know that?

15

After Julia and Cami solved the mystery of the code, the couples went to dinner at a nice Italian restaurant. Cliff and Julia split the homemade gnocchi with gorgonzola cheese, shrimp and mushrooms. Sammy and Cami ordered their own pasta dishes.

About halfway through the meal, Cami said to Cliff, "That's too bad you didn't catch that woman the other night. The one you were chasing. Any idea who she was?"

"We don't know," Cliff said, letting out a noticeable sigh. "I guess she's the killer we're looking for. She left behind a shoe. The crime lab wasn't able to get a DNA or fingerprint match."

"That's a shame," Cami said.

"There wasn't enough DNA left on the shoe to pull a sample," Sammy explained. "Maybe she wore stockings or something. All we have in the way of fingerprints is a partial palm print. Not enough to confirm it's her one way or the other."

"Did you get a good look at her?" Cami asked.

Cliff had just taken a bite of food and waited until he finished chewing to answer. "Pretty good look, I guess. It was dark out."

"What did she look like?" Cami asked.

Cliff took a sip of his tea and swallowed.

"Kind of like you, I suppose. About your height. Slim. Really fit."

No one said anything so Cliff added, "I'm going to take a sketch artist down to the bar next week and see if we can get an artist rendering of the suspect. Maybe someone will recognize her."

They didn't talk about the Clown Slayer the rest of the evening.

***

Two days later

Information was coming in fast and furious. After receiving the second set of letters from the Clown Slayer, the Lieutenant lit a fire under the crime lab, and they were turning around DNA test results as fast as Cliff had ever seen it.

The next morning, Cliff pulled the Joseph Alexander box full of evidence out of the cold case files. Then went to the medical examiner's office and found the stored samples of all the DNA gathered at the crime scene. He took them to the crime lab and already had the results.

They were a match. The Clown Slayer killed Joey Alexander. No big surprise there. The mystery of victim number eleven was solved.

Cliff chuckled to himself. He felt somewhat vindicated. The Clown Slayer had challenged his detective skills. He wished she knew he'd discovered the identity of victim number eleven. At some point, the Lieutenant might call a press conference and announce it to the public. More than likely, he'd want to keep it under wraps for the time being.

So, he'd just have to revel in his own satisfaction. Although, admittedly, he wouldn't have identified the victim without the killer's help. For that matter, he couldn't have done it without Julia and Cami's assistance in solving the code.

Arrogance had no place in a police investigation anyway. A good detective kept his nose to the grindstone. The job would knock you down a peg in a moment's notice. Cliff certainly had nothing to celebrate.

He knew the identity of the eleventh victim, but that's about it. He was no closer to finding the Clown Slayer than the day he joined the investigation team.

That wasn't exactly true. He'd been within a few feet of her. Came within a stone's throw of capturing her. That thought gave him a burst of energy. He had a lot of things on his things-to-do-list.

Thinking about what might-have-been wasn't one of them.

The first thing on the list was to go through the Joey Alexander murder files. What he found in the file was interesting. The forty-two-year-old man was killed two months after the Clown Slayer's first murder. As far as Cliff could tell, Alexander was her second victim.

The investigator working the case at the time never linked the two murders together. In his defense, he had no reason to. The Clown Slayer didn't start leaving red lipstick at the scenes until she killed her third victim more than three months later.

Cliff flipped through the pages of the murder book and looked at the autopsy results. Joey Alexander was found in his home with his wrists slashed. The cause of death was initially ruled a suicide by the medical examiner. Because of that, the investigator was satisfied and closed the file, even though DNA from an unknown source was found at the scene.

Upon the insistence of the Lieutenant at the time, the cause of death was changed from suicide to suspicious, but nothing further was done. No DNA tests were run on the samples.

In the investigator's opinion, the DNA likely came from a maid who was at the house earlier that day. The illegal had disappeared and couldn't be found, so getting a DNA sample from her wasn't possible.

So, the investigator filed the case away and never looked at it again. It eventually moved to the cold case files. Somebody, someday, might've pulled it out of the files and taken a look, but for all practical purposes, the case was essentially buried.

Even if somebody were to look at it later, they would've reviewed the file and closed it without giving it a second thought or seeing a need to pursue it. That's what Cliff would've done. There wasn't enough information in the file to waste time on an investigation on a probable suicide.

The Joey Alexander file would've never been on anyone's radar had the Clown Slayer not basically confessed to it in her letter to Cliff. Maybe the woman wasn't as smart as she thought she was. Her arrogance might be her downfall.

Cliff flipped the pages to a section he really wanted to see. What he found caused his heart to skip a beat.

Joey Alexander was a Tier III convicted serial sex offender. He'd been in and out of jail since his teenage years and, at the time of his murder, was out on bail awaiting trial for the rape and murder of a college coed at Northwestern University.

The investigator had concluded that Alexander was guilty of that crime and killed himself so he wouldn't have to go back to prison. Cliff now knew that wasn't the case. The Clown Slayer killed him.

Why?

The man's criminal history sent huge alarm bells going off all at once in Cliff's mind. The Midway Butcher and Joey Alexander were both men who raped and murdered women.

Was that the connection?

Cliff closed the Alexander file and proceeded to do the tedious work of going through every file of every Clown Slayer victim and pulling police records on all of them. What he found was downright shocking, even though he halfway suspected it.

Every single victim of the Clown Slayer had been accused of a sexual assault at some point in their lives. Several had gone to jail. A number of them were accused of murder. Some had beaten the rap and others had done time. Almost all of them were awaiting trial at the time of their murders for additional charges of sexual assault.

Cliff could barely contain his excitement. He'd found a connection. Random killings were impossible to solve without a break. Serial killings where the victims had a meaningful connection were difficult to solve, but at least Cliff had a road map. Instead, of eight million people possibly being the next victim, the universe had shrunk considerably to a few hundred. Maybe a couple of thousand.

It felt like he was making progress.

Cliff organized the information and went to the Lieutenant's office to fill him in. Sammy had taken a few days off and left with Cami for a short vacation. Cliff was left to work on everything by himself. Which was fine by him. He'd spent most of his career working alone and preferred it.

For all practical purposes, Cliff was the lead investigator now, and the Lieutenant came to him when he needed information and updates. Even the Lieutenant could see that the investigation was more organized and gaining momentum. He'd be pleased by the latest developments.

Cliff was pleased to tell him. He needed to show progress after the fiasco in the bar.

"I found a connection between the victims," Cliff said, after the Lieutenant invited him to sit in the chair across from his desk. Cliff sat on the edge of his seat with the files in front of him on the desk. The Lieutenant leaned forward. Fully engaged.

"What's the connection?" he asked.

"I think she sees herself as some kind of Joan of Arc," Cliff explained. "All her victims were bad dudes. They all had a record. I linked every one of them to some kind of violent sexual crime."

The Lieutenant's eyebrows raised as his eyes widened. He leaned back in his chair, and his eyes shifted back and forth as he contemplated that information. A faint smile formed on his face.

"That's interesting," he said. "You can work with that. Those above my pay grade won't worry about solving it as much if they know she's ridding Chicago of some lowlife scum."

Cliff expected that reaction. While he understood it, he didn't quite see it that way. Not all victims were created equal in some people's minds. Like when prostitutes were murdered. Some felt like they got what they deserved. Not that they deserved to be murdered but that they shouldn't have put themselves in that position.

When gang members were killed in a drive by shooting, some investigators didn't care as much as they did when an innocent person was killed. Cliff did. He wanted to solve every murder regardless of the character of the victim. It's just how he was wired.

The Lieutenant shared Cliff's views of law enforcement. Pursue every lawbreaker with the tenacity of a bulldog. The Lieutenant was simply making an observation about what others might think. The fact that it'd take some of the pressure off both of them was a bonus. Most of the pressure Cliff felt in an investigation was self-imposed.

Cliff ignored the Lieutenant's comment and continued to explain. "I think that's the reason for the name, Requiter. I think the Clown Slayer sees herself as some kind of vigilante. Requiter means avenger. It means to give someone what they deserve. That's what she thinks she's doing."

"Apparently, she thinks they all deserve the death penalty," the Lieutenant said with a slight chuckle, which Cliff didn't take as derisive. Just another observation.

"Yep. But in our system of justice, we leave that to the judge and jury. That motive doesn't make her any less a murderer. It just helps me understand her motivation."

The Lieutenant nodded. A point not worth belaboring.

"Have you discovered a pattern?" the Lieutenant asked. "When do you think she'll kill again?"

"In the first letter to the press, she said she'd already picked out her twelfth victim. I'm going to start looking for men accused of sexual assault crimes who are awaiting trial. Then expand the list to all registered sex offenders."

The Lieutenant chuckled. "Good luck with that. There are more than 2300 registered sex offenders in the city of Chicago. That doesn't include all the ones in jail. Just those out on bail or those awaiting trial. You could be talking about thousands of potential victims."

"Still a lot less than looking for someone out to kill any Tom, Dick, or Harry."

"That's for sure."

"I have to start somewhere," Cliff said. "It narrows my focus. What I need to figure out is why she targets those men. Was she a victim at some point? Is this her way of getting revenge?"

"That would explain the gruesomeness of the crimes. We already knew she had a deep-seated hatred for men."

"Yeah. But how does she identify her victims? Take the Midway Butcher. She knew he was a serial killer. How? We didn't even know it."

"That's why we pay you the big bucks," the Lieutenant said with a smirk.

"Just so you know, you can't pay me enough to work on another serial killer case," Cliff said.

"You don't like it?"

"Not at all. I'd rather have a root canal. I like to work on catching normal murderers."

"That's an oxymoron. Normal murderers. No such thing."

"You know what I mean. Seriously. I want to finish up this case and get back to my normal job."

"I need you on this. You're doing good work, Cliff. Keep it up. If I hadn't assigned you to the case, Sammy would still be chasing his own rear end."

"Sammy's a good investigator," Cliff said. "He just accepted what was in the file at face value. I didn't."

"That's why I assigned you to the case. Now go prove me right."

"I will."

Cliff went back to the strategy room. With a sense of satisfaction. The Lieutenant would be happy with him for a few hours. Maybe a few days.

He looked over his checklist to see what was next.

Cliff dialed the number for the *Hideaway Saloon*. The bar wasn't open yet, but he knew the owner would be there. He answered the phone on the fourth ring.

"This is Detective Cliff Ford. I'm calling about the incident at your bar last Thursday night."

"Yes. Detective. What can I do for you?"

"I wanted to set up a time to meet with the bartender on duty that night. Charlie. I want to have a sketch artist talk to him and try to come up with a drawing of the suspect."

"I haven't seen Charlie. He hasn't been to work since Thursday night."

Cliff's heart started beating faster.

"Did he call in sick?"

"No. Like I said, I haven't heard from him. Payday is every Friday, and he didn't even show up to pick up his check. It left me in a bind. I had to cover his shift."

Cliff's heart sank.

The Clown Slayer must've gotten to Charlie before Cliff could.

Was he victim number twelve?

16

The case of the missing bartender from *Hideaway Saloon* was solved by Cliff before a missing person's report could be filed simply because he bypassed his Lieutenant and took matters into his own hands. Technically, Cliff should've waited for a relative or friend to report Charlie Wilson missing.

If he had, the matter would've been turned over to someone in the missing person's division to investigate. If a dead body was discovered, a homicide detective would take over. If the detective found a link to the Clown Slayer killings, then, and only then, would Cliff get involved.

Instead of waiting for those dominoes to fall, Cliff pulled Charlie's address from the driver's license database and drove to it. Under the pretext of interviewing a witness in the Clown Slayer case. Something certainly in his purview to do.

On the way over, Cliff developed a strategy. If Charlie answered the door, Cliff would question him about seeing the woman with the red lipstick in the bar. Why did he call in the tip? How was she acting suspiciously? Did he get a good look at her? If it seemed like he did, then Cliff would arrange a meeting with the sketch artist.

The best possible scenario. Charlie was alive and they would have a composite drawing of the Clown Slayer.

That didn't seem likely. Why didn't Charlie show up for work on Friday night? More importantly, why didn't he pick up his paycheck?

Cliff assumed the worst.

If Charlie didn't answer the door, Cliff wasn't going to drop it. It didn't mean Charlie wasn't there. He could be inside the house, dead or dying. Cliff wasn't going to leave there without knowing for sure.

The modest house was easy to find and showed no signs of activity. Cliff went all the way around the outside of the house, peering in windows and checking the doors. All were locked.

Cliff was within his rights to check the handles. At any time, if a detective or police officer observed something suspicious, they could go as far as to enter a house as long as a reasonable person would've done the same thing.

Cliff decided not to force his way in.

Not yet anyway.

Instead, he walked toward the detached garage. He wanted to know if Charlie's car was there. That might be a good enough reason to enter the residence.

The door to the detached garage was ajar. At least that was Cliff's story, and he was sticking to it.

Once he opened the door, he smelled the odor of a decomposing body and called it in.

The various forces descended on the home over the next thirty minutes.

Charlie Wilson's body was discovered in his vehicle. His throat had been slashed with what appeared to be a surgical instrument. From left to right if facing the victim which was interesting.

The Clown Slayer was presumed to be right-handed.

The killer was likely sitting in the back seat, behind Charlie. There's no doubt who the killer was. Written on the windshield of the car in red lipstick were the words, *Tag You're It*.

More taunting.

Cliff couldn't help but think that the words were for his benefit.

If this were a competitive game, Cliff was losing. If killing were a sport, he had to give the woman credit for being good at it. It wasn't easy to kill twelve people and get away with it. Although, the annals of history were filled with serial killers who'd killed more.

Ever since Cliff started working on this case, he'd been reading about serial killers. Trying to learn as much as he could about their techniques, motives, and how they were eventually caught.

The horrifying stories had given him a few nightmares.

Why did so many serial killers come from Chicago?

John Wayne Gacy. H. H. Holmes. William Heirons, better known as the Lipstick Killer. The Ripper Crew. Richard Speck. On and on and on. No telling how many unknown numbers of people were killed by Chicago mafia leaders and their henchmen.

John Wayne Gacy was from a northern suburb of Chicago. He killed at least thirty-three people. Maybe more. Ironically enough, his moniker was "Killer Clown" or "Pogo the Clown." So named for his community work as a clown at children's functions. He's quoted as saying something to the effect that it's easy for clowns to get away with murder.

The Clown Slayer might be thinking the same thing. The thought caused Cliff to smile nervously. The killer he was tracking obviously didn't like her name very much.

The crime scene in the garage was secured, the inside of the house was searched, and proper procedures followed from that point on.

According to the forensic examiner, Charlie Wilson was likely killed last Thursday night. The same night Cliff chased the woman from the bar.

How was that possible?

The timeline didn't make sense. How did the Clown Slayer get from the bar to Charlie's house? Sammy and Cliff hung around the parking lot until everyone left. Cliff remembered the bartender being one of the last ones to leave.

The last time Cliff saw the Clown Slayer, she was on foot and disappearing over the fence and into the darkness. What did she do next? She obviously had transportation. And motive to kill Charlie. He had seen her face. She might've even deduced that Charlie was the one who called the police on her.

So, she came to his house and killed him.

But how did she know where he lived?

From looking at the scene, it appeared that the Clown Slayer surprised Charlie. In the garage. She forced him back in his car. Got in the back seat and slashed his throat. With her left hand.

A couple of scenarios scrolled through Cliff's mind. Only one made sense. She followed him home from the bar.

But then it didn't make sense.

How did she get in the garage before Charlie? For that matter, where was she hiding at the *Hideaway Saloon*? How did she watch Charlie exit the bar and leave for home without Cliff and Sammy seeing her?

A second thought occurred to Cliff.

He left the crime scene and went back to the station. First, he showered and changed. He couldn't go home to his wife and daughter smelling like a dead body. After bagging his clothes and filling out a form to have them dry cleaned and washed, Cliff returned to his desk.

Once there, he logged into the database and found what he had suspected. Charlie Wilson had a record. For sexual assault. He was awaiting trial for a fourth offense. He'd beaten the rap on two others.

Not only was Charlie Wilson an eyewitness—he was also a target. The Clown Slayer didn't have to follow him home from the bar that night. She probably already knew where he lived and that he lived alone. She was at the bar to seduce him. Get him to take her back to his house. Then kill him.

When things went south and she had to flee, she adjusted her plan on the fly. She went directly to Charlie's house. There she waited for him in the garage and killed him. Skipping the drugging and all the other rituals.

Killing two birds with one stone, figuratively and literally speaking. Eliminating a potential witness and furthering her aim to kill deviant men.

Cliff set up a new file and murder book for Charlie Wilson.

Victim number twelve.

He filled out the proper paperwork so DNA tests could be run. Then sat at his desk and thought about what to do next.

He had several options. Two seemed the most obvious. Both time consuming, but necessary. One was to load the DNA of each Clown Slayer murder victim into the database and see if they could be linked to any other crimes. Particularly cold cases. Unsolved rapes and murders.

Cliff was diligent in that way. If DNA or fingerprints were part of any one of his files, he always checked them against the database. To see if he had a match. Any number of cases had been solved that way. Even ones not related to his.

The second line of investigation he was considering might prove to be the most productive. To go back through the files and find the names and contact information for all the women assaulted by the men killed by the Clown Slayer.

A DNA sample of every victim would be in medical storage. Cliff wanted to check to see if any of the victim's DNA matched the Clown Slayer's.

A working theory had emerged in his mind. The killings were her way of avenging a crime against her. Perhaps she was assaulted by one of the men she murdered. Maybe the man beat the rap, or the punishment didn't fit the crime in her mind, and she wanted to exact some retribution of her own.

At the very least, Cliff had a thread to work on.

The crime lab wasn't going to be happy. Cliff was keeping them busy as it was. Coupled with the directive from the Lieutenant that the Clown Slayer case was a priority, they were getting behind on their other work and some of the other detectives were beginning to complain. Now he was going to have them cross check as many as twenty to thirty victim's DNA. Maybe more.

Cliff didn't worry too much about that. Every detective thought their case was a priority and complained about the pecking order of all the limited resources available to the departments. Budget cuts had only made things worse. Cliff's cases didn't make it to the top of the list of priorities very often, so he'd enjoy it while it lasted and use it to his advantage.

Satisfied he'd done all he could for one afternoon, Cliff called it a day, and headed home. The twenty-minute drive gave him time to think about the latest developments and his new theory.

He might even discuss it with Julia. She would have some ideas.

By the time he pulled into his garage, he was convinced his theory was well founded. The Clown Slayer had an agenda. She tortured and killed men who assaulted women. In her own mind, they deserved it.

Cliff remembered something she said in her letter. *I'm not evil.* The woman didn't see herself that way.

Of course, most serial killers didn't. Cliff had read the quotes. John Wayne Gacy claimed he was innocent even though he killed all those young boys. He famously said that all anyone could ever get him for was operating a funeral home without a license.

Richard Ramirez, another famous serial killer, said that what he did on a small scale, was what governments did on a large scale. His way of rationalizing his behavior.

Maybe the Clown Slayer was more like Aileen Wuornus. She was a sex worker. She'd been beaten and raped by a number of her clients. At some point, she snapped. She began to rob and kill some of her clients. She said that she killed them cold as ice and would do it again. The opposite of remorse. Her exact quote was *I killed them because I've hated humans all my life.*

The Clown Slayer might be driven by that same bloodthirsty lust. A hatred so strong, that she had lost all moral compass. Maybe she started out seeking revenge. Now she killed for the thrill. Like it was her right.

The Clown Slayer was evil, whether she recognized it or not.

Cliff always saw his job as good vs. evil. Never more so than now.

He couldn't remember reading about one serial killer who had remorse. Most reveled in it. The fact that the Clown Slayer taunted him, made him think that she was enjoying it as well. She loved that he couldn't catch her.

It's like she wanted him close to her.

Cliff shuddered.

The Clown Slayer could be watching his house right now. Probably had been at some point.

She could be anyone. No telling how close she was to them.

Time was of the essence. She'd continue killing until Cliff caught her or killed her.

Sammy said to catch a serial killer that Cliff had to think like they thought. He was starting to understand what he meant, and he didn't like it.

Of all the serial killers he'd read about, she was one of the more vicious. The Clown Slayer made the crime scenes so gruesome that she was obviously sending a message.

Peter Sutcliff was another serial killer who killed prostitutes. He said they were littering the streets. Killing them was his way of cleaning up the place a bit. The Clown Slayer was ridding Chicago of low life scum in her own mind, while also making their houses as horror-filled as possible.

Cliff felt like he needed to take another shower.

He shut off the car and went into the house. Seeing Julia and Rita would help get his mind off serial killers and bloody images.

He stepped through the door and into the kitchen. As soon as he saw Julia's face, he knew something was wrong.

17

Julia had Rita in one arm resting on her left hip, some papers in her right hand, and a pained look on her face.

"What's wrong?" Cliff asked.

About that time, Rita lunged toward Cliff, and he took her from her mother. The little bundle of joy squealed with delight and laid her head on Cliff's shoulder. He couldn't fully enjoy her until he knew what was troubling his wife.

"What's the matter?" Cliff asked again.

Julia frowned, then grimaced. She thrust the papers in her right hand in his direction. "I got my DNA test results back today," she said.

"What in the world are you talking about?" Cliff asked.

"I meant what I said. I got my DNA tests back today."

At first, he thought he misheard her. Cliff had DNA on the brain. Considering his day had been overwhelmed by DNA tests, Charlie's murder, and Clown Slayer frustrations.

"My DNA test said that I'm seventeen percent Irish!" Julia said with exasperation.

Cliff laughed. He thought she was going to tell him someone had died.

"It's not funny," Julia said.

"I'm sorry. But I have no idea what you're talking about."

"I'm talking about my DNA results. You of all people should know what those are."

DNA results?

Cliff's mind wasn't processing the words coming out of her mouth. Rita was also playfully slapping him in the face, putting her fingers in his mouth, which was distracting him from the conversation.

Whatever it was, Julia was clearly upset. If he continued to be flippant about it, she'd be upset with him.

"I know what DNA tests are," Cliff said tersely. "I don't know anything about you taking a DNA test. Can you start at the beginning?"

Julia took Rita from Cliff's arms.

"Thank you," he said. "I just got home. Let me get settled and we can talk about what is upsetting you."

Julia stood to the side so he could come further into the house. Cliff placed his keys, and wallet on the kitchen island, then took off his jacket and draped it over one of the bar stools. He disappeared for a moment to put his gun in the safe. Then returned to the kitchen area.

Since he took a shower at the station, he only needed to change into something more casual and comfortable. He could do that later.

Julia was crowding his space. Hovering over him like a bear over a cub. Waiting impatiently. Something about these tests had clearly upset her. Cliff rolled his shoulder to loosen them.

He moved his head from side to side, faced his wife, looked her in the eye, and said sincerely, "Okay. Tell me about these DNA tests."

She handed Cliff the papers in her hand.

He stared down at them. The heading said *DNA Results Summary for Julia Ford*. Cliff was still confused. When did his wife take a DNA test? Where did she take it? Who did she get the test results from? Why would she even take a DNA test?

His investigative nature formed questions in his mind faster than he could ask them.

Upon further inspection he saw that the results came from *Generation Tree*. The ancestry site. Things started to make sense. Julia had been building a family tree on that website. She hadn't mentioned it in over a week, so he'd almost forgotten about it.

"Tell me what I'm looking at," Cliff said.

"You know how I am building my family tree on *Generation Tree?*"

Cliff nodded and prepared himself for a long and drawn-out answer to his simple question.

"I know. You showed it to me."

Julia went through a long explanation of facts he already knew. He didn't interrupt or ask questions. Just feigned interest for as long as possible until she got to the part he didn't understand. When she finally paused and took in a deep breath, he figured they were getting to the good part.

"*Generation Tree* has a service where they check your DNA."

"I think I've heard of that," Cliff said.

"They advertise the DNA tests on their website. They say it's really accurate. They check something like two thousand regions. It's really comprehensive. You can find your relatives, uncover your family history, and help build your family tree. All those things. It's fascinating."

"Sounds like it."

Cliff genuinely meant it. DNA testing had been valuable in his line of work. He wasn't sure how detectives solved crimes years ago without it. While he'd heard the tests from the private sector weren't reliable, he didn't know enough about it to throw cold water on the conversation.

Julia seemed genuinely excited about having her test run. Even if she were upset about the results for some reason. He was also curious to look at the results. DNA profiles fascinated him.

Rita was back in his arms again, distracting him. Demanding his attention which was now divided.

"I ordered one of the tests." Julia's head and neck shrunk back in embarrassment.

"I didn't know that."

"I didn't tell you. It was supposed to be a surprise. Anyway. . . I got the test kit in the mail and sent it back in."

She paused, waiting for a response, and continued when Cliff simply nodded.

"I got the test results today," she said with disgust in her voice. "They emailed them to me."

"Okay. That was fast."

"They promise a quick turnaround."

That seemed incredibly fast considering Cliff sometimes waited six months for test results from the crime lab.

"The test said I'm seventeen percent Irish!" Julia said.

"You don't look Irish."

"I know!"

"You're Cuban."

"The test says I'm only forty-two percent Cuban. Not even half!"

Every sentence was said with as much emphasis as Julia could muster without sounding crazy. His wife shuffled the papers in the air, then threw them on the kitchen island in disgust. Within seconds they were back in her hand, and she talked about the results faster than Cliff could keep up.

She read from the papers. "It says I'm seventeen percent Irish, including Scotland and Wales. I'm six percent European South. That's Italy and Greece. I'm seven percent European West. That's France. It says I'm one percent Portuguese!"

Cliff could not help but laugh even though he knew it wouldn't be helpful.

"I guess your mother has some explaining to do," Cliff said jokingly.

Julia glared at him.

"I'm kidding. There must be some kind of mistake. You look like your father. He's definitely a hundred percent Cuban."

Julia had all her dad's features. Including the heavy eyebrows. The dark jet-black hair. High cheekbones. His fiery personality.

"Those tests aren't always accurate," Cliff added. The only thing that came to mind that might make his wife feel better. Somewhat relieved that the issue was minor. At least to him.

"They guarantee its accuracy," Julia retorted. "How can I be less than half Cuban?"

"I don't think you can. That's what I mean. Both of your parents are from Cuba. You have to be a hundred percent Cuban."

He put his free hand on her shoulder. "Take the test again. Maybe the results will be more accurate a second time."

Cliff didn't know about *Generation Tree*, but results from a crime lab were supposed to be near foolproof. Accurate enough to send a man to prison for the rest of his life on nothing more than a DNA match. The company shouldn't sell tests to the public if they weren't proven to be accurate.

"It must be reliable," Julia said. "It matched me with Anna."

Anna was Julia's sister who lived in New York.

"What do you mean by *matched* you to Anna?"

"*Generation Tree* somehow knows that Anna is my sister. Look at this."

Julia showed him the second page of the results. Under the heading "Possible Relative Matches" was her sister Anna's name. Next to her name were the words, *high probability she is your sister*.

"How would they know Anna is your sister without her DNA profile?" Cliff asked and genuinely wanted to know. His curiosity was beyond piqued.

"Anna took the test. Months ago."

That made sense.

"I called her as soon as I got my results today," Julia continued. "Her tests were similar to mine. She's nineteen percent Irish! Even more than me. Neither of us knows where that came from."

Rita was starting to get fussy. Julia let out a huge sigh and took their daughter back in her arms. The little girl was being passed back and forth like a hot potato.

"Let me get changed and we'll talk about it some more," Cliff said.

"Okay. I'll get dinner on the table."

"Sounds good."

Cliff changed and met Julia back at the dinner table. She served grilled cheese sandwiches with sliced tomatoes on top along with chips. A light meal, but one of Cliff's favorites. Julia knew just how to grill the bread with the right amount of butter on it.

Cliff downed everything on his plate with a glass of iced mint green tea. Then ate half of a second sandwich. They finally got back to discussing the tests.

"Being Irish isn't all bad," Cliff said. "Aren't the Irish supposed to be lucky?"

He said it with his best Irish accent. Which wasn't good at all. It sounded to him like a cross between Australian and hillbilly.

"Why am I not surprised that you would make a joke about this?"

Cliff felt a grin building on his face. "A frog got his DNA back."

"Don't even!"

"He was confused about his results as well. Like you are."

"Do you want to sleep on the couch tonight?"

"Don't you want to hear his results?"

"No."

"The frog is part Irish, part Scottish, and a tad Pole."

Julia let out a discernable groan. "That's a horrible joke, Cliff. Did you just make that up?"

"How many Irishmen does it take to change a lightbulb?" Cliff asked.

"I'm ignoring you."

Julia refused to make eye contact. Her head was turned away from him and she was focused on feeding Rita.

Undeterred, he said, "It takes two Irishmen to change a lightbulb. One to change the bulb and the other to drink until the room starts spinning."

Julia turned toward him. The disgust returned to her face. "That's also proof I'm not Irish. I don't even like beer!"

"When the Irish say drink responsibly, they mean, don't spill your beer."

"How long are you going to keep this up?"

"I could go all night."

"How was your day?" Julia said in an obvious attempt to change the subject.

"I'm sorry about your test, honey. I really am. I don't think it's that big a deal."

"It is a big deal to me."

"The results are obviously not right. They're still trying to perfect those things. You are clearly a daddy's girl. Cuban through and through."

"I'm proud of my heritage. I've always identified as Cuban American. That's what I've always told people. Am I supposed to tell them I'm Irish now?"

"You should be proud of your heritage. No one can take it away from you. No cheap test can define who you are. I love who you are."

"I love you, too. You're right. I was shocked when I saw those results. They can't be accurate."

Rita was mostly playing with her food. Throwing some on the floor. Moving it around on her highchair. Julia was clearly getting frustrated. The test results had her on edge and less patient with their daughter than she usually was.

"Anyway. You asked about my day. I'll tell you about it after we put Rita to bed."

Julia nodded. She knew what that meant. A murder had occurred that day. They'd decided that when Cliff had a murder, they wouldn't talk about it in front of their daughter. Before long, she'd be old enough to understand the words and the nature of the conversation. Better to get in the practice of sheltering her now.

Julia did the dishes while Cliff took Rita into the living room and played with her on the floor. For the next two hours, their baby consumed all their attention. They gave her a bath and put her to bed with several bedtime stories. When she was finally asleep, they collapsed onto the couch in the living room.

It hardly seemed like a good time to discuss the murder of Charlie Wilson, but Cliff had no choice. Julia would insist. She said it was her way to stay connected to him and she didn't want them to have separate lives.

Cliff filled her in on the details. Going to Charlie's house. Finding his body in the car. The red lipstick on the windshield. The connection between all the cases. The sexual assaults committed by the men she murdered. His theory that she's on a vendetta.

"Honestly, I spent most of my afternoon poring over DNA test results," Cliff said with a chuckle.

Julia's eyes suddenly widened, and her mouth gaped open. She bolted straight up.

"What?" Cliff asked.

"What if you did the DNA test?" she asked enthusiastically.

He wasn't sure why she was so excited.

"I guess I could. I mean. But I know who my parents are. You know Ford is an Irish name. My ancestors came from Ireland. I'm sure that's what the test results would show."

"Not you, Cliff. I don't mean for you to take the test. I mean for your case. What if you sent the DNA results of the Clown Slayer to *Generation Tree*? They can compare them to their database. What if they found a match? Then you'd know who the killer was."

Cliff sat up on the couch this time.

Now fully engaged.

A few seconds before, he was thinking about going to bed. Now it'd be several hours before he got that tired again.

His wife was on to something. Again.

18

Julia suggested to Cliff that he send the Clown Slayer's DNA profile to *Generation Tree* and see if they found a match. A good idea that could blow the case wide open if the ancestry company was able to find one. Cliff tried to think through all the ramifications. So many came to mind it was hard to process them all.

His Lieutenant would have to sign off on it. That wouldn't be a problem. His boss was as anxious to solve the Clown Slayer murders as anyone and would do almost anything if it sounded reasonable and within the law.

Had this ever been tried before?

Surely some law enforcement office somewhere had thought of it. Maybe not. Cliff hadn't, so maybe no one else had either. If he remembered correctly, the technology had only been available in the private sector on a retail basis for a short period of time.

How big was the company's database? Was it a wide enough net to catch the Clown Slayer? Cliff's net wasn't that wide now anyway. The only way the Clown Slayer would show up in his DNA national database was if she had committed a crime, been arrested, and processed through the system.

The ancestry company probably had a broader reach than that. Or at least would soon enough. The possibilities were mind boggling. This could solve hundreds if not thousands of cases nationwide.

What a great idea Julia had.

He smiled at her warmly. It seemed like she knew the intent behind it because she blushed slightly.

As soon as optimism began to take root, doubts began to creep in as it often did in Cliff's analytical and skeptical mind.

Would *Generation Tree* give them the results?

He could see them refusing. Would his office go to court to force them to release the information? Of course, they would. And they'd win. What judge in his right mind would let a serial killer remain free when *Generation Tree* knew her identity?

Stranger things had happened. *No. They'd definitely win.*

Cliff tried to dampen his enthusiasm. He was getting way ahead of himself.

What if he didn't ask for permission? He could send the information to the company under a fake name. He had plenty of samples of the Clown Slayer's DNA. If he didn't get a match, then no harm no foul. If he did, he knew the identity of the killer. The rest would be easy.

But would the information be admissible in court?

No way. Not in a million years. Not if he secured it under false pretenses. He could ruin the whole case. Could even get fired from his job.

He'd better not risk it. He needed to go through proper channels.

"What are you thinking about?" Julia asked. She must have seen the concern on his face.

"I doubt the Clown Slayer would be stupid enough to send in her own DNA to *Generation Tree*," Cliff said with a hint of resignation in his voice. The optimism had left as quickly as it came.

"Maybe. Why not? She hasn't always been a killer."

"She started killing two years ago. At least that's what we know of. She could've killed someone in another city and moved to Chicago. Anyway, that's when the killings started here. I don't think the technology has been around that long. Surely, the Clown Slayer would not willingly send her own DNA to an ancestry website to put it on the public record."

"She might not send in her own DNA test," Julia retorted, "but what if one of her family members did? I didn't know Anna had taken the test. I only found out about it after I sent mine in. Maybe a sister or mother or cousin took the test. If any of them did, they'd find a family match. Like they did between Anna and me."

"That's possible. You're right. That'd be amazing. It might not tell me who the Clown Slayer is right away, but at least I could narrow down the suspects to a specific family."

"Well, yeah. If I were a killer and you had my DNA and you sent it to *Generation Tree,* it'd say that Anna is my sister. All you would have to do is find out how many sisters Anna has and there are your suspects. She has one. Me. Case closed."

"Julia. That is a brilliant idea," Cliff said, as the optimism returned. Not as strongly as before, but enough for him to feel it. If nothing else, he couldn't wait to tell the Lieutenant and score some points with him. The Lieutenant would think it was a great idea. He liked it when his investigators thought outside the box.

Cliff's mind spun like a merry-go-round in a playground full of kids.

More objections flooded his mind, cooling his optimism again.

"I'll have to run it by the Lieutenant," Cliff said, thinking out loud. "There may be privacy issues. But the woman is a serial killer. I would think that'd trump privacy issues."

"It might help you solve the case."

"I can't get my hopes up. There are steps to go through before I can make that happen. It's a good idea though. Thank you."

"I'm happy to help."

"I knew there was a reason why I love you so much."

"I thought it's because I'm the mother of your child. Or that I cook all your meals. Clean your house. Wash your clothes. Have sex with you."

"I like those things, too."

Julia rolled her eyes.

"Seriously," Cliff said, "I think you may be onto something."

"I know," she said proudly.

She laid her head on his shoulder and settled in. He pulled her closer. His shoulders finally relaxed for the first time all day. He wished his mind would.

He needed a distraction. Something to get his mind off the Clown Slayer, DNA, and murders. The whiff of Julia's hair and the faint scent of lavender was a good start.

"I've done all those things for you today except one," Julia blurted out after a couple of minutes of silence had passed.

"Done what things?" Cliff asked. He wasn't sure what she meant.

"We were just talking about it. All the things I do for you. The list of why you should love me. Let's go over it again. The first one is that I'm the mother of your child."

"Yes, you are. My little *Irish* baby looks just like you."

Julia pinched him under his arm without lifting her head off his shoulder..

"Oww!" he said in an overly dramatic tone.

It didn't hurt, but he could pretend it did. He couldn't see Julia's face, but she probably rolled her eyes again.

"I cooked your meals today," she added. "Breakfast and dinner anyway."

"They were delicious."

"I washed your clothes."

"Thank you."

"I cleaned your house."

"I appreciate it."

"I solved your case for you."

"I hope so."

"I haven't done that other thing."

"What other thing?"

Julia was sitting up now, looking at him with a sly grin. "Think Cliff. I mentioned all the reasons you should love me. I've done all of them, except one."

Cliff scrolled back through the conversation and suddenly knew what she meant. His eyes widened. She matched it and smiled seductively.

"I haven't had sex with you today," Julia said. "Not yet. But I will."

When she said the words, desire pulsed through Cliff's entire body, and sent chills down his spine. He was suddenly overwhelmed with desire for his wife.

Their faces were close now. He took her head in his hands and stared into her eyes. She looked back at him longingly.

Julia was so beautiful. It almost took his breath away. He struggled to get it back for what came next.

She tilted her head to the side and closed her eyes slowly. Invitingly. He kissed her gently. Then more passionately. Neither of them eased up on the intensity or pulled back for nearly a minute. Maybe two.

Time stood still. Or at least it seemed like it did.

It felt good.

"Do you want to go to the bedroom?" Julia asked.

That feeling now went all the way from the top of the head to the end of his toes.

"Well, yeah! Of course, I do."

Thirty minutes later, they were both completely spent. Physically and emotionally. The lights were down low, and a peaceful calm had settled over the room. The stress of the day was momentarily lifted.

Work was the last thing on Cliff's mind.

He remembered something.

A surprise for Julia he'd been working on for months.

"*Besarte es como ver las estrellas,*" Cliff said softly and with a Cuban accent. At least the best one he could muster.

Julia's head rested on her pillow. She lifted it up. Her droopy and tired eyes widened noticeably.

Cliff looked deep into them and said it again. The second time doing better with the accent.

She still looked like she was in shock. Speechless.

"It means kissing you is like seeing the stars," he said gently.

"I know what it means," she said, matching his tone. "I didn't know you knew any Cuban words."

Cliff chuckled. "I know the words, but I'm not sure what they mean. How is kissing like seeing stars? It sounds romantic, though."

"It is romantic. It's very sweet. Where did you learn it?"

"*Cada dia te quiero mas*," Cliff said, ignoring her question. This time it didn't come out right. It sounded butchered. He was kicking himself. He'd practiced these phrases a hundred times in front of the mirror and in his car while driving to work.

"That's so sweet," she said. "Each day I love you more, too, sweetheart."

Julia seemed genuinely touched. Since he was on a roll, he kept going.

"*Tu eres mi alma gemela.*"

"You just said that I'm your big fat pig!"

Cliff's heart skipped a beat. How could he have gotten that wrong? "Oh no! I'm so sorry!" he said apologetically. "That's not what I meant."

"I'm just kidding," she said after letting out a big laugh. "I know what you said. You said that I'm your soulmate."

"Yeah! That's it. You had me going. That wasn't funny."

"I know. I'm sorry. It was kind of funny though."

Cliff repeated the phrase. He scooted closer to her in the bed and said it in a deep Cuban accent. He couldn't help but laugh. She giggled.

"Now you're just showing off," she said.

"You are my soulmate," he said in a normal tone. Then kissed her.

"Yes, I am. You never cease to amaze me, Cliff Ford. I didn't know you knew any Cuban. I'm impressed. Seriously. When did you learn those phrases?"

"Several months ago. I looked them up on the internet and memorized them. I practiced them in front of a mirror. I learned them for you. I wanted you to be impressed."

"I am. I appreciate the effort. How long have you been waiting to use them?"

"A little while."

He saw her shoulders slump.

"I know. I'm sorry, Cliff. Things have been a little dry in that area since Rita was born. Really since I got pregnant. I'll try to do better."

"You don't hear me complaining. I've been distracted with work. It's easy to do. We need to take a trip sometime. Keep the spark going."

"I thought the spark was pretty good a few minutes ago."

"Me too. It was wonderful."

"I'll try and make it happen more often."

"You're doing fine. We're both getting older. And tired."

"When do you want to have another baby?" Julia asked out of the blue.

Cliff thought it would've spoiled the mood, but it didn't. Rita had put a crimp in some things, but he couldn't imagine their life without her. He tried to picture what it'd be like to have two of her running around.

His first thought was surprisingly positive. It warmed his heart to think about having another baby. Especially after they lost the first one in the riot. He almost lost Julia as well. Life was precious and fleeting. Maybe they shouldn't put it off.

Julia sat up and began to make her case. "Even if we started now, Rita would be almost two by the time the next baby is born. That seems about right. I don't want them to be too far apart in age."

"I guess. Me either. She might need a younger brother to protect her."

Julia laughed. "I don't think Rita's going to need anyone to protect her. She might be the one protecting her little brother."

"We might as well have them while we're young and have the energy to keep up with them."

"I already don't have the energy to keep up with Rita."

"Wait until she starts crawling. And walking."

"Don't remind me. Won't be long. They grow up so fast."

The conversation ground to a halt.

"*Yo quiero tener a tu bebe,*" Julia said, in Cuban.

"I think I heard the word baby in that sentence."

"I said that I want to have your baby." She pulled out her deep Cuban accent.

"You know. You really shouldn't be speaking Cuban," Cliff said.

He could feel the wide smile on his face. A renewed energy had come to the room.

"Why not?" Julia asked.

"Because you're not Cuban. You're Irish!"

She punched him in the arm.

Cliff formed a frown on his face.

"What's wrong?" she asked.

"I'm disappointed."

"Why?"

"I thought I was marrying a hot Latin girl. I'm sad to learn I married an old Irish woman."

"I'll show you that I'm still a hot Latin woman!" Julia said as she threw the covers off of them.

She did show him how hot she still was. For a second time.

They hadn't done that since before she was pregnant with Rita.

Afterwards they both were out of breath and out of energy, and Julia had effectively proven her point.

The next thing Cliff remembered was the sun peeking through the curtains. Right after the alarm clock sounded the following morning.

19

The attorneys for the Chicago P.D. sent a warrant to *Generation Tree* requesting they conduct a search of their files and turn over the names of potential matches they found in their database. Direct or familial.

The company's response arrived sooner than expected. In the form of a two-paragraph letter. Not only did they deny the request but were belligerent in doing so.

Dear Sirs,

We are in receipt of a request for information regarding the DNA profile of one of our valued customers. It is the policy of Generation Tree not to cooperate with law enforcement requests unless compelled by a valid court order and only after a trial by jury and the exhaustion of all appeals.

Not only will we not share the information with you, but we will also fight all efforts on your part to force us to do so. Our client's privacy is of utmost importance. Such a disclosure of privileged information to a third party would be a significant breach of the foundational trust our customers put in us. Such an action would be dangerous to our democracy and constitutional safeguards and would be beyond alarming.

We hope this settles the matter.

Sincerely,

Alfred Minion,

CEO, Generation Tree

Logan Hough, the attorney for the Chicago P. D. was livid. "This doesn't settle the matter at all!" he said with vitriol.

Cliff, Sammy, and the Lieutenant were in his office. Hough had received the response earlier that morning and called them in to discuss the next steps.

"What can we do about it?" Cliff asked.

"I'm going to file an emergency motion in court later today or first thing in the morning," Hough said. "We'll request an expedited hearing on the matter. We *will* force them to turn over the information. It won't be by a jury. We'll get a judge to grant the warrant. They'll have to comply."

"They said they'll appeal," Cliff said.

"Let 'em. That'll only delay the inevitable. We'll get those records one way or the other. It might take a few extra days, but we'll get them."

"It seems to me like they must've searched the database and found a match," Cliff said.

"Why do you say that?" the Lieutenant asked.

"If they ran the search and found nothing, they'd say so. Save the legal battle. Why come to Chicago and fight a warrant if they don't have the information anyway."

"I agree with Detective Ford," Hough said. "Those S.O.B.'s have the information and they're trying to hide behind some constitutional right to privacy that doesn't exist."

Cliff's heart did a somersault. The thought of knowing the identity of the Clown Slayer was beyond exhilarating. A competing emotion was also boiling inside of him. Anger. Borderline rage. He couldn't believe a company would be so flippant about helping to find a cold-blooded killer.

Cliff thought of something.

"When my wife submitted her DNA test to *Generation Tree*," he said, "they sent her a report matching her profile to her sister Anna. Using their logic, how is that not a breach of Anna's privacy?"

"That's a good point," Hough said. "We'll certainly make it. The bigger issue is community safety. We have a serial killer on the loose in Chicago. Someone who will kill again if not stopped. That supersedes any so-called privacy issues."

"When will the hearing be?" the Lieutenant asked.

"I'll let you know," Hough said. "We'll have to serve *Generation Tree*, so they have notice of the hearing. Then we'll get it on the judge's docket. I'm sure he'll want to hear this right away."

"How's the judge?" the Lieutenant asked.

"He's tough, but fair," Hough answered. "A stickler for rules and procedures. That should help us."

"Let us know what we can do," the Lieutenant said.

"I want your men at the hearing," Hough answered. "I'll need one of them to testify."

"That'll be Cliff," the Lieutenant replied. "I'll make sure he's there."

Cliff nodded.

The meeting ended. The wheels of justice were spinning. They'd have to wait for the next step. While Cliff hated waiting, he knew how the court system worked. These things took time.

He was more optimistic than he had been at any time in the investigation. Convinced that *Generation Tree* found a match. He couldn't wait to get his hands on that information.

This might be the break he'd been hoping and praying for.

***

Sunday afternoon
The day before the hearing

In an attempt to get their minds off the *Generation Tree* hearing scheduled for the next morning, Cliff and Sammy decided to take Julia and Cami to play a round of miniature golf. Unfortunately, the topic of the Clown Slayer and the DNA hearing came up, and an argument ensued between Cliff and Cami.

Since their little spat at the first dinner together, Cliff had mostly avoided any hot topics with Cami and the two had gotten along fairly well. She wasn't a person he'd choose to spend time with, except that Sammy was his partner and he felt an obligation.

If they kept having these blow ups, Cliff might have to avoid interacting with them on a personal level altogether.

It started when they were driving over to the miniature golf course. Cliff and Julia were in the backseat. Sammy was driving. Cami was in the passenger seat. The exchange between them had been heated.

Both of them raised their voices to the point of nearly yelling.

Julia frowned at Cliff and squeezed his hands in a clear attempt to get him to calm down.

Cami was facing forward now. Seconds before, she'd been turned toward the back seat. Straining her neck so she could see Cliff who was sitting directly behind her. She was so angry Cliff could see the veins bulging in her forehead.

The silence was welcoming although the tension still lingered in the car like the smell of a skunk they'd just run over.

Julia hadn't participated in the argument. She and Cami started out on a fast track to becoming good friends. After a few outings together, the relationship had cooled somewhat. Julia diplomatically said that they didn't have that much in common and used that as the excuse.

Julia was married with a baby. Cami was single. Cami worked. Julia was a stay-at-home mom.

Something that seemed to irritate Cami.

Cliff thought it went deeper than that. Cami was opinionated. She had a hard time keeping those opinions to herself. She seemed to have a chip on her shoulder towards men. She viewed Julia staying home and taking care of the baby and Cliff as some kind of subservient role. Julia was happy in her role. She saw it as a privilege. In her mind, her responsibilities in the family were as important as Cliff's. Only different.

Really, in her most honest moments, Julia admitted that she felt uncomfortable around Cami. The woman had a temper that occasionally reared its ugly head. She was strong-willed and opinionated. That part didn't bother Julia so much, except that Cami had a hard time dropping things, if someone disagreed with her.

And Cami always seemed to want to talk about the Clown Slayer murders. She seemed obsessed with it. Cliff had given Julia strict instructions not to discuss details of the investigation with anyone. Sammy clearly told Cami everything, but every time they were together, Cami would bring it up. Julia would try to change the subject, but it always seemed to come back to the case.

Which was happening today. Cami brought it up again. That's what led to the tension in the car. They were arguing the merits of the warrant served against *Generation Tree*. A touchy subject with Cliff anyway. In his mind, the company was obstructing justice. While he understood their right to fight it in court, he didn't understand why they would.

Cami held the opposite view. She agreed with the company that they shouldn't release the records and didn't mind saying so, even though Cliff was right there in the car and her boyfriend had a lot riding on the outcome of the case.

Her attitude still had Cliff fuming. She'd struck a nerve in him, and he had to speak his mind even though he knew he shouldn't.

"Aren't people innocent until proven guilty!" Cami said piercing the silence, in a more confrontive tone than Cliff would've liked.

Sammy, as usual, was oblivious. Driving the car with the uncanny ability to tune them out.

"Everyone has a presumption of innocence when they are in court and have been charged with a crime," Cliff argued. "Not when I'm doing an investigation. I can draw whatever conclusion I want. In fact, that's my job. To decide if someone committed a crime. I don't arrest someone unless I think they're guilty."

"Many people are in jail today because the investigator thought they were guilty and they got it wrong."

"I don't disagree with that," Cliff said, trying to soften his tone after Julia gave him another glare. "We're not infallible. That's why DNA is important. It is conclusive."

"Not always. DNA tests aren't a hundred percent accurate."

"Close enough to be admissible in court. That's why *Generation Tree* should turn over what they have in their database. So we can find the killer. She'll be afforded an attorney who can make whatever argument he wants to make to defend her."

"*Generation Tree* is a private company. They shouldn't be forced to help law enforcement with anything."

"They are a private company with information that will help solve a crime. They have a responsibility to turn it over."

"I vehemently disagree! People have a right to privacy. It's scary to think that law enforcement can look at my personal information anytime they want."

"If you haven't committed a crime, then you shouldn't be worried about it."

The debate was reaching a fever pitch. Each was responding to the other faster than they could catch their breaths.

"Someone should only have to give their DNA sample voluntarily," Cami argued.

"We can make someone give a sample now if they are the target of an investigation."

"That may be true, but an individual who gives a DNA sample to *Generation Tree* is not consenting to have their test used for law enforcement. They consent for it to be used privately."

Julia interrupted them in a calmer tone. "I could see why the company would be worried about it and would want to fight it. If people knew that their DNA might be turned over to law enforcement, then they might not be willing to buy the test. That would hurt their sales."

Cliff nodded but then rebutted, "Like I said. If you're innocent, you shouldn't care."

"It's unethical and should be illegal," Cami said.

"What's unethical about it? The woman killed twelve men. Don't you think that's unethical?"

"It's unethical to go behind someone's back and use their information against them without their consent."

"Even if they're guilty! You can't be serious."

"I'm dead serious."

"What if we use the service to identify human remains?" Cliff argued. "Let's say we find a Jane Doe. We have no idea who she is. Don't you think the family has a right to know that their loved one is dead? If *Generation Tree* can help us identify that person, then they should."

"That's different. That's for the greater good."

"You don't think getting a deranged serial killer off the streets is for the greater good."

"You don't know that she's deranged! Why do you keep saying that?"

"The woman is a sicko. You'll never convince me otherwise."

"You don't know that!"

Cliff didn't respond. The statement didn't justify a response. He didn't understand why Cami was always defending the Clown Slayer. It was getting annoying.

"I hope you lose the hearing tomorrow," Cami said.

"I don't think we will," Cliff retorted, not willing to hide the disgust in his voice.

"I want to go to it," Cami said.

"Me, too," Julia said.

Cliff looked at his wife in surprise.

"What?" she said to Cliff. "It's fascinating. I want to see you on the stand. To support you. I can get a sitter. I'd like to hear the arguments."

"It's open to the public," Cliff said. "Both of you can go. We'll save you a seat on our row."

"Do you think you'll win?" Cami asked. She bit her lip as she said it.

"I do," Cliff said. "I think the company has a match. Either the killer or one of her family members. I think we'll know the name of the killer tomorrow in court."

"I hope you lose."

"Yeah. You said that already," Cliff said angrily.

"Can we just agree to disagree?" Julia asked. "You guys aren't going to settle anything by arguing about it. The whole idea of today was for us to have fun. It's ruining the afternoon."

"I didn't bring it up," Cliff said.

Julia glared at him again.

"I'm sorry," Cliff said, even though he wasn't.

He did prefer not to talk about it. He and Cami were like oil and water. They didn't mix well together. Cami turned back around facing forward with her arms crossed. Not hiding that she was upset about the conversation but was willing to drop it.

Sammy reached over and tapped Cami's knee. Cliff did understand what Sammy saw in Cami. She was beautiful. Smart. Had a good job in the medical profession. She was a likable person as long as they didn't discuss certain topics. She stood up for herself. Julia was that way. Cliff liked that in a woman. Except that his wife was more diplomatic. Less confrontational.

Thankfully, they arrived at the miniature golf place and everyone's mood improved. Once they were out of the car, Cami was back to her usual cheery and playful self. Cutting up. Cracking jokes.

Amazing how she had the ability to turn it on and off.

They went inside to the counter. Cliff paid for everyone as a peace token for Cami. They each chose their color of golf ball. Julia chose purple, her favorite color. Sammy chose black for the Chicago White Sox team colors. Cliff chose blue. Cami chose red. That seemed to be her favorite color. She always wore red lipstick and had it on her lips that day.

They each picked out a putter.

"Do you have a left-handed one?" Cami asked the kid behind the counter.

"We do."

He handed her one from underneath the counter. Cami tried it out by simulating a couple of putting strokes.

"I didn't know you were left-handed," Cliff said.

"I'm ambidextrous," Cami said. "I'm proficient with both hands."

They exited the building and Cami let out a groan.

The first hole had a huge clown in the middle. An obstacle between them and the hole. They had to putt through or around it.

Cliff cracked a Clown Slayer joke and Cami was angry again.

20

The courthouse was abuzz with activity. A standing room only crowd packed into the room not constructed to hold that many people. Half of those present were reporters. Even the major networks had taken an interest in the hearing. All the local stations and the cable news networks had interrupted normal programming to televise it.

Logan Hough, the attorney for the Chicago P.D., said the case was groundbreaking with far reaching implications. He wouldn't be surprised if the outcome, whatever it was, made its way all the way to the Supreme Court of the United States. A number of complex legal theories were in question. Right to privacy being one. Right to freedom. Proportionality.

Hough was nervous about their position. Catching the killer was for the greater public good. Did that trump the right to privacy for the innocent? He would argue that the innocent would be unharmed. No inconvenience would come to them whatsoever. In his mind, the biggest obstacle to overcome would be probable cause.

Cliff didn't care about those things. He just wanted the name of the killer so he could stop her from killing again. The lawyers and judges could resolve the legal issues. If there were any. In his mind, the issue was cut and dried. If *Generation Tree* had information to help catch a killer, they should hand it over. Case closed.

Unfortunately, he didn't get to make that decision.

The sound in the courtroom was slightly below a loud din. Cliff and Sammy sat directly behind Hough on the front row along with

Julia and Cami. The Lieutenant sat next to Hough at the Plaintiff's table.

The first row adjacent to them was lined with a dozen attorneys seemingly in the same blue designer suit, white shirt, and red tie. They represented a number of interested parties. Mostly civil liberty groups who had filed briefs in support of *Generation Tree's* position. It remained to be seen if the judge would let them speak.

One lone attorney sat at the defense's table. Jacob Culver. A slick looking lawyer with perfectly coiffed hair, designer cufflinks, and a haughty look on his face. He seemed confident. Arrogant even. In a chair behind him, sat a frazzled navy blue pants-suited assistant with a stack of papers in her lap and what looked to be law books sitting on the chair beside her.

The clock on the wall crawled painstakingly slowly toward ten o'clock when presumably the judge would enter the courtroom. Hough said Judge Howard Stevens was a stickler for time and would not be one second late.

It couldn't come soon enough for Cliff.

He had a lump in the pit of his stomach. Some might attribute it to nerves, but Cliff knew otherwise. His mind was elsewhere. Something about the case bothered him. Many things, but one in particular. A sixth sense. It had come upon him yesterday.

He was missing something and couldn't pinpoint what it was. The nagging feeling started the day before at the miniature golf course. It continued through the evening. Hounded him all night as he tossed and turned until he fell asleep shortly after two in the morning. He woke up with the same angst.

It had to do with something in the file. Evidence that would crack the case if he could figure out what it was. He could feel it. Over the years, he'd had this same feeling a dozen or so times. Early on in his career, he ignored it. Now he knew better. The answer to solving this case was in the evidence room. He racked his brain trying to come up with the clue.

Somewhere deep in his subconscious he knew who the killer was. Or at least he knew how to find her. Trying to figure it out was driving him crazy. He tried to put it out of his mind. Worrying about it now was counterproductive. He needed to clear his mind of any distractions.

He'd be on the stand testifying soon. With all the cameras around, he wanted to be on top of his game. Hough said the opposing attorney was formidable.

The clock struck ten.

Cliff's thoughts were interrupted by the opening of the door from the judge's chamber.

"All rise," the bailiff said.

The murmuring in the crowd immediately died down to the point that not even a piece of paper was being shuffled around.

Judge Howard Stevens was younger than Cliff had imagined. Late forties. Slight graying around the ears. Level of fitness hard to determine under the large and flowing black robe, although Hough had said Judge Stevens was an avid biker, so Cliff assumed a trim body was underneath.

The judge sat down and began to speak. Orate would be a better description. Cliff despised the man immediately. The judge spoke for ten minutes on things that had nothing to do with the matter at hand. Like he was the Solomon of the Bible. Letting everyone know how wise he was right from the start.

Finally, the judge completed his remarks which were obviously intended for the viewing audience. The attorneys of record for both sides made their introductions and opening remarks. The formalities that ensued allowed Cliff's mind to wander back to the evidence room.

He should be focused on his testimony, but mentally, he scrolled through the files back at the office. The DNA tests. The victims. The dark figure of the woman he chased out of the bar and through the industrial complex.

The shoe.

What was he missing?

He felt a nervous smile form on his face when he thought of the story of Cinderella. Cami had brought it up after golf, at dinner the night before.

"Round up all your suspects," she said, "make them sit in a chair and try on the shoe. If it fits, you got your girl. Like Cinderella."

"The problem is that we don't have any suspects," Cliff said, soberly.

Cliff didn't think the shoe was the key to solving the case. The shoe was a size eight and a half. The most common shoe size among women in the United States. Sammy and Cliff even assigned one of the staff to research stores in and around Chicago that sold the shoes. It didn't take long to learn what they already knew. Thousands of those shoes were sold every year in Chicago. Not only that, but they were available online. They could've come from anywhere.

Cliff looked around the courtroom at all the cameras. Certain the Clown Slayer was watching the hearing. More nervous than Cliff would ever be.

What was she thinking at that very moment?

Probably dreading the ruling. With one stroke of the judge's gavel, the whole investigation could turn in his favor. Cliff's greatest worry was that if they did win, the Clown Slayer would disappear. Maybe leave the country. She couldn't stay in Chicago. He'd find her in no time.

She had to know Cliff was close. Closer than he'd been since that night at the bar when he was within a few feet of her.

Would he ever be that close to her again?

He strained his neck and scanned the courtroom for women wearing red lipstick. How ironic would it be if the woman were actually in the courtroom?

Julia smiled at Cliff reassuringly. Cami sat next to Julia. She leaned forward, caught Cliff's eye and smiled at him. He nodded back. A truce had formed between them, but a smile would be impossible to form at that moment.

The preliminaries dragged on for more than thirty minutes. The Lieutenant warned about that. With the cameras in the courtroom, the attorneys had their fifteen minutes of fame and would milk every last bit of facetime out of it. The judge had set the tone, and the lawyers weren't about to let the judge upstage them.

It only served to give Cliff more time with his thoughts which were finally interrupted when he heard his name called.

Cliff stood. He suddenly felt millions of eyes on him. His knees were weak. His heart raced. He almost tripped over Cami's foot getting out to the aisle.

Was he holding his breath?

If so, he needed to take one in before he felt lightheaded.

The rest of the walk to the witness stand was a blur. When he got to it, he plopped into the chair making a loud noise that echoed through the courtroom.

He suddenly felt angry. He wasn't like the judge and the attorneys. He didn't welcome these fifteen minutes of fame. This was *Generation Tree's* fault. They should've turned over the information without creating this spectacle.

Cliff was sworn in and took his seat in the witness chair. Hough questioned him first. They had rehearsed the questions, so Cliff knew what to expect. Hearing Hough's voice helped to calm his nerves somewhat.

The questions had to do with the investigation and the murders. Meant to lay a foundation. Even though the entire country knew about the woman serial killer, Cliff couldn't discuss anything in court related to making *Generation Tree* turn over her DNA until they provided evidence to the court that she even existed and that a crime had been committed.

It seemed silly, but that's how the rules of procedure worked in a courtroom.

Cliff skillfully answered the questions, and his nerves began to subside somewhat. He knew the case backward and forward and the questions coming from Hough were easier than slow pitch softball. Maybe as easy as hitting a tee ball.

Hough finished, then turned things over to the *Generation Tree's* attorney. If there were to be fireworks, they'd start now. More than likely, Jacob Culver would hit on the issue of probable cause.

It didn't take him long to do so.

But not before he tried to get under Cliff's skin with an inappropriate opening question.

"Detective Ford, why are you asking my client to do your job?"

"Objection, argumentative."

"Sustained," the judge said coolly. "Restate the question, Mr. Culver."

"Sorry, Your Honor," Culver said. "But it goes to the heart of this case. Why should my client have to turn over their customer's DNA when the detective hasn't made a case against our customer? He doesn't even know her identity!"

Culver looked at the camera when he said it. More pandering to the audience of public opinion than for the judge's benefit.

"Objection," Hough said again. "Is that a question for Detective Ford or is Counselor wasting the court's valuable time with rhetorical questions?"

"Limit your questions to those you want the detective to answer," the judge said firmly.

"Yes, Your Honor. Detective Ford, what is probable cause?"

Another softball question. Cliff took a deep breath. Then let it out after making a mental note to speak slowly and not rush his answers.

"It's the standard we use to determine whether to detain a suspect, make an arrest, or search a residence."

"I understand what it is, but how is it applied?"

"When there's a fair probability that the search will lead to evidence that a crime has been committed."

Homicide 101. Cliff tried not to sound condescending.

He shifted in the hard wooden witness chair. He hadn't realized his feet and rear end had been frozen in one position and were starting to fall asleep.

Culver nodded, then stood to the side of the podium that contained his notes. He probably wouldn't stray too far away from the microphone because he'd want his voice heard on the television.

"There are limits to searches even if there's a fair probability that a crime has been committed, are there not?" Culver said in a lawyerly voice.

"Yes, sir."

"If you searched every home in Chicago, there's a fair probability that you'd catch your killer. Would you agree with that statement?"

"If the killer lives in Chicago. Yes. Probably."

"Why don't you search every home in Chicago?"

Cliff chuckled. Knowing where the smooth talking lawyer was going with the question. Cliff wasn't going to fall into his trap. He'd look for an opportunity to set one of his own.

"First of all, we don't have the manpower."

"I realize that. But even if you did, you're not allowed to conduct such a broad search, are you?"

"No, sir. We are not."

"Thankfully. Why not?"

"We need probable cause to search someone's residence."

"You can't even search every home in a neighborhood or a city block, can you?"

"We can canvas a neighborhood. But we can't enter a residence without probable cause or the homeowner's consent."

"Yet you're asking in this warrant to search *Generation Tree's* entire database. That's over two million people. How is that different from searching every house in Chicago?"

A thought suddenly popped into Cliff's mind. Culver had made a mistake.

"It's very different," Cliff said.

"How so?" Culver asked skeptically.

Cliff was glad he asked. He had a response ready. He'd thought of it seconds before.

"Let's say that a murder occurs," Cliff said, gaining confidence. "And a witness sees the killer run into his house across the street. I have probable cause to search that house."

"That hypothetical doesn't apply here. In this instance, you don't know who the killer is. Do you?"

"No, sir. But you do."

"Why would you say that?"

"I find it incredible that you don't want to tell us who the killer is even though it would almost certainly save lives. Everybody in this room wants to know the name. Why won't you give it to us?"

A gasp went through the courtroom.

If the attorney could pander to the court of public opinion, so could Cliff.

"I object, Your Honor." Culver was back behind the podium now. Clearly flustered by Cliff's last question.

"Are you objecting to your own question?" the judge asked.

"I object to the response. The Detective is stating facts not in evidence. And is non responsive. He's asking me questions. I never stated that my client knows the identity of the killer."

"Yes, you did," Cliff interjected.

Hough stood up to enter the fray but sat back down. Probably deciding Cliff was doing fine on his own.

"I did no such thing," Culver argued.

"Would you like for me to explain?" Cliff asked.

"No," Culver said. "It's not responsive to my question."

"I'll hear the explanation," the judge said.

Cliff couldn't stop the grin from forming on his face. He quickly tamped it down, but the cameras likely caught it. If he handled it right, he could blow the entire defense's argument out of the water.

"You asked me, and I quote, 'Why should my client have to turn over their customer's DNA when the detective hasn't made a case against our customer?' That's an admission on your part that you have a customer who is a match."

"That's not what I said."

"That's exactly what you said. Word for word. Maybe the court reporter should read it back to jog your memory."

"Let me get back to my questioning," Culver said.

"I'd like to clarify further, if I may," Cliff replied.

"I haven't asked a question," Culver retorted roughly.

Hough stood to his feet. "I think the detective should be able to clarify his answer."

"I agree," the judge said. "This is a hearing. There's not a jury present. A little informality won't hurt anything. Please continue, Detective."

"Thank you, Your Honor." Cliff liked him slightly more than he did earlier.

Cliff spoke at a faster pace. "Counselor is right that I can't search every home in Chicago. But if I get information that a particular home contains evidence pertinent to my investigation, then that is probable cause, and I can search that home. Within reason. Counsel for the defense asked why his client should have to turn over the DNA for one of his customers. That tells me that he already has the evidence in his possession. He knows who that customer is. The killer."

Cliff paused for effect and to let the words sink in.

"That's the probable cause necessary to get that information. Even if the judge were to reject the argument that we could search the entire database, *Generation Tree* has already done so, so it's a moot point. Now it's just a matter of them turning over the evidence."

"You are mischaracterizing my words!" Culver practically shouted.

Hough stood to his feet. "Can counsel for *Generation Tree* characterize his words for us? Does his client have a customer whose DNA profile matches that of the Clown Slayer killer?"

"That's a fair question," the judge said. "How about it, Mr. Culver? Care to clarify?"

Culver was clearly squirming. He didn't answer right away.

"If not, then why are we here?" the judge asked.

"I request a sidebar, Your Honor," Culver said.

The judge motioned for the two attorneys to approach the bench. Cliff could hear them talking.

"Do you have the information, Jacob?" Hough asked their attorney. "I'd like to know. We all would."

"My client shouldn't have to answer that," Culver pleaded with the judge. "Not until you make your ruling."

"Given that answer, I'm going to assume that you do," the judge said. "Would you like to go on the record?"

Culver hesitated.

"Yes, Your Honor," Culver said barely above a whisper. "My client did find a DNA match."

Cliff about fell out of his chair.

21

During the hearing, an anonymous call came into the tip line.

"I think I just saw the woman," the man's voice said excitedly. "You know. The one killing all those men in Chicago. She's on television right now. She almost killed me, but I got away. I saw her go into the courthouse. Her name is Macy."

The staffer recorded the information in the log along with dozens of other calls that came in that morning.

***

Courthouse

The sidebar had turned into a raging debate.

Cliff was still in the witness chair within earshot of the entire scene unfolding before his eyes in a real-life courtroom drama. One in which lives hung in the balance.

The counsel for *Generation Tree* had admitted his client had discovered a DNA match. The judge acted like he was about to rule against the ancestry company and order them to turn the information over to the Chicago P.D.

Culver tried desperately to prevent that from happening. His arguments seemed to fall on deaf ears.

Cliff was almost beside himself with anticipation. With the identity of the Clown Slayer, he could focus his investigation on finding her.

Would the judge make them turn over the evidence today?

Would Cliff walk out of there with it?

How soon could he find her?

Would they have to wait for an appeal?

Questions swirled around in his mind like a tornado on a prairie.

Cliff turned his head in the opposite direction so the judge and lawyers wouldn't think he was purposefully listening to them. Although, they seemed oblivious to him. The only consideration they gave was to keep their voices high enough for the court reporter to hear but low enough that the television cameras wouldn't pick up their words.

Culver sounded desperate. Hough kept the pressure on.

"The Detective's argument makes sense, doesn't it?" Hough argued. "If you know the killer, then there's probable cause for you to turn over that specific information. In essence, the warrant is specific to the killer. Not the entire database."

Culver ignored the argument and didn't even try to rebut it. He threw out something that didn't even make sense to Cliff.

"I'm going to rule for the Plaintiff," the judge finally said after Culver finished with his nonsensical argument. "The Plaintiff's warrant is well founded, and I find probable cause to grant it. Your client has information that will catch a murderer. You must turn it over."

"Your Honor, I have a motion prepared for your consideration," Culver said.

"What? It's too late for that now," Hough said. "The judge is ready to rule."

"We should have the opportunity to make a motion to the court," Culver said. "I think you'll find it dispositive."

Cliff knew dispositive meant definitive. What kind of shenanigans was the lawyer trying to pull? Some kind of legal trick?

"Why am I hearing about this now?" the judge asked.

"This was an emergency hearing. We didn't have a lot of time to prepare."

"Make your motion," the judge said.

"I'd like to make it in your chambers."

Judge Stevens paused, then said, "Step back."

The two attorneys walked away from the bench and back to their positions behind their respective tables.

Cliff was confused. He thought the case was over. What was this last-minute motion? What could they possibly have that would be dispositive?

Cliff tried to remain optimistic. Culver was only throwing out a desperation ploy. Something to buy time. An attempt to snatch victory from the throes of defeat. Mostly, he was probably just getting his motion on the record for appeal purposes.

The judge seemed locked into his decision.

When the attorneys were back at their tables, Judge Stevens picked up his gavel and slammed it a couple of times on the bench. "The court will be adjourned for fifteen minutes. Detective Ford, you may step down with the thanks of the court."

Cliff was beyond exuberant. On such a high, he practically floated back to his seat. They were going to win. He could barely contain his enthusiasm. The Lieutenant gave him a thumbs up as he passed by the Plaintiff's table.

Everyone stood and Hough and Culver followed the judge out of the courtroom and into his chambers.

Julia's lips were twisted to the side with a confused look on her face. "What's happening?" she asked.

"They're going back to the judge's chambers to discuss something," Cliff said, barely above a whisper so the people around them wouldn't hear. "I think the judge is going to rule in our favor. Their attorney basically admitted that they know who the killer is. I think the judge is going to grant our request and give me the name of the killer. Probably today."

Cami looked like she'd seen a ghost. Her face was white as a sheet.

Julia gave Cliff a slight reassuring tap on the arm. Sammy clasped Cliff's elbow in excitement.

"Good work, buddy," he said.

Sammy slapped his hands together. Gave Cami a big hug. Then patted Cliff on the back.

"You were amazing," Julia said to Cliff. "You were so cool under pressure. With all the TV cameras and all."

The Lieutenant was now beside them. Cliff filled him in on the developments. He was clearly pleased.

When Cliff turned back around, Cami was gone. Cliff scanned the courtroom for her.

Julia must've sensed what Cliff was thinking because she said, "Cami went to the lady's room."

Cliff nodded. His mind was doing cartwheels. Mental gymnastics. A celebration was going off in his head.

These were the days that made it all worthwhile. When he crossed a threshold in a case. He could work for hours and hours. Searching for clues and suspects. Then the big break happened, and the case was blown wide open. Those were the most satisfying of times.

A case had three such instances. When the guilty party was identified, when he had enough evidence to make an arrest, and when the suspect was found guilty and hauled off to jail. It's what Cliff lived for. Why he risked his life.

While they were a long way from a conviction, he felt like they were close to the first step. Knowing the identity of the Clown Slayer. He wanted to shout from the rooftop to all the reporters and protesters below.

Cliff's worst nightmare had been that this case could take years to solve and he'd be stuck on this merry-go-round of a case for months and months with no way to get off. Now, if things went well, he could be back to his old job within days.

He could hardly wait.

Fifteen minutes passed and the lawyers were still not back in the courtroom. Cliff thought about leaving and going to the restroom but wanted to be present when the judge returned. He had to be there when the judge ruled in their favor. To see the look on Culver's face.

It seemed like everyone was thinking the same thing, as the courtroom was still packed. More people were in the courtroom now if that were even possible.

Cami was still gone. Sammy kept looking back at the door for her.

Thirty minutes later, the lawyers appeared. The wait had been excruciating. Cliff wondered if he'd have to go back on the stand.

Probably not.

Hough had a stern and serious look on his face. His jaw was clenched, his lips pursed, and his forehead furrowed.

Cliff wasn't sure how to take it.

The judge entered moments later. After the room was seated, the judge spoke one sentence.

"This case is dismissed. On the grounds that the warrant was not properly served."

The entire room collectively gasped.

The judge pounded the case closed, stood to his feet, and left the room quickly. Before those in the courtroom even had a chance to rise for him.

Cliff sat in his seat completely stunned. His mouth agape in disbelief.

What just happened?

The words had appeared out of thin air like a bolt of lightning and had struck at the core of his being. How could the judge dismiss the warrant?

On a technicality!

Cliff wanted to shout out in disgust but was speechless. Not even sure what he'd say. He put his hands over his eyes and rubbed them roughly.

Stay cool.

Culver exited the room quickly. Almost before his assistant had a chance to gather her things together. Cliff wanted to follow the attorney outside but resisted the urge. The cameras were still rolling. He didn't care if they saw his expressions of disgust but they couldn't see him act out toward their lawyer.

Improper service!

The judge had blood on his hands.

What a load of crock!

The lawyers for *Generation Tree* had found some deficiency in the warrant. The wrong address was probably listed.

Hough was slumped down in his chair. His head was down like he'd just lost game seven of the World Series. Struck out with the bases loaded. The case was won. Then it wasn't.

How did Hough let Culver steal it from him back in the chambers?

The Lieutenant was clearly angry. He and Hough carried on an intense conversation for several minutes. Cliff decided not to interrupt them. He'd know what happened soon enough. He just fidgeted around in place. Unable to believe the sudden turn of events.

All they could do was stand around and wait. Julia, Sammy, and Cliff. Together on the first row. The courtroom had cleared. The only ones left were workers disassembling the cameras and cables. One loan sketch artist sat on a chair in the back.

Cami still wasn't there.

Sammy had his phone out and had turned it on. Phones weren't allowed in the courtroom, but it didn't matter now.

"I got a text from Cami," he said a few seconds later. "She's not feeling well. She went home."

"She'll be happy with the outcome," Cliff said bitterly. "Too bad she missed it."

"I'm going to text her to see if she's okay," Sammy said. His massive fingers typed away on the cell phone.

That nagging feeling returned. The one where Cliff felt like the answer was right in front of his face. That he didn't need *Generation Tree*. If he were a good detective, he should have already solved the case.

What is it?

He couldn't really think about it. The reality was hitting him between the eyes like a matador's sword pierces the bull. The powerful animal confident right up to the point of death. Like he had been.

Cliff had been that bull. Counted his chickens so to speak. He was back to square one. No closer to catching the killer than he was yesterday. For the second time, the Clown Slayer had slipped through his fingers. He'd come so close to catching her and yet he was so far away.

Culver probably had the name in his briefcase. Less than a dozen steps away from Cliff.

What was this feeling?

Cliff had to get back to the evidence room and start poring through the documents again. Maybe something would knock the memory loose.

"I guess I'll go home," Julia said, interrupting his thoughts. "I'm sorry, Cliff. I was hoping for a better outcome."

"We all were," Cliff said, feeling the anger leave him momentarily.

Julia kissed him on the cheek. Her smile was so sweet. Her eyes so loving. Genuinely feeling the same hurt he felt.

He didn't think he could love her more. In times like this, he realized he could. He did.

"You did a great job on the stand," she said sweetly. "I'm proud of you. It's not your fault. You'll catch her."

"I know. This is a hard pill to swallow. I can't believe they know who she is but won't tell us. It's okay. You go home to Rita."

"Are you going to be late for dinner? I understand if you are."

"No. I'll be home at the usual time."

Cliff anticipated going to the evidence room, poring over the documents, and leaving frustrated. Going home was the only thing he looked forward to.

Cliff kissed Julia on the cheek a second time. Then she left.

By that time, Hough and the Lieutenant were standing. Hough abruptly turned and left the courtroom without saying anything to

Cliff. Probably to go express his outrage to the press. Win or lose, the show must go on.

Cliff wanted to do the same thing, but knew it was for the better. He wasn't in the right frame of mind to face the questioning of the press. Hough would be diplomatic. Cliff would give them a piece of his mind. Tell the world how much he disagreed with the decision.

Not a good idea.

The Lieutenant filled Cliff and Sammy in on the details. As Cliff had already deduced, there was a deficiency in the warrant. It wasn't served to the proper corporate office. Hough would fix it.

"How long will that take?" Cliff asked.

"Six to eight weeks and we'll be right back here. Three to four months if things don't go as planned."

Back to square one.

Maybe not. Cliff was going to go back to the station and find that piece of evidence.

It had to be there.

22

Two days later
Wednesday

Julia didn't tell Cliff her latest off-the-wall theory related to the Clown Slayer case. Something her intuition was telling her.

What if Cami were the killer?

The hair-brained idea came to Julia while driving home from the courthouse after the huge disappointment at the hearing. Several times, she'd thought about telling him her idea, but chickened out.

Tuesday night, she almost told him. Until he started complaining incessantly about all the crazies on the tip line calling in the most absurd and outrageous tips. Wasting their time.

Julia didn't want to be lumped in with them.

She couldn't quit thinking about the hearing, though. Everything about that morning seemed strange. The huge throng of reporters. Television cameras in the courtroom.

It sounded like a good idea to go to the hearing and support her husband when Cami suggested it. Then and now, she wasn't so sure.

What Julia found when she got there that day was nothing less than a media circus. A dangerous situation in retrospect. Hundreds of protestors had gathered at the courthouse. Representing both sides. The threat of a riot was real.

Julia had been seriously injured in a riot once. While she didn't remember the actual riot because of the head injury she sustained, she knew she didn't want to put herself in that situation again.

Going down to the courthouse had not been a good idea.

Cliff and Sammy went in through a backdoor with the Lieutenant and their lawyer, so they were able to avoid the mess outside. Cami and Julia had to fight their way through the throng of people to get inside the main entrance. Security was tight and they almost didn't get in.

Controlled chaos was the only way to describe it.

Inside the courtroom was equally weird. Cliff testified and did a good job. It looked like the judge was going to rule in their favor. Cliff had been so excited only to have his hopes dashed like a sinking boat on the rocks. With one bang of the gavel, the judge reversed himself and did the unthinkable—let a murderer continue to remain free to murder again because of a technicality.

Maybe it made sense to some people who understood the law, but not to Julia. Protecting society from bad people should be the number one job of law enforcement and the courts.

As unbelievable as it all was, what seemed stranger was Cami's behavior. As soon as it looked like Cliff was going to win, she disappeared. Said she was sick. Left the courthouse and went home without telling anyone.

The whole time, driving over and then at the hearing, Julia couldn't help but notice how nervous Cami was. She was constantly fidgeting. Wringing her hands. Crossing her legs. Uncrossing them. Then crossing them again all in one motion.

At first, Julia thought Cami was nervous for Sammy. Standing by her man like Julia was. In retrospect, it seemed like she had more riding on the outcome than what appeared on the surface.

Her reaction didn't fit the circumstances. Julia was nervous for her husband as well, but this was only one case. Cliff had had many ups and downs over the years. Win some, lose some. While this case was important, it wasn't the end of the world.

Maybe it was to Cami. Almost like it was life and death to her.

That's when the thought occurred to Julia. If Cami were the Clown Slayer, she had a lot riding on the judge's decision.

Perhaps even a worst nightmare.

What if Cami's name had been revealed right there in the court-room?

That made sense as to why Cami wanted to get out of there as quickly as possible. Probably planning a getaway.

Predictably, when Cami learned the judge had ruled against them and wasn't going to turn the killer's name over to Cliff, she was sud-denly okay. Communicating with them again. Like nothing had ever happened.

It all seemed suspicious.

How incredible would it be if Cami were the killer?

Julia gasped and put her hand over her mouth.

The woman had been in her home. Held her baby. They'd been together an unknown number of times. For lunch and dinner.

Julia shuddered.

She'd let a cold-blooded killer inside her home.

Once the idea was in her head, Julia couldn't get it out. Her imag-ination began to run wild. Connecting dots that might only be a co-incidence.

The red lipstick.

The most obvious connection. Julia searched for it on the inter-net. Red and pink were the most common colors worn by women. Hardly definitive. In reality, Cami wore the most commonly sold lip-stick in America.

Julia felt foolish.

Some detective she was. She'd even worn red lipstick herself on occasion. Did that mean she was a suspect?

Still the thoughts continued.

Cami was an anesthesiologist.

Cliff said the Clown Slayer drugged her victims. Cliff was convinced the killer had medical training. Julia conducted an-other search. More than two thousand anesthesiologists worked in Chicago. Tens of thousands of medical professionals.

Was Julia grasping at straws? Trying to create an elephant out of an ant.

Cliff would laugh her out of the room if she brought it up to him. Actually, he wouldn't. Cliff was too nice. He'd just politely nod his head, dismissively, and go about his business trying to do the work of a real detective.

She'd be embarrassed.

He'd think I'm crazy.

She probably was. But she couldn't get it out of her mind.

She couldn't control herself. The evidence was mounting.

Cami was off on Wednesdays and Thursdays. All the murders were committed on those nights.

Julia passed the point of no return. She wasn't going to drop it. The popcorn was in the microwave. No way to unpop it.

Her heart ached for Sammy. He would be devastated. Another clue popped into her mind.

How the two met was suspicious.

Sammy said Cami was outside his doorstep on his way to work one morning.

Coincidence?

Not a chance!

Seems too convenient. Staged. Sammy had just started working on the Clown Slayer case. Cami planned the meeting. Pretending it was a chance meeting.

How ingenious to start up a romantic relationship with the investigator. Weasel her way into the inner circle so she knew every aspect of the investigation.

Julia felt angry.

Sammy loved Cami. Another thing Julia noticed and had even commented to Cliff on. Cami didn't seem to be as into Sammy as he was into her. He was head over heels in love. She was effusive but guarded. Cold even at times.

It made sense now. Cami wanted to be close to the investigation.

That's why she asked so many questions. Constantly. Always drilling Julia for answers. *What was Cliff thinking? Did he have any suspects? Tell me everything you know.*

Cami was constantly hounding Julia for information. Now she knew why.

Julia felt used. Manipulated.

And the name!

Clown Slayer. Cliff and Cami had argued about it.

Cami hated that name. Thought it was disrespectful. Why would you show respect to someone who killed men?

At the time, it seemed like a difference of opinion between Cami and Cliff. Now Julia knew that the disagreement was personal. Cami was offended by the name.

Because it was her.

Julia let out a noticeable gasp. Rita was the only one in the room to hear it.

Julia thought of something.

Cami's sister.

Julia remembered the conversation like it was yesterday. According to Cami, her sister was tragically killed. At the time it seemed like a rare show of vulnerability on Cami's part. She wouldn't talk about it in detail, but it sounded horrible, and deeply affected Cami's psyche.

The FBI profiler said the Clown Slayer had a deep hatred for men. Cliff said he thought the Clown Slayer was a victim of violence from a man in her past. Or maybe a relative was.

Cami's sister must've been killed by a man. Murdered. Under tragic circumstances.

"I have to tell Cliff."

Julia was talking to herself out loud now. Which she often did when she was alone.

"I don't have enough evidence."

"I just know it's her. I feel it in my gut."

Cami was ambidextrous. The Clown Slayer killed men with her left and right hand.

I know it's her. I can feel it.

Cliff was a detective. He didn't go by feelings. He relied on facts. The two of them were opposite in that way. That's why they made a good team.

Shouldn't she at least tell him what she was thinking?

No. He'd say something to Cami. Or to Sammy.

What a horrible accusation to make against their friend.

Cliff's partner's girlfriend.

If Julia was wrong, she'd ruin everything between them. Cami would never speak to her again.

Julia needed more evidence.

So she did something stupid.

She picked up the phone and called Cami. That Wednesday morning. Cami's day off. Right after she secured a sitter for Rita.

"Hi, it's Julia," she said to Cami.

"Hey, girlfriend," Cami responded cheerfully. "What ja doing?"

"I'm getting Rita dressed. Are you feeling better?" Julia asked.

"Much better, thank you. I don't know what came over me at the courthouse. I guess all the excitement. I'm better now."

I know what came over you.

Julia could feel the vitriol building inside of her. She tamped it down so it wouldn't come across in her words or tone.

"I have a babysitter for Rita," Julia said. "How about some girl time? Are you free for lunch? I'm buying."

"I am."

"Great."

"I just got back from a run," Cami said, "so I'll need to hop in the shower. I can be ready in an hour or so. Is that enough time?"

Perfect.

Julia had a plan.

"Sure. That sounds good," Julia said. "I'll pick you up."

Julia wanted to look in Cami's closet. At her shoes. See what size they were. She wasn't sure how she was going to distract her so she could do so, but she'd figure it out when she got there.

Julia might even find murder weapons if she looked hard enough. The thought sent tingles down her spine.

She'd never actually been inside Cami's house. Another fact that was suspicious.

A panic suddenly came over her.

What would she do if she found murder weapons? What if she got caught?

Cami might kill her.

"No. I'll meet you at your house," Cami said.

"Are you sure?" Julia whined, even though she was breathing a sigh of relief on the inside. "It's on my way."

"I'm sure. I've got a few errands to run anyway. I'll drop by your house. I'll drive."

"Okay. I'll see you in a few."

Julia hung up. She bent over and put her hands on her knees to catch her breath. To keep from hyperventilating.

She may have dodged a bullet. Literally. Or a scalpel. If Cami caught her snooping around her house, she could kill her.

The woman's good.

Julia was suddenly angry that Cami had successfully kept Julia out of her house.

"She doesn't want me anywhere near there," Julia said aloud. She was talking to herself again.

"Cami murdered twelve men. There's probably evidence in her house. Of course, she doesn't want me to go there."

Allegedly, she heard Cliff's voice in her head say. *She allegedly murdered twelve men.*

"This is stupid," Julia said aloud. "The woman is dangerous. She could kill me and cut up my body and Cliff would never know what happened to me."

Another gasp.

"What if Cami finds out I'm onto her? What if she figures it out while we're together?"

Julia wasn't good at lying or keeping secrets. She wore her emotions on her sleeve.

"What if she drugs me?"

Julia would be paranoid to take another sip of a beverage around her. Cami could knock her out, kill her, then kill Cliff. Then Rita.

Tears welled up in her eyes. This wasn't worth the risk. What she was doing was insanity. Cliff would be so mad if he found out she was even considering it.

Julia was in over her head. This was a bad idea. How could she call Cami and get out of it?

"Breathe, Julia! You're overreacting. Cami only kills men."

"I don't know that! Who knows what she's capable of?"

That was a scary thought. The Cami they knew was a façade. An actress playing a role. Underneath the warm exterior was a cold-blooded serial killer.

Julia was suddenly filled with doubts. Bordering on panic.

It's too dangerous.

Too late.

Her curiosity was piqued.

Cami would be there soon. She needed to take the risk. For Cliff and the investigation.

Julia spent the next hour coming up with another plan. Once she was satisfied, she rushed to get ready. The babysitter arrived which gave her more freedom to do so.

The whole time, anxiety kept building inside of her like a volcano about to erupt.

Julia literally jumped when the doorbell rang.

Cami!

Julia was in the bedroom. She heard the babysitter answer the door.

Was she putting her babysitter's life in danger as well?

"This may be the stupidest thing I've ever done in my entire life."

23

Cliff hadn't checked the tip line log since last Friday.

Had it been that long?

It had. He was off on Saturday and Sunday. Monday was the disastrous hearing. The rest of Monday and all-day Tuesday were spent poring over the files looking for that elusive clue. The hunch he knew was there. The rabbit hole he had obsessed over for two days. He'd chased the snake into the weeds but never found him.

Her in this instance.

He finally gave up and went back to real detective work. Investigating. Searching for more clues. Not searching for a needle in a haystack when he didn't even know if the needle existed.

The call log was well maintained. A staffer entered the date and time of each call into a log and a quick summary. The call was assigned a number. Each call was meticulously transcribed and placed in a computer file by number.

None of the calls over the weekend looked promising. After the hearing, the calls increased by a multiple of twenty. Crazies from as far away as other countries had called in tips. The volume was so overwhelming that Cliff decided to have a staffer sort through them. He focused on the tips that came in on that Monday. During the hearing. Maybe someone somewhere saw something that jogged their memories.

One in particular looked interesting.

The call log read, *Tip: he saw killer at hearing.*

Cliff wrote down the log number and went to the transcript.

He read through it. Twice. It rang true. For whatever reason. Back to instincts again. Reading between the lines, he could draw some conclusions. The caller said he was attacked by the killer but got away. That meant there must be a police report.

The caller was anonymous, but they tracked every call. Cliff looked up the area code and prefix. The number was from the twin cities. St. Paul, Minnesota. That's where he'd begin his search for a police report.

The tipster said the woman's name was Macy. No last name, but something to go on, nonetheless. They even had a phone number. Cliff would call it back. Hopefully, it wasn't from a burner phone and the person who left the tip would answer. He could get more details that way.

The man also said he saw the Clown Slayer at the hearing. Cliff had instructed the staffers to record all the news footage from that day for this very reason. It wasn't unusual for a serial killer to inter-ject himself or herself into the case in some way. Attend a victim's funeral. Or a press conference. Loiter at the scene of the crime after-wards to watch the police activity.

Attend a hearing.

He went to find Sammy. They'd spend the rest of the afternoon going over that footage. Looking at every person who entered the courthouse that day.

Maybe they'd see her. It felt like the investigation was gaining momentum again.

***

The Shoe Spa
Downtown Chicago

Julia was determined to find out if Cami was the Clown Slayer. Either rule her in or out. She had two ways to do it. By finding out her shoe size and/or by getting a sample of her DNA.

Cliff said the shoe left behind by the Clown Slayer that night at the bar was not much of a clue. Actually, worthless without a suspect.

If they had a person of interest, it could be useful for one purpose. Having the person try it on. If the shoe didn't fit, then she obviously wasn't the killer. Cliff had chased her through the industrial buildings. No one could run like that wearing high heels that were too small or too big.

If the shoe did fit, it didn't necessarily mean that the suspect was the killer. All it meant was that they needed to find additional evidence. Combined with other facts, it could very well help bolster a circumstantial case or lead to something more definitive.

Julia desperately wanted to find out Cami's shoe size. She could come right out and ask her, but if Cami were the killer, then she'd be suspicious. The killer knew Cliff had one of her shoes.

Julia had to be more subtle.

So she took Cami shopping for shoes. It couldn't be just any old shoe store. It had to be someplace where Cami would willingly take off her shoes.

Julia had racked her brain coming up with the plan in the short time she had to think it up. A lot of things could go wrong. What if they got to a shoe store and Cami didn't want to try on shoes?

That's when Julia got the idea to take Cami to *The Shoe Spa*. A high-end specialty shoe store in downtown Chicago that also did massages and pedicures.

At the shoe spa, Cami would have to take her shoes off. Julia paid for a package for the two of them complete with pedicure, a foot massage, and a customized shoe fitting.

Julia made reservations. Fortunately, she was able to get them in on short notice.

She was petrified.

The reality was hitting her between the eyes with the precision of a hammer hitting a nail.

The whole drive over, Julia kept her hands clasped so Cami wouldn't see them shaking. If her instincts were right, she was in the car alone with the most notorious female serial killer in the history of Chicago.

It's all Julia could do to act normal.

She had to. She needed to be courageous. Keep her wits about her. Follow through with the plan.

Confirm the shoe size. If Cami wasn't an eight and a half, then Julia would say a silent apology to herself. Honestly, she hoped that happened and Cami was innocent. For a lot of reasons. Their friendship. Sammy. Even Cliff. While it'd be good to solve the case, it'd be better if it wasn't someone they'd let into their inner circle.

If Cami was the right shoe size, Julia would be forced to go to step two. Take her to lunch and get her DNA. On something. Preferably a glass. Something her lips had touched so the red lipstick would be on it. Cliff could run a test and see if there was a match.

Julia had already screwed up the first shot at getting Cami's DNA.

Right after Cami arrived at their house, Julia offered her a drink filled with Cami's favorite liquid. Cherry lemonade. Julia started to fill the glass and hand it to her.

Cami waved her hand in the air, shooing it away.

"I'm good. I just put my lipstick on. I don't want to have to refresh it."

Julia's heart sank. This wasn't going as planned.

Oh well.

There'd be plenty of opportunities to get Cami's DNA. At the restaurant. Julia would have to figure out a way to steal the glass without getting caught.

On the drive over, Julia asked Cami about her sister. Cami seemed hesitant at first so Julia talked about her own sister. An FBI agent. Killed by a drive by shooter. A gang member. The Strikers. Cliff caught him. The murderer was in jail. Cliff always catches the killer.

She threw that in for good measure.

Rita's death was still painful.

Cami was surprisingly forthcoming. Her sister was raped and murdered. Everyone knew who did it but he was never arrested. Never tried.

Julia could hear the bitterness in Cami's voice. It didn't mean anything. Julia felt that same disgust for Rita's killer.

Julia even got a name. Chloe.

It might be a made-up name. Julia had gotten cynical about everything that came out of Cami's mouth.

Was Cami even her real name?

Julia didn't know what to believe. Cliff said don't believe anything in an investigation until it's proven.

Cami drove to the shoe spa. Julia couldn't help but think that Cami's DNA was all over that car. She had to be patient. Wait for the right moment. Lipstick on a glass was the best idea.

They arrived at the spa and were greeted by a perky woman in hot red high heels holding two glasses of champagne in her hand. Wearing bright red lipstick.

It reminded Julia of how far in left field she might actually be. Not everyone who wore red lipstick was a killer.

"I'm Charise," the salesperson said. "I'll be your personal assistant."

Personal Assistant?

The place was more upscale than Julia had imagined.

If Cami wasn't a serial killer, they were about to have a wonderful time.

Cami took a big swig of her champagne and Julia realized she could kill two birds with one stone. Get the shoe size and the DNA if she could figure out how to steal the champagne flute without getting caught.

Cami let out a satisfying moan. "That tastes good," she said.

Julia barely took a sip. She wanted to have her wits about her and not relax too much. When she thought about slipping the expensive flute into her bag while the personal assistant wasn't looking, she took a bigger swig.

She'd need it to get up the nerve.

The thought almost caused her to laugh out loud. Imagine if she had to call Cliff to come bail her out of jail. How would she possibly explain it? He would already hit the ceiling when the four-hundred-dollar charge showed up on his credit card. Julia had insisted on treating so Cami would have no choice but to cooperate.

Cami downed her entire drink and Charise took the flute from her hand and set it on the table at the front desk. The red lipstick was clearly visible on the rim of the glass. Julia thought about walking over to the desk and slipping it into her purse. While everyone was distracted.

She didn't get the chance. Within seconds, one of the employees of the spa had the flute in her hand and disappeared through a door that almost certainly led to the back of the store.

Darn!

So much for that idea. She'd have to try later.

Charise led them into a room behind a curtain. It reminded Julia of an airplane and the curtain that separated first class from coach. The main showroom was off the street and full of people. The spa was in the back behind the curtain.

Charise led them through it and closed the curtain with a purpose. Like the have-nots weren't allowed to even look upon the special people in the spa area. In this case, Julia was one of the privileged. The lesser people being the shoppers in the main part of the store.

Julia felt guilty. For one, being there when they were under such a tight budget. Two, putting on this entire ruse for her friend.

She quickly forgot about it.

They were now in the main spa which was bustling with activity.

Within seconds they were offered more drinks. This time they had a choice of beverages. Wine. Soda. Water. Something stronger. Cami chose wine. Julia sparkling water. Both served in more fancy flutes.

Along both sides of the wall were spa chairs with attached foot baths. Charise led them to two open chairs where they sat down. The personal assistant turned on the massage features on the chairs and explained the controls.

Two spa employees prepared the foot baths. After placing a liner in the basins, they turned on the water. Then kept checking to make sure the water was the right temperature.

If Julia weren't so nervous, she'd be enjoying it.

She looked over at Cami who had her eyes closed and a satisfied smile on her face. Her glass with lipstick sat on the table between them. Julia eyed it like a tiger eyeing a prey.

She wanted to snatch it and put it in her purse.

She had to wait.

As the water filled the basins, the doubts came rushing in like a flood.

Cami didn't look like a killer. The woman was beautiful. Actually, Cami was one of the most gorgeous women Julia had ever met. She had a rich shade of dark brown hair. Sultry eyes that glistened like the sun off a golden pond. Long black eyelashes. Julia would kill for eyelashes that perfect.

The thought made her laugh, releasing some tension. Julia would never kill anyone. Not for eyelashes or for anything else. Cami wouldn't either. Surely this charismatic and genteel model-like creature wasn't capable of the atrocities Cliff had described.

Cami's nose was petite. The best plastic surgeon in the world couldn't duplicate its perfection. Her cheekbones high. Her lips were full. The red lipstick accented her perfectly white teeth.

Julia looked at her perfectly manicured hands. Were those the hands of a killer? *How is that possible?*

Julia stared at her lips. Red was the right color for her to wear. The perfect accent for the perfect woman. Of course, she wore red.

She began to doubt herself even more. She couldn't picture it. She couldn't see Cami carving up men like a butcher carved up a cow.

She was wrong. Cami wasn't the Clown Slayer.

She felt so foolish.

The plan was stupid. She needed to drop the idea of trying to get Cami's DNA. Let Cliff solve the crime. He was the detective.

Julia sat back and closed her eyes. She'd just enjoy the spa treatments. Like Cami was.

They finished the pedicure then asked to choose the color for their nails. Cami chose red. Julia chose millennial pink.

The two most common colors. Julia was kicking herself for letting her imagination go so off the rails. While their nails dried, the spa attendants massaged their legs and calves. It felt heavenly. Cami thanked Julia several times for the thoughtful surprise.

It's the least I could do. Considering I thought you were a murderer.

Afterwards, Charise led them to a private room. A number of different stylish shoes lined the wall. In the room was a red bench and two red chairs. Fittingly. They each took a seat.

The shoes were stylish and high end. The kind that didn't have price tags on them. Julia was afraid to ask how much they cost. She suddenly felt the pressure to buy a pair. Cliff was going to have a fit. Why was she buying designer shoes when their baby needed shoes?

Because I was trying to solve your case for you!

The argument was raging in her head.

Charise asked for their shoe sizes.

"I'm an eight," Julia said.

"Eight and a half for me," Cami said.

Julia's heart skipped a beat.

The Clown Slayer wore a size eight and a half shoe.

Cami really is the killer!

24

"How was your day, dear?" Julia asked in a sweet and sincere tone.

Rita was asleep and Cliff and Julia were in the bedroom and dressed for bed. This was the first real chance they'd had to talk about their days.

Cliff had to be careful. Sometimes his work was frustrating. Rarely more so than today. But he couldn't just get into bed and spew out all his discontentment on his wife like a man sickened with food poisoning.

At the same time, he had to be honest. Julia would see through any pretense. Cliff let out a deep sigh and thought of the best response. "Today wasn't great."

He wanted to leave it at that. Knowing Julia, she wouldn't let him. True to form she said, "Tell me about it. What happened?"

"We got a call on the tip line. The caller said he saw the Clown Slayer at the hearing. Sammy and I pored over news footage for hours."

Julia was sitting up in the bed with her legs crossed under her. Wide awake. Cliff was already under the covers even though the lights were still on. What he really wanted to do was kiss her goodnight, turn over, and go to sleep. Not relive the frustrations of the day.

"Did you see anything?" Julia asked inquisitively. More than with just a passing interest. He wasn't going to sleep anytime soon.

Something was up with Julia anyway. He had noticed it earlier. She was acting strangely. Like she wanted to tell him something but was hesitant. Cliff didn't feel the need to ask about it. Most things didn't have to be pried out of Julia. Based on her demeanor, she'd tell him before the lights went out.

Cliff answered her. "Yeah. I saw a lot of things. Did you know that a bunch of the protesters were wearing red lipstick? Men and women."

"I saw that."

"This woman is becoming a cult figure. It's almost like some people are rooting for her. Wearing red lipstick is somehow in her honor."

"I saw some people dressed up like clowns. I thought I was at a circus."

Cliff nodded. "I hate working on this case. I despise it. It's such a waste of my time."

What he voiced now had been building for a while. Ever since he was assigned to the case. He loathed working serial killer cases and would never do it again.

"I could've solved three murders today," Cliff said roughly. "Instead, it's been weeks since I made an arrest. I want to go back to my old job."

"This case is important," Julia said. "That's why they need their best investigator on it."

"I suppose." He appreciated the subtle, best investigator compliment meant to make him feel better even though it didn't.

"I saw you and Cami on the news footage," Cliff continued. "The cameras caught you going into the courthouse."

Julia's eyes widened and her lips twisted to the side in a distorted frown. She looked off in the distance. Like she was deep in thought.

What's going on with her?

She rubbed her forehead. Then changed positions on the bed. Clearly uncomfortable. What about the conversation was bothering her?

Something was brewing. He'd been to this rodeo before. Julia wanted to tell him something but was afraid to. Whatever it was, she desperately wanted to blurt it out. Julia looked like a kid who needed to go to the bathroom but was afraid to ask permission, and just stood there squirming.

She couldn't hold still but still didn't spill the beans. Prying it out of her was becoming necessary.

"What are you thinking about?" Cliff asked.

Julia hesitated.

"What?" Cliff sat up in the bed to let her know he wasn't going to let it go. A kernel of curiosity had popped up inside of him as well.

"What if Cami is the Clown Slayer killer?" Julia blurted.

As soon as she said it, she put her hand over her eyes. Like she didn't want to see Cliff's reaction.

"Why would you ask that?"

She leaned forward. Toward him and put her fists on the bed to hold herself up. Legs still crossed. Her eyes were filled with excitement. Glistening with exuberance. Like she'd just found a present under her pillow.

"Hear me out. Don't you think Cami has been acting kind of strange?"

Cliff shrugged. Then chuckled. "The woman is strange."

"I mean stranger than normal."

"I guess, I've noticed."

"I think she's the Clown Slayer."

Cliff paused before reacting and dismissing it out of hand. It's not like he hadn't considered it. Any time he did, he quickly convinced himself the thought was ridiculous. Cami was weird. So was Julia sometimes.

Not that Cliff didn't have his idiosyncrasies. Everybody had them. That was the point. Acting strange didn't make someone a suspect. If it did, he'd have them lined up around the block.

And Cami was his partner's girlfriend. Sammy was an investigator. Not the best, but good enough. If Cami were the Clown Slayer,

Sammy would've figured it out by now. Seen something suspicious. Noticed her behavior.

Maybe not.

Love was blind sometimes. Cami did have a charm about her. That was an understatement. The woman could charm a king cobra into letting her pet him. So, Cliff shifted to detective mode and allowed himself to consider it. Julia's discernment had been right on more than one occasion. What else did he have to go on?

Nothing.

He might as well humor his wife.

"Tell me why you think she's the Clown Slayer."

"Cami wears a size eight and a half shoe," Julia said in a matter-of-fact tone.

"How do you know that?"

"We went shoe shopping today."

Cliff felt his eyes widen. "I didn't know that you were with Cami today."

Julia waved her hand in the air. "It was a last second thing. We went to the *Shoe Spa*."

"I've never heard of a shoe spa."

"It was nice. We got manicures. I bought a pair of shoooeees."

Julia drew out the last sentence, like she'd done something wrong. Cliff didn't care if Julia bought a pair of shoes. She knew their budget as well as he did.

"Show them to me," he said, which was the appropriate response.

Julia hesitated and looked back toward the closet. "I'll show them to you later."

That was strange. Julia never turned down an opportunity to show Cliff what she bought shopping.

"Anyway," Julia continued, "I found out at the shoe store that Cami wears eight and a half!" Julia said it with emphasis like it was the evidence that solved the case. "Same size as the Clown Slayer."

"So do half the women in Chicago," Cliff retorted.

"Not half. Sixteen percent. I looked it up."

"Okay. Sixteen percent. So one in five women wears size eight and a half shoes. That doesn't mean anything."

"Sixteen percent is not one in five," she said defensively.

Julia was annoying when she got exacting like this. If he didn't state things with precision, she always felt the need to correct him.

"Whatever. Sixteen percent. One in... whatever." He couldn't do the math that quickly and shouldn't be forced to. What difference did it make?

"Actually, seven is the most common size shoe sold in America." Julia laughed. "Eight and a half is the most common size for women's feet."

"That's weird. Why would women buy shoes too small for their feet?"

"Because they're embarrassed. They buy shoes too small, so they don't feel bad about having big feet."

"That's the dumbest thing I've ever heard in my life."

"The point is that Cami wears the same shoe size as the Clown Slayer. What are the odds? Sixteen percent is not that big a percentage."

"I don't know. Now you've got me doubting the shoe size. Maybe the Clown Slayer has size ten feet but buys a shoe too small because of it. Maybe she really is a clown."

Cliff thought the joke might ease the tension in the room somewhat.

Julia gave him a playful glare. Then her nostrils flared, and she was dead serious again.

"Think about it, Cliff. The red lipstick. Her unusual behavior. Cami had a sister who was raped and murdered. She met Sammy out of the blue. You said so yourself. Cami has an obsessive interest in the case. She's ambidextrous."

Julia was speaking at a rapid pace now. Trying to get her point across before he could rebut each point.

"I need more proof than that."

"I have proof."

Cliff sat up now. "What kind of proof?" he asked hesitantly. Not sure he wanted to know the answer.

Julia's head sagged.

"What?"

"I may have did a thing," she said, sheepishly.

She wasn't making eye contact. Instead, acting like a kid who'd been caught with her hand in a place it wasn't supposed to be.

"What did you do?" Cliff said sternly. He didn't want to sound fatherly, but couldn't help it.

"Don't be mad at me."

"How can I promise not to be mad at you, if I don't know what you did?"

The whole conversation sparked an anger inside of him, he was trying hard to contain. He'd hold it back until he knew all the facts.

Julia bounded off the bed. She left the room. His eyes followed her out. She was wearing short shorts and a skimpy tee shirt.

Hard to be mad at her when she was dressed like that. Did she do it on purpose? He wouldn't put it past her. This wouldn't be the first time she had used her feminine wiles to manipulate him.

He hoped she kept doing it.

When Julia returned, she had something in her hand. An object wrapped in a napkin. She sat it on the bed. Cliff reached for it.

"Don't touch it!" she practically shouted.

Cliff pulled his hand back.

"What is it?"

Julia pulled the napkin away slowly. The object was a drinking glass with red lipstick on it.

"Will you tell me what's going on?"

"That's Cami's glass. From lunch."

"Why is it on our bed?"

"I stole it from the restaurant."

Julia squealed. Her hands were over her eyes again.

"You stole it!"

"Yes. I slipped it inside my purse when no one was looking."

"Julia!"

"I know. I'm a bad girl."

"I can't believe you shoplifted a glass and a napkin from a restaurant."

"I didn't exactly shoplift it."

"What would you call it?"

"I left twenty dollars on the table. The glass isn't worth that much."

It wasn't worth arguing over. What was done was done. The bigger question flew out of his mouth like a burp.

"Why did you take the glass?"

"So you could run Cami's DNA."

"And why would I do that?"

"To rule her out as a suspect."

"She's never been a suspect."

"I think she should be. I think she's the killer."

He about fell over in the bed.

"Are you serious?"

"Dead serious. Run the DNA. You'll see. Cami is the Clown Slayer. I know I'm right. You can also check the shape of the lips on the glass. See if you have a match. Her fingerprints are on it."

"I can't just run her DNA without probable cause. You heard my testimony at the hearing. I need some proof. I need her fingerprints or DNA at the crime scene."

A bolt of adrenaline shot through Cliff like a lightning bolt.

A bell went off. His whole body jerked. Like Pavlov's dog did when he heard a bell ring.

More of a siren. An alarm. A bullhorn shouting for him to think.

It didn't come to him right away. Cliff bolted out of bed and began to pace around the room. The rush of adrenaline was what he needed to jolt his mind into gear to figure out that elusive clue. The one that had been nagging him all week long.

He knew what it was. Or was so close to knowing. He could practically touch it. If it were a fire, it'd sear his hand.

"What is it, Cliff?"

"Give me a second," he said as he continued to pace.

DNA tests. Victims. Pictures. Murder book. Tip line.

What did Julia say that had lit the spark?

"What was the last thing you said?" Cliff asked, snapping his fingers at Julia.

"I said that Cami's fingerprints are on the glass."

The lightbulb went off.

Cliff knew.

It came to him like a heavy rushing wind.

"Of course! Why didn't I think of this earlier? Julia, you are brilliant."

He leaned over and kissed her hard. "Cami is the Clown Slayer!" he practically shouted.

"I know!"

"No. I mean, she really is the Clown Slayer!" He said it in a quieter voice so as not to wake Rita.

"That's what I've been saying."

Cliff was on the bed now. Sitting next to Julia with his legs crossed under him. Holding her hands.

"Do you remember when you and Cami showed up at the station one night? You wanted to take Sammy and me to dinner. You surprised us. The Lieutenant was in the room."

"I remember."

"Do you remember what happened when the Lieutenant left?"

Julia shook her head.

"We had just gotten the second letter from the Clown Slayer. That same day. The one where she was mocking me. Do you remember what happened?"

"Vaguely."

"The cryptogram letter. Cami picked it up and held it."

"I remember. You yelled at her to put it down."

"I can't believe I didn't see this sooner!"

"See what? Help me understand."

"Cami's fingerprints weren't on the letter. What I mean is. . . they were on the letter, but they weren't. Does that make sense?"

"No it doesn't."

"The crime lab ran DNA and fingerprint tests on the letter. They only found the Clown Slayer's DNA and fingerprints. They didn't find a second set of prints. That's because Cami is the Clown Slayer."

"I think I understand."

"I didn't see it sooner because there were several sets of prints and DNA on the envelope. Because a number of people handled it. Postal workers. Our mail sorters. But they only found one set of fingerprints and DNA on the letter. Which was inside the envelope. No one touched it without gloves. Except Cami."

"Which means her fingerprints and DNA should be all over it."

"Exactly. And they are. Which gives me enough probable cause to run a DNA test on the glass that you stole from the restaurant."

"I'm glad I became a criminal to help you solve the case," Julia said proudly.

"Don't do it again," Cliff said playfully.

Then his demeanor changed as his head was suddenly filled with potential problems.

"Is the glass even admissible?" he said aloud, but more to himself than anything.

He rubbed his eyes roughly. Then left the room and went to his office where he found an evidence bag. He returned and deposited the glass and napkin in the bag, careful not to touch it.

The glass was a problem. Cliff was concerned that the glass had been stolen from the store. By his wife. A defense attorney would have a field day tearing apart that evidence and the chain of custody.

The last thing he wanted was for a judge to throw out his case on another technicality. Surely, he wouldn't. But after what happened on Monday, Cliff could never be sure.

For that matter, Cami touching the letter would be problematic. Why was Sammy's girlfriend even in the room, much less handling evidence? Maybe she touched a lot of things. Maybe none of the evidence gathered would be admissible.

He needed more. He needed to catch Cami in the act.

"What's tonight?" Cliff asked.

"Wednesday."

He looked at the clock. The red numbers showed eight thirty.

"I need to go to Cami's house," Cliff said. "See if she goes out tonight."

"I want to go with you."

"What about Rita? We can't leave her home alone."

"No. Silly. She'll come with us."

"I can't take our baby to a stakeout."

"You're right. She's sleeping anyway. I'll stay home."

Cliff started getting dressed. After he donned his shoes, he kissed Julia on the cheek and said, "I'll be back. Don't wait up."

"You be careful. You don't know what Cami's capable of."

Cliff thought of the Midway Butcher crime scene and how Cami carved the man up like a cooked turkey at Thanksgiving.

"I know exactly what she's capable of," Cliff said soberly. "That's why I have to stop her."

25

The red lipstick was always the last thing to go on.

Cami looked at herself in the mirror. Satisfied with what she saw. Although, her Bible toting mom, and her hellfire and brimstone Baptist preaching father would not approve of the sexy outfit. Strappy, cold-shoulder black top, sequined tight-fitting jeans, and wedge sandals with three-inch heels.

Of course, she was on her way to kill a man. They wouldn't approve of that either. Her mom and dad would fall over and die of a heart attack if they knew their sweet straightlaced honor roll homecoming queen little girl had become a serial killer.

Cami hardly believed it herself. Growing up, this wasn't her life plan. It just turned out that way.

Most days she felt normal. Good job. A good-looking boyfriend who treated her well and thought she hung the moon. Nice home and fancy car. Everyone who knew her thought she had it all together.

On Wednesday and Thursday nights, she morphed into a monster. Someone she hated but had grown to accept.

She'd just gotten off the phone with Sammy. He was as clueless as a mouse gnawing on a piece of cheese on a mousetrap.

"Do you want to come over and watch a movie?" he asked.

"I can't tonight. I got things to do. How about a raincheck?"

He sounded disappointed, but agreed. How could he know that the thing she had to do was track down a man and gut him like a fisherman gutted the day's catch.

Cami stared at herself in the mirror as she applied the last swipe of lipstick. Then said aloud to herself, "Oh Sammy. You are so naïve."

Not a day went by that she didn't feel bad about what she was doing to him. She felt sorry for him. While she was fond of Sammy, she wasn't in love with him. He'd be devastated if he found out about her.

When he found it.

Dating Sammy was strategic. Nothing more, nothing less. Necessary. That's why she followed him home from work six months before, when she learned he was assigned as lead detective on the Clown Slayer case. Once she knew where he lived, the rest was easy. Dress sexy, run into him right outside his house, bat her eyelashes a few times, and he'd be hooked. Typical gullible man.

Meeting Sammy and getting him to fall for her had been a godsend. Within a week, she was able to find out his passcode into the Chicago P.D. database. That's how she found her victims. By looking up cases in the files. Men who had committed sexual assaults and murders. Reprobates who hadn't been punished properly. Some hadn't even been caught. As in the case of the Midway Butcher, and the man who'd meet his demise tonight.

It also got her close to the investigation. She could keep track of it that way. Had Sammy remained the lead investigator, she'd never get caught. Cliff Ford, on the other hand, was making her life difficult. Pursuing her like an obsessed bulldog. He'd almost caught her several times.

The clock was ticking. Now it was only a matter of time until he got the DNA from *Generation Tree*. Her days of being a free woman were numbered. That's why she moved up the timetable on tonight's kill.

As soon as the DNA came back, that'd be it for her.

Not her DNA, but her sister Carly's.

Carly was the one who first signed up for *Generation Tree*. Was all excited about it. She built a family tree. Took the DNA test. The test that'd be Cami's downfall. Cliff would know that Carly's DNA was a familial match. That Carly's sister was the Clown Slayer killer.

A little investigation would show that Carly had two sisters. One was dead. The other lived in Chicago.

Even Sammy could connect the dots.

Cami's heart felt a sharp pang when she thought of Chloe. Her little sister was murdered at age sixteen.

It was her fault.

Her mother said it wasn't. But Cami blamed herself. Her father wouldn't come right out and say it but he blamed her too.

Her father was right. Cami was the older sister. Responsible for her little sister. Cami was the one with the car and always drove Chloe to school and back.

Except on that fateful day.

Fifteen years ago.

Cami remembered it like it was yesterday. She was hanging out with a boy after school. Making out with him at the park. Smoking cigarettes. She should've been picking her sister up from school. She lost track of time. Forgot to pick Chloe up. Her sister left the schoolyard and started walking home.

They didn't know exactly what happened after that. Apparently, Chloe accepted a ride from a local man. Or he forced her into his car. Either way, Chloe should've never been on the street alone. She wouldn't have been if Cami had picked her up like she was supposed to.

The twenty-three-year-old man's name was Bobby Durbin. Cami was in a sheer panic when she got home and Chloe wasn't there. She finally told her parents who called the police. They didn't find Chloe's body for three days.

When they did, the autopsy showed that she'd been raped and brutally murdered. Beaten. Her head smashed in. According to investigators, she didn't die right away. Which meant she suffered.

Everybody knew Bobby did it. He even bragged about it to his friends. But it was never proven. He was questioned several times but never arrested.

Cami killed him with a knife. So driven with rage she stabbed him more than forty times.

The police came and asked her a few questions. She lied. Over the next few weeks, Cami kept expecting to be arrested. The police never came back. Bobby's murder was still unsolved. The knife in the bottom of the local lake.

Cami got a taste for vigilante justice, and it felt good. There were more Bobby's out there. Men who preyed on young girls and got away with it. Either were never arrested, beat the rap, or got out of jail after a few short years.

Their victims couldn't avenge their deaths. So Cami did it for them.

She never killed anyone who didn't deserve it.

Like the man tonight. E. B. Combs. Probably the worst of them all. Combs owned an old hotel in downtown Chicago. He had purchased an abandoned building several years before and renovated it. Actually ran it as a hotel although few people actually frequented the establishment. Mostly prostitutes and people with something to hide. Like an affair, gang, or drug activity.

E. B. Combs had his own secret. The hotel was just a front. Something sinister was going on inside. Cami knew because she'd been following the man for four months.

Combs prowled the seedy areas of Chicago and preyed on young women and girls. Runaways. Prostitutes. Vagrants. Homeless drug addicts. Young girls who no one would ever know went missing. Or if they did, they didn't care.

Ironically enough, Cami discovered Combs through an ancestry company. She was scrolling around the Chicago P.D. database when she found a cold case. A fourteen-year-old runaway was missing. Kidnapped at a bus stop. Her backpack was left behind.

The killer's DNA was found on a piece of the girl's torn shirt found at the scene. DNA tests were run, but a match wasn't found in the national database. The investigators had no suspects, and the case grew cold. Cami found the DNA profile in the file.

She composed a letter on Chicago P.D. letterhead and sent the profile to a website called *Me and My Shadow*. An ancestry company similar to *Generation Tree* but one that cooperated with law enforcement. The letter came back to her post office box with a match.

A third cousin to the killer.

Cami did some detective work and found out that E. B. Combs was a relative and lived in Chicago. She put two and two together and began following the hotel owner.

On more than a dozen different occasions, Cami saw him pick up young girls from homeless camps, street corners, and under bridges. He took them back to the hotel. They never came out. Cami checked and the girls were never reported missing or somehow fell through the cracks.

Tonight he was going to get his.

Combs made things easier for Cami with his predictability. He followed the same routine. He went out between nine and ten o'clock. After the streets started to thin out. He drove to the same part of town. He wasn't hard to follow.

Cami left her house and drove to the hotel. She parked out of sight but with a clear view of the exit. She'd done this dozens of times.

She waited.

He wasn't hard to spot. Combs drove an older model faded black limousine with dark tinted windows and shiny silver hubcaps.

Tonight was no different. Like clockwork, he pulled out of the hotel and onto the main thoroughfare around nine thirty. Cami followed, staying far enough away not to be seen. Not at all concerned about losing him. If she did, he'd be easy to find. He always cruised the same areas.

He'd go up and down the thoroughfare until he spotted a young girl alone. Preferably one who was tipsy or strung out on drugs. Sometimes asleep on the side of the road. Other times staggering down the sidewalk.

Another of his preferred targets was a girl standing on a street corner, trying to flag down men to turn a trick. Combs ignored them unless they were alone.

The homeless shelter was another target. The girls came in and out of there with frequency. Usually, he avoided the area because of all the activity. Sometimes, when he struck out in the other areas, he waited outside the shelter until a girl emerged on foot, then he followed her. Looking for an opportunity.

Those girls were vulnerable. They'd do almost anything for a few bucks to buy some drugs.

Tonight, Combs went directly to one of his favorite jaunts. Underneath a railroad trestle. A debris littered, hell hole that the rats would be disgusted by.

A girl who couldn't be older than sixteen leaned against a girder. Her face was drawn and vacant. Her arms skinnier than broom handles. Probably hadn't had a decent meal in weeks. When she did get money, she no doubt spent it on drugs and not food.

Barely a hundred pounds sopping wet. Cami's heart was broken for the girl.

The pain Cami felt was soon overcome by the rage building inside of her. The girl was probably close to Chloe's age when Bobby Durbin kidnapped and killed her sister.

"Don't get in the car," Cami pleaded. "He'll kill you."

Cami was determined not to let that happen if she did. The other nights, Cami had to sit back and watch it happen. Tonight, she would rescue the girl and send Combs to hell where he belonged.

For whatever reason, her thoughts turned to her father. Why wouldn't he approve? She'd sat through any number of his Old Testament eye-for-an-eye sermons.

Cami was doing the world a service.

Combs rolled down the window to the car. The girl staggered over to it. Then got in. He probably offered her drugs or money in exchange for sexual favors. Once the girl was in the car, Cami knew Combs would take the girl back to the hotel. He always did.

Cami reacted quickly.

She sped away.

She had to get back to the hotel before Combs did. He'd drive straight back.

The hotel had an underground parking garage. Cami found it while staking out the place. She'd seen Combs come and go out of it many times. The entrance to the garage was in an alleyway behind the hotel. Cami had figured out a way to get in. If she could beat Combs back to the hotel, she could hide in the garage and follow him inside the hotel.

She raced to the hotel, careful not to get pulled over by a cop. Combs was a slow driver. She had timed it and could get back to the hotel, park several blocks away, and run to the garage and get into position by the time he arrived.

Things went as planned. Cami was in the alleyway and there was still no sign of Combs.

She pried the side door open and snuck in carefully closing it and locking it behind her. The parking garage had space for a dozen or so cars. It was moldy and damp. Lit by only one light above the door that led into the basement of the hotel.

Cami hid in the shadows.

Her heart was beating so fast she could hear it pounding in her ears.

She jumped when a couple of minutes later, the garage door began to open filling the garage with a sound of gears grinding. The metal door opened from side to side. Combs drove through it and into his parking space.

He got out of the vehicle and looked around. Cami retreated further into the shadows even though she was certain he couldn't see her. Combs pushed a button in his hand and the garage door closed.

He walked around to the passenger side door and opened it. The young girl got out. Combs took her arm and roughly led her inside.

She tried to resist. Combs was a big man. Likely six four or five. Two hundred pounds. Big boned. Full beard. A full head of hair for someone in his mid-fifties.

The young girl didn't seem to have all her wits about her. Her knees were weak as she walked. He might've already given her some drugs. She tried to pull her arm away but he strengthened his grip.

"You're hurting me," she heard the girl say, and Cami's heart broke a second time.

Rage burned inside of Cami like a raging bonfire. All common sense was melting down faster than a nuclear reactor.

She hated Combs. He would suffer and die a slow and painful death. She always drugged her victims. Not this time. Bobby Durbin didn't drug Chloe. Her helpless sister had to suffer. Why shouldn't Combs?

What she needed was hidden in the pockets of her jeans. She touched them for reassurance.

Scalpel. Knife. Clamp. To control the bleeding.

Cami snuck up to the door leading inside and pressed her ear against it. Not that she could hear anything through the massive iron antique door that was at least four inches thick in the center.

Cami didn't hear anything, so she opened it slowly and crept inside. It led into a hallway.

She felt a rush of panic. Which way did they go?

She heard a noise to the left and headed toward it.

It sounded like a door shutting.

Her breathing was labored. She tried to calm it so she wouldn't make so much noise.

Cami rounded a corner and it led to another hallway. At the end was a closed door. That felt like where the sound had come from.

Cami crept up to it. Not daring to breathe. Careful not to cause the floor to squeak.

She heard sounds coming from inside the room. Then something like chains rattling. A girl screamed. It sounded like a metal door closing. Like a prison door.

Cami took a deep breath. The stale moist moldy air sickened her. It smelled like death. Burning flesh.

She considered bursting in the room. Cami had the element of surprise on her side. She contemplated how to use it. A full out assault didn't seem wise. She waited for Combs to leave the room. She'd ambush him on the outside.

She also had some fighting skills she'd learned in a self-defense class. She never carried a gun. Instead relied on her scalpel that was sharp enough to slice the skin off a man. It was now in her hand.

She heard another door shut. This time silence. It sounded like Combs had left the room.

Panic turned to resolve. Courage. Anger. Fury. The face of the young girl was now seared in Cami's mind.

She opened the door slightly. What she saw caused her to gasp. On the right side of the room was a makeshift prison cell. The young girl was inside it. Disoriented. Sitting on a pallet on the floor. Chained to the wall.

The room was hot. Cami started sweating almost immediately. She smelled the fire.

What looked like an incinerator took up most of the back wall. The kind of thing she'd seen before on television. At a crematorium. The realization hit her. That's what he did with the bodies. That's why the girls never left the hotel and were never found. He killed them, then burned their bodies.

She held back another gasp. Combs had to be nearby and she didn't want him to know she was there.

Where had he gone?

She needed to act now. Set a trap for Combs when he returned.

She held the scalpel in her right hand. Left the door ajar in case she needed to escape out of it.

She walked toward the girl.

"I'm going to get you out of here," Cami whispered.

She suddenly saw movement. Behind her and to the right

Cami raised the knife and spun on a dime, but the angle was wrong.

Too late. The object in his right hand was headed for the side of her head.

Then everything went black.

26

When Cami woke up, her head was throbbing. She reached for it, but her arms and legs were bound to a chair by leather straps.

It took a few seconds for her to clear the fog and remember where she was. When she saw Combs standing in front of her sharpening a knife with a wicked smile on his face, it all came rushing back to her.

She instinctively looked to the right for the young girl and saw her sitting on the floor of her cell, sobbing. A sense of doom immediately came over Cami.

The realization felt like a building collapsing around her. Not only did she fail to save the girl, but this was how her life was going to end.

Combs was going to kill her.

The room was hot and sticky. It felt like a sauna. Only hotter. Her clothes were soaked from the sweat. Mixed with blood oozing from the wound on her head.

Then the smell. It filled her nostrils. The chemicals burned her eyes and her throat when she sucked in air. Burning wood and foul residue of ashes. Human remains, she suspected.

The horror pulsed through her veins with every heartbeat.

The incinerator was going full blast and created a loud roar in the room. Like a locomotive was bearing down on them. Cami felt the chair shake slightly, like they were having a minor earthquake.

Combs had a smug satisfying smirk on his face.

All her senses were heightened within seconds. A cacophony of sound challenged her mind to assimilate it all. The whirr of the incinerator. The sobbing of the girl. The steel clank of the knife sharpener. She could even hear the tick of a massive clock on the wall.

And the laugh. The diabolical laugh. More of a deep-throated gurgle of a madman.

Combs sharpened the knife with a purpose. Then he'd laugh. Sharpen some more. Look at Cami and let out a groan of pleasure. Each disgusting look sent cold chills down her spine.

From his eyes, she believed him to be insane. That's how they were different. Cami hated killing people. She did it for the satisfaction of seeing the low life scum get what they deserved. Maybe she was kidding herself, but she felt morally superior to Combs. He did it for sport. Bloodthirst.

Her shoulders shuddered. From the looks of things, her end wasn't going to come quickly enough.

Surprisingly, Combs set the knife down and scooted a chair in front of her, but didn't sit down. He wiped the sweat off his face. Even though it was like a furnace in the room, he wore a heavy wool suit coat and tie. Thick shoes with heavy soles that made a thudding sound with each laboring step.

Cami took in the room. To look for any lifeline. To her left was a desk. Above it a chalkboard. Next to it was a file cabinet. The desk was cluttered. Combs walked over to it and picked up a clipboard and pen. Then sat down in the chair across from Cami and stared at her.

Without a word, he sat back in the chair and crossed his legs, like a psychiatrist about to counsel a patient. She held her tongue even though lots of thoughts pressed against her lips trying to get out.

After nearly a minute of awkward silence, Combs said, "I'd like to start by asking a few questions. Who are you?"

Cami didn't answer. She was testing the straps, pressing her arms and legs against them. Not concerned that he would notice. They had little to no give in them. Getting out of there would be next to impossible.

Combs clearly knew that and seemed unconcerned by her lame attempts to escape. Nothing but a waste of valuable energy.

"Why are you here?" Combs asked in a monotone, emotionless, voice. Almost like he was interviewing her for a job at his hotel.

She forced her lips shut. Hard to do since she didn't dare breathe through her nose. Inhaling through her mouth was the lesser of the two evils considering the smell.

"Don't want to answer?" he asked.

Cami remained silent. Kept her eyes fixed on his face. As if staring would somehow intimidate him. She had no such hope. Instead, she was memorizing every detail in case she somehow lived to tell about it.

If she didn't, at least she had these last few moments of hate which he couldn't take away from her.

Combs let out a sound of disgust. Then another.

"Dear child. You don't want to cooperate. I understand. No matter. You will answer me. Eventually. I'll make sure of it. You can save yourself a lot of pain by humoring me."

Combs seemed to be speaking in a fake British accent.

Did he see himself as a Jack the Ripper wannabe?

It almost caused her to smile. She might have if the situation weren't so dire.

"You obviously came here to kill me," Combs said, not hiding his first expression of anger. "I found your scalpel. Are you a doctor?"

Cami stared straight ahead. Trying to maintain eye contact, but Combs kept looking down at his notes.

"I'll ask a second time. Don't expect a third. What's your name, dear?"

I'm not your dear.

Cami decided to speak, "Powerful people are going to come looking for me," she said, trying to sound confident and serious which meant keeping her voice from cracking. "When they do, they're going to arrest you."

She couldn't think of any other form of bravado that made sense.

He chuckled. Not taking her any more seriously than she expected him to when she said it. No one was coming for her. No one knew where she was. He must've sensed it because he didn't seem the least bit concerned.

"They'll come to your hotel looking for me," Cami said with more intensity.

"What are they going to find? By morning, you'll be nothing more than a pile of ashes."

He pointed to the incinerator. Then let out another deep throated laugh that sent chills down to the ends of her toes.

The scene was playing out like a horror movie. Only in real life.

For the first time, Cami felt sheer terror. Not only for herself but for the young girl in the makeshift prison cell. Cami deserved her fate. In a roundabout way. She could accept it. Combs had gotten the best of her. The young girl didn't deserve what was going to happen to her.

Cami rattled the bands and bounced her chair up and down for effect. Combs didn't even respond like he knew her efforts were useless.

He pointed at the incinerator. "Do you like my invention? I designed it myself. I'm a mechanical engineer. Did you know that? Pretty clever, isn't it?"

Cami didn't know what to say. So she took the most direct approach she could think of.

"I know who you are. E. B. Combs. You kill young girls. The police have your DNA. Like I said, they will come looking for you."

"Dr. Combs. I insist that you call me doctor."

"I'll call you whatever I want. You don't deserve the title of doctor. Doctor's take an oath. Not to harm people."

A jolt of guilt pierced through her stomach. She could be speaking of herself. The ultimate hypocrite. She'd taken the same Hippocratic Oath. She'd done harm to twelve men. Thirteen if Combs would have given her the chance. She also had taken offense to the moniker, Clown Slayer. It seemed trivial at the moment.

"You're not afraid of me," Combs said. "I like that."

Cami was petrified but took some satisfaction in knowing she was successfully hiding it. Of course, belligerence would make things worse, but she couldn't help herself.

"But you have it wrong. I'm not a medical doctor," Combs retorted. "I'm a professor. Are you impressed?"

"Not really."

He frowned. Then looked her up and down lustfully which sent a wave of disgust through her. Any fear she felt was replaced with anger. She'd rather feel the cold steel of the knife than his scaly slimy hands.

"Do you know what I call this place? The Murder Castle. Rather ingenious don't you think?"

Why did he care what she thought? Did he think she'd be impressed?

"You're a coward, Combs," Cami said with as much disgust in her voice as she could muster. "You prey on defenseless girls. Loosen these straps and make it a fair fight. A fight to the death. We'll see who comes out on top. My scalpel against your knife."

"I'll be on top of you soon enough," he said disgustingly. "Anyway, you had your chance. I won the fight. I outsmarted you. You should've watched your back."

He had a point.

"I found you, Combs," she retorted. "So will the police. You may kill me. But your days are numbered."

"Hardly matters. When they finally catch me, and they will, I'll gain the notoriety I deserve."

Combs pointed to the wall. A chalkboard had a number on it.

236.

"That's how many girls I've killed. You'll be number 237. The girl over there will be number 238. I am the best serial killer who ever lived."

"Hardly something to be proud of. You're a weak man, Combs. You prey on the most helpless in our society. You think it's some kind of badge of honor. I pity you. You couldn't make anything of your life, so this is what you resorted to. You're the best of the worst. There's a hot place in hell for men like you."

She was one to talk. How could she judge him with what she'd done? She'd be in hell with him. Only she'd get there sooner.

Something she said set him off. Combs' eyes suddenly burned with rage. He stood up and slapped her across the face. She tasted blood. Her cheek felt like it'd been stung by a hundred wasps.

As quickly as he stood, he sat back down. The matter-of-fact manner returned.

"Now, I need you to answer my questions for the file. You are trying my patience. A famous serial killer once said that he killed so many people he couldn't keep them all straight. I will not make that mistake. I must document who you are for posterity."

He adjusted his position in the chair.

"I like to document all my victims. Make it easier for the police. To prove I really did kill this many people. The history books will record all my victims. Your name will be preserved for posterity as well. Aren't you proud that I have afforded you that opportunity?"

"You're a sick man."

"I won't argue with you there. I'm the devil in disguise. Hell is my future home. I look forward to it."

His eyes were vacant. Cold. Like he didn't have a soul. It sent a chill through her, even though the room was getting hotter by the minute.

Cami felt like she was looking at pure evil.

Did my victims have the same feeling right before I killed them?

How ironic that she would experience both sides of the depravity?

Her heart suddenly felt heavy.

Combs' words had struck a chord. A memory. Her father's sermons. On hell. Reserved for the worst sinners. Eternal torment. However horrible the next few hours were going to be, they were nothing like what things would be for her when she died and spent an eternity in hell.

She'd never really paid attention to the sermons. Actually, she must have. She remembered almost every word as they came rushing back into her mind, searing her conscience.

Was it too late for her?

Would God forgive her?

Her father said it was never too late. Anyone could come to Christ at any time. Even on their deathbed.

Death chair as it were.

Cami didn't deserve God's forgiveness. The guilt and shame overwhelmed her. If God didn't condemn her, then she'd condemn herself. She deserved it.

"Why don't you just get on with it?" Cami said bitterly.

"In due time. I need your information first. You'll save us a lot of time if you give it to me voluntarily."

Cami didn't want her name associated with him. In some ways, this would be better. She would just disappear. No amount of torture would make her tell him her real name. She didn't carry ID on her for this reason.

She thought of her parents. They were about to lose a second daughter. Hopefully, they'd never know the horrible things she'd done.

She hoped and prayed that Cliff Ford didn't figure it out.

Sammy would think she was kidnapped. A victim. He'd file a missing person's case. They'd look for her for weeks. Maybe months. How could they know that she'd been incinerated, and they'd never find her?

She prayed to God for the first time in years.

"God please don't let Sammy find out I'm the Clown Slayer." She even used the name like she had now accepted her real identity.

The prayer caused her to chuckle. Even in her death, she was more worried about protecting her reputation than her eternal destiny.

My sister.

Carly. She'll lose a second sister to a violent crime. She'll be alone. Having never known what happened to her. Which would be worse? Knowing Cami was a killer or never knowing her fate?

Cami suddenly felt regret for the things she'd done. Remorse even. She should've chosen a different path in her life. After what happened to Chloe, she'd become so consumed with hate that she wasn't thinking clearly.

This wasn't the way to avenge her sister. She had thought it'd make her feel better, but it never did. She always felt worse after each kill.

She saw the same hate in her eyes that she saw in Combs at that moment. Like she was looking at herself in a mirror. It's who she had become.

She despised Combs. Hated him. Hated herself just as much.

A tear formed in her eye. It escaped and fell down her cheek.

Combs noticed.

"Don't think I'm crying because of you," Cami said roughly. "I feel sorry for myself. For the things I've done. I've killed twelve men. I'm only sorry I didn't kill thirteen."

Combs' mouth gaped open in surprise.

"That's right. I'm a serial killer," Cami said. "I came here tonight to kill you. I should've killed you when I had the chance."

Cami pounded the chair up and down. She was able to lift it off the floor slightly. She made her arms taut, trying to supernaturally break the bindings. She envisioned herself doing so, grabbing the knife out of Combs' pocket and stabbing him with it.

Even now, she couldn't contain the anger that burned inside of her like a raging wildfire.

When she was exhausted, she gave up. Slumped in the chair. Defeated.

Then found the energy to scream at him, "Get on with it. Just kill me. I deserve it."

A loud bang.

Behind her.

At the door.

Combs jumped. Cami's heart skipped a beat. Who was it? She didn't have a clue. The door had been left slightly ajar. It burst open. She could feel the presence of a person behind her.

She strained to look back and see who it was.

Movement. A flash. A person moving quickly and stealthily. To her right.

Combs reacted. He stood to his feet quickly for a man of his size. He had the knife in his hand.

Cami screamed.

Combs raised his hand to throw the knife. At her? Or at the threat in the room? She didn't know.

"Drop it," the familiar voice said.

Cliff?

Combs reared back. Too far. It took too long. Two gunshots rang out before he could release the knife out of his hand.

Time slowed down. Cami saw everything in slow motion. She felt the breeze of the bullets whizz by her head through the thick hot air.

Combs' eyes widened in surprise when the bullets hit him. He didn't fall right away. He put his hand to his chest. Then looked at the blood on it.

He let out a gurgling sound. Then fell to the floor.

A pool of blood began to form under him.

The man who saved her life was now in front of her.

Cliff.

Their eyes met.

She should be excited.

All she could feel was shame.

27

No amount of training could've prepared Cliff for the horror he saw unfolding before him. When he burst into the basement of the *Castle Hotel*, the first thing he saw was Cami strapped to a chair.

His mind processed the irony quickly. She went there to kill another man. The tables had obviously been turned on her. Not unlike how she had turned them on the Midway Butcher.

As if it couldn't get any weirder.

Directly in front of him on the back wall was a large stove-like contraption in the shape of a crematory. The room was hot and had the stench of death. It took all of his self-control to keep from gagging. He'd been around decomposing bodies before, but nothing like this.

To his right were bars attached to the wall like a cage or prison cell. A person appeared to be lying on the floor, but Cliff didn't have time to look twice to see.

A more direct threat had captured his full attention.

A tall man with a thick beard stood over Cami brandishing a knife. When the man raised the weapon, it appeared that he intended to throw it at Cliff.

Cliff instinctively fired two shots. Dead center. Striking the man in the chest.

The knife wielding assailant staggered but kept his feet. The knife fell to the ground, so Cliff didn't fire again, but kept his hand on the trigger ready to act if the threat wasn't contained.

The man clutched his hand to his bloody chest and looked at Cliff with widened eyes of disbelief. Several seconds later, he collapsed to the floor with a loud thud. His head cracked on the concrete floor sending an eerie echo bouncing off the walls.

Almost certainly dead.

Cliff moved his gun from right to left, several times. Rapidly, scanning the room for any more threats. Seeing none, he walked over to the man, bent over him, and checked for a pulse, keeping the gun in his hand just in case. He felt a faint pulse, although it might've been Cliff's own heart which was pounding out of his chest. He could feel every heartbeat race through his arms to the tips of his fingers.

Cliff stood and turned toward Cami. Tears poured down her face. Her cheeks were as red as her lips and the right side of her mouth was swollen. Her hair was matted with blood.

"Are you okay?" Cliff asked.

She nodded.

"Check on... the girl first," she said between sobs.

He considered releasing Cami from the bands holding her to the chair and handcuffing her but decided against it. At the moment, she was contained. He checked the leather straps holding her to the chair and she was securely restrained, so he left her to check on the person in the cell.

What he saw broke his heart.

A young girl. Maybe fifteen or sixteen. Concentration camp emaciated. Cowering against the wall. Chained like a dog. Filthy. Her eyes sunken. Clearly a girl of the streets. Drugged out. Probably got the money for the drugs by selling her body.

Somebody's daughter. Sister maybe. How did she get in this condition? *God only knows.* Cliff didn't work sexual assault cases for this very reason. He didn't have the stomach for it. He could feel the emotion welling up inside of him. He didn't know to what extent she was a threat or a victim, but he had compassion for her.

Cliff took a deep breath, immediately regretting it because of the stench of the air that burned his nostrils and sickened him. He made a conscious effort to tamp down the emotions and go into investigative mode. Trying to wrap his mind around what had just happened.

He had gotten to Cami's house just as she was pulling away. He followed her to some seedy areas of Chicago. Resisted the urge to pull her over when he saw her following a black limousine.

He didn't really know what was going on, so he decided to let it play out. He figured she was stalking another victim. Someone he assumed had a criminal and violent past.

She quit following the limousine and led him to the hotel. He followed her on foot to a back alleyway. Hid in the shadows so she wouldn't see him.

Now here they were.

He didn't expect this.

A makeshift prison in the basement of a hotel.

Who was the dead man lying on the floor?

It didn't take much of an investigator to figure it out. The man kidnapped young girls. Locked them in the cage. Did despicable things to them. When he was finished with them, he cremated their bodies and destroyed any evidence that they ever existed.

Cliff had arrived outside the door of the room just in time to hear the man mention a number, 236. He said it was the number of girls he'd killed. It seemed almost impossible to believe. Cliff had waited outside the door until the right time to enter. Hoping to gain more intelligence.

"Please don't hurt me," the girl pleaded with Cliff, snapping him back to reality. She scooted as far away from him into the corner as the chains allowed.

"I'm not going to hurt you," Cliff said gently. "I'm here to help you. You're safe now. What's your name?"

She didn't answer. Just sat there shaking.

Cliff bent down next to her. To assess her wounds. Other than the obvious neglect, she didn't seem to be hurt. He tried the chains, but they were secure. Older and rusty, but Cliff wasn't strong enough to break them with his bare hands.

"I'm going to leave you for just a second, but I'll be right back," Cliff said in a reassuring tone.

She nodded, but her eyes begged him not to leave.

"I'll be right back," he said again.

He wanted to take her in his arms and hold her. To comfort her, but he didn't want to destroy evidence that might be on her person and it wouldn't be appropriate anyway.

In a way, he wished Julia was there. She ran a shelter for young girls and women who had been abused. She'd know how to help the girl. Of course, he was glad Julia wasn't there. No one should ever have to see what he was seeing.

Cliff reluctantly left the cell and searched the dead man's body and found a key to the chains. He came back quickly and opened the locks.

The girl still didn't trust him. She scooted away and curled up in a ball in the corner.

Cliff was concerned that she might run away if given the chance, so he decided to leave her in the cage until more help arrived.

He took out his phone and called for an ambulance and to find out who was already at the scene. Earlier, when he had gotten to the garage, he called for backup. He probably should've waited for them to arrive but entered the premises anyway. Concerned that Cami might kill someone before help arrived.

It turned out to be a good decision. Who knows what would've happened had he waited.

As it turned out, backup was already in the lobby. They weren't sure what to do. He didn't know how to tell them how to find him, other than to come down toward the basement.

Normally, he'd call Sammy, but decided against it. He'd be no help processing this situation. He'd only give Cliff another thing to worry about. He'd go ballistic if he saw Cami strapped to the chair.

No way Sammy would be able to control his emotions. Cliff was having a hard enough time as it was.

Cliff decided to leave things as they were until the paramedics and backup arrived. Everyone was safe and he didn't want to disturb the scene. He wanted them to get pictures of everything just as he found it.

He did check the man on the ground again for a pulse. Nothing.

Since it was now an OIS, Officer Involved Shooting, an IC needed to be called. An incident commander. Someone who could take over the scene from him and investigate the shooting. See if Cliff had acted properly.

Cliff would not give up control of the investigation of Cami. So many things needed to be done.

He looked over at her.

She looked like she'd aged ten years. The once gorgeous woman seemed like a shell of herself.

He didn't feel sorry for her. That was for others to do.

Cami's lips contorted. A frown formed. She obviously had as many questions for him as he had for her.

"What are... How did... you find me?" she asked. Her voice cracked as she said it. Slightly slurred from her swollen cheek and lips.

"I've been following you," Cliff replied.

If she was surprised, she didn't show it.

"You saved my life."

He nodded. "Doing my job."

Her shoulders slumped. "You've been following me? So you know who I am?"

"Yes."

Her head drooped, and shoulders sagged further in shame. She avoided looking at him.

"You are the Clown Slayer."

Cliff felt no emotion. He was numb, going through the motions. It didn't seem real. He'd just killed a man and still didn't know all the facts. Cami was the Clown Slayer. That much was certain. Whatever doubts he had before were gone.

It seemed like she even nodded when he said it.

Thankfully, she didn't ask any more questions.

He checked Cami's wounds again. It seemed strange. Two weeks ago, this person was in his house. Playing with his daughter. She was his wife's friend. His partner's girlfriend. Now he had to treat her like a killer.

Not willing to release her bands for fear she might kill him and escape.

He couldn't even begin to process all the fallout that was going to come from this. The best thing to do was keep sorting through the facts.

"Who is this man?" Cliff asked, pointing to the dead man on the floor.

"E. B. Combs. He's a serial killer."

Cliff had deduced as much. When he followed Cami to the hotel, he watched her enter the garage. He started to follow her inside, but that same black limousine pulled up before he could. The garage door opened and the limousine pulled in. A man was driving. The garage door closed behind it.

He didn't see a girl. He didn't know if she came in with the limousine or was already there.

Cliff tried to enter the garage, but the doors were locked. He finally kicked one in, risking making the noise. He didn't know what was happening inside but figured time was of the essence.

Once inside, Cliff didn't see Cami or the man.

It took him a while to find them. He followed the sound of conversation once he heard it. The door to the room was slightly ajar and he could hear everything from the hallway.

He could hardly believe the words coming from inside the room.

"I heard him mention 236 people he's killed," Cliff said.

He remembered the man mentioning a chalkboard. Cliff scanned the room until he saw it. Written in chalk was the number 236.

It was almost unfathomable.

"He cremated the bodies, so no one would ever find them," Cami said. "I was trying to stop him."

Cliff considered giving her a lecture about taking the law in her own hands, but what was the point? Cami's motives would be sorted out in a court of law.

He heard sounds coming from the hallway.

Cliff shouted to them so they'd know where he was. Six beat cops entered the room. Cliff began barking instructions.

"I need a man at each entrance and exit of the hotel. No one goes in or out. Hold everyone for questioning. Get more people down here. Call in everyone who is available. I want the hotel searched. Every room. Make sure there are no more victims. Be careful not to disturb any evidence. Note anything you see that might be helpful to the investigation. Call forensics. And get the paramedics down here. Now!"

The cops sprang into action.

Cliff searched the room, careful not to touch anything. He didn't have gloves or booties with him.

The paramedics arrived shortly thereafter. Cliff gave them instructions as well.

They attended to the young girl first, per Cami's insistence. The girl was loaded onto a gurney and taken to the hospital by ambulance. Probably dehydrated. High on drugs. Otherwise, she had no noticeable injuries.

Cliff instructed a policeman to follow them and stay with the girl. Provide her with protection but also to detain her for questioning.

The paramedic examined Cami. She might have a slight concussion from the blow to the head, but she was well enough to take down to the station. They treated her wounds and Cliff handcuffed her.

"You're under arrest for murder." He read her her rights.

She was compliant. Stood there silent, completely frozen. Numb. Resigned to her fate.

Cliff gave instructions for an officer to take Cami to the station and put her in an interview room. He'd handle the questioning and the booking.

As they were taking her away, Cami looked at him.

"I'm sorry," she said.

Cliff nodded.

He didn't care. A lot of people were sorry after they were caught.

Once she was gone, Cliff had things to do at the scene. He donned gloves and began poring over the files in the cabinets.

Combs had been right.

He was meticulous in documenting each victim.

Cliff counted 236.

28

The next morning

Cliff hadn't slept. He texted Julia to let her know he was okay. He also let her know he had arrested Cami without giving her any details other than that she was the Clown Slayer. Julia had been right.

He spent most of the night questioning Cami in Interview Room A. She was cooperative. He videotaped it to cover his bases. By the time he was done, they were both exhausted. Physically and emotionally. He'd never been so personally involved in an interrogation before. The entire process was painful for both of them.

Cliff grabbed a bite to eat and some coffee and took a shower at the station and changed clothes. He got something for Cami to eat and drink and gave her a chance to freshen up in the shower under the supervision of a female detective. After she'd gone through booking and had her DNA taken from her body and clothes.

She was given an orange jumpsuit to wear and taken back to the interview room where she was no longer handcuffed. He afforded her some privileges because of their relationship and her cooperation. He was also immensely thankful that she'd helped him solve all those crimes and even told her so.

Cliff went back to his desk and waited for the Lieutenant to arrive. When he did, his boss already knew something was up. He mentioned a swarm of reporters outside the station and cursed them under his breath.

Sammy still hadn't arrived. Cliff expected him to get into work early.

Cliff was dreading telling him about Cami.

He was happy to see the Lieutenant though. His boss would be pleased with him.

The Lieutenant motioned for Cliff to come into his office and then invited him to sit down.

"What's going on?" the Lieutenant said. "The press is already gathered outside the station. And a swarm of 'em are at the Castle Hotel. Tell me you have good news."

"I arrested the Clown Slayer."

The Lieutenant nodded stoically. Cliff didn't expect any more re-action than that. Any celebration would come later. The Lieutenant had probably already deduced as much.

"Are you sure it's her?" he asked.

"A hundred percent. She confessed."

"Tell me you mirandized her."

"Of course. I have it on tape. She waived her rights to a lawyer and spilled everything. It seemed like she wanted to. Like she was unburdening herself."

Part of the confession had been self-serving. Trying to justify her actions. Most of it was sincere. It seemed like she felt genuine re-morse.

By the time they were done with the interrogation, Cliff didn't feel sorry for her, but did pity her. What happened to her sister was horrible. Had it never happened, Cami probably would've lived her whole life having no interaction with law enforcement other than a few traffic tickets.

As it were, she was going to jail for the rest of her adult life.

"Who did you kill then?" the Lieutenant asked out of the blue.

The Lieutenant had obviously been notified of the OIS, but prob-ably didn't know the details.

"E. B. Combs," Cliff answered. "He's the proprietor of the hotel. He's also a serial killer as well. I solved 236 murders last night while you were sleeping."

The Lieutenant's eyebrows raised so high they would've flown off his head if not attached.

Cliff could feel his face beaming proudly as he said it. The one thing about handling serial killers was that he could solve a lot of cases at one time. It'd take him two or three years to solve this many individual homicide murders. That didn't mean he wanted to be transferred. He'd rather have his nails ripped off than go through this nightmare again.

Made worse by the personal connection.

"Tell me how you did that," the Lieutenant said, almost in disbelief.

Cliff explained everything. The Murder Castle. The incinerator. How he came to be there. He followed the Clown Slayer. Rescued the young girl. Killed Combs. Arrested the woman.

He felt a sudden urge to defend Cami. Even though the Lieutenant didn't know her identity yet. He'd hit the ceiling when he found out.

"We wouldn't have caught Combs if it hadn't been for the Clown Slayer," Cliff said. "She did us a service. I was right. She only targeted sexual predators and murderers."

That was the extent he was willing to go to bat for Cami.

"Who is she? Anybody on our radar," the Lieutenant asked.

"Come see for yourself. She's in Interview Room A."

Cliff probably should have told him right then and there but wanted to see his reaction. For maximum effect. Cliff didn't lead him directly into the room but an adjacent room where they could see her through the one way mirror.

Cami had her head down on the table. She couldn't see or hear them.

The Lieutenant noticeably gasped. Cami's head was on her arms but her face was turned toward them so she was easily recognizable.

"Is that who I think it is?"

"It is."

"Sammy's girlfriend is the Clown Slayer?" the Lieutenant said incredulously.

"Yes sir."

"You're freaking kidding me!"

"Nope. Hardly believed it myself. Actually, I had my suspicions. That's why I followed her last night. Sammy doesn't know."

"That stupid boy! Thinking with his you know what and not his head."

"Cami was a good liar. She had me fooled for a while, too. I wouldn't be too hard on Sammy. He was blinded by love. She used the name Macy to kill her victims. Those are the same letters. Cami rearranged them. She just changed the i to a y."

"Does Sammy know that she's the Clown Slayer?"

"He knows I made an arrest. But he doesn't know it's her. He should be here any time now."

"Are you sure he wasn't covering for her? If he did, he'll be going to jail with her."

"I don't think so. She made a point to say that he didn't have a clue."

"Either way, he's got some explaining to do."

Cliff wasn't sure what was going to happen to Sammy. He'd breached protocol. Letting a serial killer that close to his investigation would most certainly result in a suspension. Cliff wondered if it would fall back on him as well. Probably not, since he'd captured three of the most notorious serial killers in Chicago's history in less than three months.

They went back to the Lieutenant's office and Cliff filled him in on more of the details. Especially the files in the basement and how Combs documented the names of all his victims. Cliff already had staffers pulling old case files and matching them up.

Sammy arrived about thirty minutes later. With a bounce in his step and a huge smile on his face. Almost giddy.

Not knowing his world was about to come crashing down.

He patted Cliff on the back and gave him a huge attaboy.

"So you caught the Clown Slayer," Sammy said with exuberance. "Who is the dragon lady? I can't wait to question her."

"Sit down, son," the Lieutenant said soberly.

Cliff stood, so Sammy could take his seat. Sammy's facial expression turned into confusion. His forehead furrowed. "What's going on?" he asked.

"Sit down."

After Sammy did, the Lieutenant said, "Cami is the Clown Slayer."

Sammy's head snapped back like he'd been punched in the forehead.

"What are you talking about?"

"He's right. It's Cami. She's in Interview Room A," Cliff said. "I brought her in last night. She's been booked for murder. Twelve counts."

"You're lying to me. What is this? A joke? It's not funny."

"I wish it were. It's true. Cami killed all those men."

Cliff didn't know any other way to say it to soften the blow.

Sammy bolted to his feet. The veins pulsed on the side of his neck. His fists were balled like he wanted to hit Cliff.

"Where is she?" he practically shouted. "You made some kind of mistake. Cami's not a killer. Why would you arrest her? Have you lost your mind?"

"She confessed," Cliff said soberly.

"What did you do to her? She wouldn't confess. Did you coerce her? What's going on here? Let her go."

"I caught her in the act," Cliff said. "I've been following her. She went to the *Castle Hotel* last night to kill another man."

Details weren't important at the moment. Sammy wasn't going to listen to reason anyway.

"This is my case! Why are you following my girlfriend and you didn't tell me?"

"Because you wouldn't believe it! I had to do it on my own. I had to get the proof."

"You went behind my back!"

"He caught a murderer!" the Lieutenant said. He was standing as well. Neither of them were sure what Sammy was going to do next.

"I'll never forgive you for this."

The Lieutenant was angry. "You let a killer get close to you. You couldn't see what was right in front of your eyes. Cliff did you a huge favor."

"She was using you, Sammy," Cliff said, as if the words would make any difference. "The only reason she dated you was to get close to the investigation."

Cliff immediately regretted the words. Nothing he could say would be more hurtful than that.

"I don't believe it," Sammy said. "We were in love. We talked about getting married."

Speaking in past tense led Cliff to believe that Sammy might be beginning to accept it and realize it wasn't a joke.

"I don't know what to tell you," Cliff said. "She's the killer. Ask her yourself."

"I will. I want to talk to her now."

"I think you should," Cliff said. "You deserve an explanation."

The lieutenant nodded at Cliff. Normally, they wouldn't let Sammy talk to her. Not right away. Since they already had everything they needed to convict her, Cliff didn't think it'd hurt anything.

Cliff led Sammy to the interview room. He let him go in alone. Another breach in protocol, but it seemed appropriate. They deserved some privacy. Although Cliff had to watch them from the other room. In case Sammy did something stupid or said something that incriminated himself.

Sammy sat down across from Cami. Tears welled up in his eyes. His jaw was clenched though. It seemed like Sammy had shifted his emotions from denial to anger. Mixed with disbelief.

Whatever hope he had for their future together had to have dissipated when he saw her in that orange jumpsuit.

"Is what they are saying about you true?" Sammy asked, soberly.

Cliff expected Cami to burst into tears, but she only nodded. She reached out her hands and touched his.

Sammy clutched her hands. His eyes were even more watery than hers.

"It's true," she said.

Cami looked directly at him when she said it, but Sammy's head slumped down, and he was no longer looking at her. He was practically sobbing. He pulled his hands away.

"So, you killed all those men?" he asked, biting his lower lip trying to regain his composure.

"Yes. I'm sorry."

"Why?"

For nearly thirty minutes, she explained. Rehashed all the details. Her sister's death. Killing the man who brutally murdered Chloe. Her way of exacting justice. When she went to medical school in Minnesota, she read about a man who raped a woman and got off. She tried to kill him but he got away.

That was the man who called the tip line.

After that, Cami left town and moved to Chicago. Afraid she was going to get caught in Minnesota. Nothing ever came of it. She read in the newspaper about a man in Chicago who raped a woman and got away with it. She killed him. It felt good. It got easier after that.

She started dating Sammy so she could access the database and find more men who deserved to be killed. That's how she found her victims. She stole his password.

"I never killed anyone who didn't deserve it," she said.

"Was anything between us real or was it all a lie?"

The hurt oozed out of him like a scab torn open. Like he'd been stabbed in the heart. In a way he had been. Emotionally, his heart was broken. Bleeding out. Cliff could only imagine what Sammy was feeling.

"I think so," Cami said sweetly. "I really care for you. I do. I'm sorry I hurt you."

For the first time, Cliff really did feel sorry for her.

For both of them.

Epilogue

Six weeks later

"How did it go today?" Cliff asked Julia.

He was home. They were sitting on the living room couch. Rita was asleep. Julia had gone to see Cami that day at the women's detention center.

"It was good," Julia said. "I mostly just listened. I think she needed someone to talk to."

Cami had requested the meeting. Cliff was skeptical, but Julia wanted to go so he didn't discourage her from doing so.

"She apologized," Julia said.

Then she put her hand in the air in a gesture to stop Cliff from responding. "I know. She's a murderer and a liar. I'm not naïve."

"I didn't say anything."

"I know what you're thinking."

"How do you know what I'm thinking when I'm not thinking anything?"

Julia twisted her head to the side and frowned like she didn't believe him. "I think even the worst killer can be redeemed," she said.

"I know you do. You try to see the good in everybody. I love that about you."

"I think Cami is truly remorseful."

"Most people are once they're in jail and facing prison. Anyway, I'm not arguing with you about it. I'm glad you went. I'm sure it was cathartic for both of you."

Julia contorted her lips again. Then shook her head from side to side.

"What?" Cliff said. "Why are you looking at me that way?"

"Cathartic? You used that word in a sentence."

"Yeah. Cathartic. It means purging."

"I know what it means. I didn't know that you knew."

Cliff sat up on the couch. "It has a Greek origin. It's where we get the word catheter," he explained. "Like someone in a hospital is purging—"

"That's enough!" Julia exclaimed. "I got the picture. You don't have to explain any further."

"I'm surprised at you," Cliff said. "I would think you'd like it when I use big words. You're such a cerebral person."

"Stop it."

"What?"

"Cerebral? Have you been studying all the words in the dictionary that start with the letter, C? Cathartic. Cerebral."

"Cerebral means intellectual."

"I know what it means," she said sternly.

He wasn't about to let up, now that he was on a roll and was annoying her.

"It's also where we get the word cerebral hemorrhaging. Kind of like the catheter of the brain. Purging blood from it."

"You're sick. What's gotten into you?"

It took all of his power to keep from grinning widely or bursting out in laughter.

"I'm just trying to improve the quality of our communication. Dumb it up. Undumb it. Er... something like that. You know what I mean."

"Dumb up? No. I really don't know what you mean."

"I mean we have a *proclivity* to simplify our vocabularies around each other. I'm trying to raise the IQ of the room. You of all people should appreciate that."

Cliff was a C student. Julia a straight A student. Something she reminded him of occasionally. Not that it bothered him. He had more street smarts. Which was more important in his line of work.

"All I'm doing is giving you the etymology of the words I'm using," he said, with a smirk she couldn't miss.

Julia rolled her eyes. "Etymology?"

"It means—"

"I know what it means!"

She had been sitting next to him, like she was going to snuggle. Now she was standing in front of the couch. "I'm going to get changed."

"Good idea," Cliff said. "I'm going to go online and pay our credit card bill. It's due tomorrow. I've been so busy I haven't even looked at it."

Julia grimaced.

Cliff wasn't sure why. She disappeared out of the room before he could ask her. He went into the office and pulled up the credit card account.

His mouth gaped open.

"Why is our credit card bill so high?" he said to himself aloud.

He pulled up the itemized statement so he could figure out why.

One charge made up the majority of the balance. To the *Shoe Spa*. For $753.48.

"What in the world?" he said aloud again even though Julia wasn't around to hear it.

Then he remembered that Julia had taken Cami to the *Shoe Spa*. That's how she figured out Cami was the Clown Slayer. It all came flooding back in his memory.

She bought a pair of shoes that day. Even wore them recently. Nice shoes, but not worth seven hundred dollars.

"How could they have been this much?" he said. "There must be some mistake."

He got up from his chair and walked back to the bedroom to find her and ask. Julia was in bed, on top of the covers, wearing that skimpy outfit again.

He hadn't seen it for a few weeks.

"Hi honey," she said sweetly. "Do you like what you see?"

He knew exactly what she was doing and told her so.

"I knew you wore that outfit on purpose!"

Oh well.

Cliff jumped on the bed. They'd talk about the credit card later.

Not The End

Thank you for purchasing this novel from best-selling author, Terry Toler. As an additional thank you, Terry wants to give you a free gift.

Sign up for:
Updates
New Releases
Announcements
At terrytoler.com

We'll send you a copy of *The Book Club*, a Cliff Hangers mystery, free of charge.

READ MORE BOOKS FROM TERRY TOLER

Jamie Austen Thrillers

Read all the Jamie Austen Thrillers. They must be good.
They've been number one on Amazon in ten different countries.
Click on the link below.

THE JAMIE AUSTEN THRILLERS (12 book series)
Kindle Edition (amazon.com)

https://amzn.to/3vmPUy7

Cliff Hangers Mystery Series

Who wants to read a good mystery? We've got you covered! Read the Cliff Hangers where homicide detective, Cliff Ford, solves crimes in Chicago, with help from his wife Julia. These books have everything Terry Toler is known for. Page turning suspense, a hint of romance, and an ending you won't see coming.

The Cliff Hangers Mystery Series (4 book series)
Kindle Edition (amazon.com)

https://amzn.to/36WX3go

About Terry

Terry Toler is an Amazon international # 1 best-selling and award-winning author. He writes clean fiction with a message and life-changing nonfiction. He's a public speaker, entrepreneur, and has authored more than forty books.

Sign up for his newsletter where you'll get free stuff, exclusive content, and news of releases and promotions. He can be followed at terrytoler.com.

If you like his books, please take a few minutes to leave a review on Amazon. We really appreciate it. It helps draw more readers to his books. Thanks!

www.ingramcontent.com/pod-product-compliance
Lightning Source LLC
Chambersburg PA
CBHW050409260626
47156CB00003B/940